Sex, Drugs &

Spiritual Enlightenment

(but mostly the first two)

Karuna Das

DIX VANOS PUBLISHING

ISBN: 978-1-955065-76-45 (paperback)
ISBN: 978-1-955065-77-1 (ebook)

For Tiffany Joy,
Whose patience, wisdom, and love
Bolster my courage and strength
To keep becoming the man I want to be

CONTENTS

AUTHOR'S NOTE

A *solo concerto*—the musical form I've adapted as an organizing principle for this literary work—is a composition, typically divided into three movements, in which a featured solo instrument is accompanied by an orchestra. The term *concerto* is thought to be a synthesis of two Latin words: *conserere*, meaning to weave or yoke together; and *certamen*, meaning a competition or fight. The structure integrates those concepts by combining episodes in which the soloist and the rest of the orchestra play, alternately, in opposition, cooperation, and independence.

"I let my pain fuck my ego, and I call the bastard art"
 — Stew, "Identity," *Passing Strange*

FIRST MOVEMENT
COCK TALES

CHAPTER ONE

SEX ON THE BEACH

"I see my sign," I said, gazing up at specks of illumination in the dark expanse.

I heard Peter take a long, slow drag. I glanced over as he plucked the half-burned joint from his full lips, which he pressed together to hold in the smoke. Curly blond locks framed the most striking feature of a chiseled visage: his neon blue eyes. I don't know if they really were a window to his soul, but they sure had proven capable of opening doors. And legs.

I fumbled the joint slightly when he passed it to me—already kinda buzzed—as I turned it around between my fingers. I brought the end toward my mouth, which I wiped with the back of my other hand, twisting my wrist at the last second to avoid giving myself a beer facial. I slid the rolled-up paper between my puckered lips. Dry as a bone. Peter was a pro.

I was merely a pretender. An imposter. At least that's how I usually felt. I took a quick hit and held it in for what seemed like an eternity, concentrating on the sound of waves rolling ashore to distract me from my burning lungs. I snuck a glance at Peter.

He *finally* blew out a long stream of smoke. "Whaddaya mean?" he asked.

I exhaled in one big puff and pointed to a cluster of stars. "There. Virgo."

"Right," he said with a smirk. "The Virgin."

I rolled my eyes, mostly at his everlasting affection for the worn-out joke, but partly at my embarrassment that for me—nearly eighteen years alive in the summer of '85—it was still a valid jibe. Sort of.

Peter chugged the final gulps of his beer, his Adam's apple pulsing. He crushed the can inside a fist and flung it aside. It landed near the pair of discarded cans—one crushed, one not—from our first round. He yanked one of two remaining cans from a six-pack yoke and dangled the last attached can toward me.

I shook the one in my hand so its contents sloshed against the sides.

"Getting warm, Madonna," he said as he let the full can drop. He sang "touched for the very first time" in his best girly voice, then cracked his fresh beer and sipped. He motioned for me to return the joint.

I passed it back and finished my tepid beer in a series of big swallows. I lobbed the intact empty toward the pile. I held the last full can down in the sand and worked the six-pack yoke from around it. I tugged on each of the plastic rings until they stretched and, after the synthetic material had turned from clear to opaque, finally snapped.

"Birds get all tangled in them," I answered Peter's quizzical stare.

He shook his head and blew smoke at me. I waved it away and finished snapping rings.

"Can you see me up there?" asked Peter out of the blue, his eyes squinting above us.

"Look south and east," I replied. I tossed the dismantled six-pack yoke in the direction of the empty cans, then pointed down and left. "That bright one with the reddish tint, Antares, that's near the head. The tail curls up just above the horizon."

"Beware the Scorpion's sting!" he exclaimed as he

2

stubbed out the roach on my forearm. The random act of aggression was normal behavior for him, if not astrologically predetermined.

"Asshole!" I cried and launched myself at him. He had thirty pounds on me, but I was scrappy for my size. Or as our wrestling coach put it when naming me varsity co-captain, I had more "fight" in me than a rabid animal. So what if I usually lost? My resolve never wavered.

And I almost never got pinned—the present moment proving an exception, as Peter flipped me onto my back. He straddled my torso, his knees trapping my arms at my sides, and rocked his hips as if humping my sternum while I twisted and kicked beneath him.

"Ooh, baby! You like it rough, huh?" he said. I ceased struggling. He reached for his beer, sipped from it, let out a satisfied "aaah," and then tilted the can over my mouth.

I opened wide. Liquid splashed off my lips and teeth before he corrected his aim and hit the back of my throat. I felt my gag reflex about to activate.

As suddenly as he'd overpowered me, Peter rolled off me and scrambled to his feet, somehow not spilling a single drop from the can. He brushed sand from his clothes and skin as he peered toward the shoreline. I looked that way and saw a sundress-clad girl about our age wandering—maybe *staggering* would be more accurate—barefoot along the water's edge.

"I'll be back for you," Peter said as he set down his beer, all business now. "I promise."

He bounded across the beach. The girl didn't see him coming until he was practically on top of her. She tried to step around him but stumbled and would've fallen had he not put his hands on her waist and steadied her. She appeared to mumble an apology. He said something in response. She laughed. Her alertness seemed to improve as they started walking and chatting. After they'd gone maybe ten yards, she reached up and rested a hand on his shoulder. He slid an arm around her lower back and pulled her close.

3

I shook my head in disbelief and a touch of admiration. I'd seen the dude work his magic before, but this had to be some kind of record.

Peter led the girl away from the water and across the sand. As they headed into the dunes, he flashed me a confident thumbs-up. I returned the gesture with mock enthusiasm.

Once they disappeared, I popped the top of the last beer, drank deeply, and gazed up at the constellation of Virgo. "The Virgin," I mused, as a memory from an earlier summer washed ashore in my mind.

I gripped the knob-headed shaft and jerked it back and forth.

On the screen in front of me, an animated frog dodged its way across five lanes of speeding traffic, hopping backwards and forwards and side to side in movements corresponding to my manipulation of the joystick.

I—or rather the frog—reached a median between road and river. I released the control and wiped my palm on my shirt. I took in a breath and then exhaled as I watched turtles and logs stream past. All I had to do was navigate my way across five rows of them to a vacant lily pad on the opposite shore—without being carried off the screen or dumped in the water by a diving turtle or devoured by an alligator masquerading as a log—and I'd be home free.

I inhaled again and ventured ahead, risking the understood but unpredictable dangers for the promise of security waiting on the other side of the rapid current. I hopped along a log and over to a turtle and onto another log. I hopped backwards onto another turtle and then forward onto the end of a new log.

A hand smacked me on the shoulder, causing me to thrust the joystick to the side. Splash went the frog. The console emitted a mournful sound as my avatar

4

transformed into a skull-and-crossbones symbol. Game over.

I scowled up at Mark, more of an acquaintance than a friend.

"Never mind that," he said. "Ever seen a hooker?"

I suspect the drastic change in my facial expression conveyed I hadn't. Not in real life anyway.

Mark grinned and nodded and indicated for me to follow. I did so, in almost trance-like oblivion to the flashing lights and ringing chimes all around me.

And then we were standing on the sidewalk around the corner and halfway up the block from the arcade. I smiled at the irony. Here I was, away from home without parental supervision for the first time in my thirteen years of life, having traveled to Kansas City from a small town in Western Massachusetts with a group of older boys—some of them college students—to attend a religious youth conference. And while I was supposed to be in the convention center listening to someone drone on about the moral challenges facing virtuous young Americans like us, I was on the street trying to catch a glimpse of a real, live prostitute. If only I'd known what was next.

The religion, in case you're wondering, was the Bahá'í Faith, which originated in the mid-nineteenth century in Persia, now known as Iran. As organized religions go, the Bahá'í Faith has a lot to recommend it. There's no clergy to come between believers and God. It promotes world peace, equality among men and women, and the eradication of racism, poverty, and hunger. In the Bahá'í ideal vision, all humanity forms one big loving family. It has too many prohibitions—alcohol and premarital sex among them—for me. But still, as organized religions go, it's not bad.

My mother declared her belief in the Faith when I was twelve, about a year after we moved from my native Midwest to New England, where she'd befriended some Bahá'ís in our new neighborhood. I was in Kansas City to make her happy. At least that's what I thought then. It

5

took me years to recognize I had already—intuitively—started my own search for the sacred.

I gazed out at the urban thoroughfare ahead of me: two lanes in each direction, divided by another one for making left turns, for a total of five. I felt a sudden impulse to dart into the steady flow of vehicles and try to make it to the other side without becoming road kill.

Before I could act, Mark grabbed my arm.

I have no idea why *he* was in Kansas City. Maybe he wanted to make *his* parents happy. Maybe, as a light-skinned Black kid from the inner city who'd been adopted by a white Bahá'í couple from the suburbs, he was on an existential quest of his own.

"There," he said, pointing to an AMC Pacer creeping toward us in the curb lane. "They keep driving around the block ... nice and slow."

I squinted at the approaching car and through the windshield saw two Black women, seemingly in their late twenties or early thirties. "Maybe they're waiting for someone to come out," I speculated aloud. "To give them a ride."

"They wanna give someone a ride all right."

An anxious laugh withered in my throat as the Pacer stopped along the curb in front of us. The passenger rolled down the window and tilted her cornrow-braided head through the opening.

"You boys looking for some fun?"

Wow, I thought. We've been solicited by real, live hookers. All I'd wanted was to *see* one. Curiosity satisfied, my mind turned to setting the high score at Pac-Man.

"How much?" asked Mark, whose curiosity apparently reached deeper than mine.

"Thirty bucks for a suck and a fuck."

I realize that sounds like quite a deal. Keep in mind it was 1981. And I wasn't thinking about how much bang I could get for my dollar. I was trying to think of a legitimate excuse not to go along with Mark's scheme.

"Most of my money's back at the hotel," I said.

"I'll front you the cash. No—what the hell—I'll *pay* for you."

"Don't you think it's kinda late to—"

A honk of the car horn cut me off. When Cornrow lifted her torso through the window and leaned forward, I gawked at her cleavage, unable to take my eyes off her chocolate skin.

"Don'tcha wanna *come* with us?" she asked.

Mark nodded and held up a finger. "Two of them and one of me," he said. "You up for it? Or are you a big pussy?"

"Fuck you," I replied. I marched toward the car.

Cornrow swung the door open.

"She'll be right back," reassured the driver, a sweet-voiced and doe-eyed beauty with straightened hair, as I stared across the parking lot toward the entrance of the Denny's that had swallowed Cornrow a few minutes before. "Aw, shit! Duck down! Duck down!"

As Mark and I scrunched low in the backseat, Straightened Hair nonchalantly adjusted the rearview mirror and touched up her lipstick with the pink tip of the applicator. Watching her, I felt a mix of fear and fascination—then pure fear when a spotlight illuminated her, its beam lingering there momentarily before passing over our heads. I peeked through the hatchback window as a police car exited the lot.

"How old you boys anyway?" asked our chauffeur.

"Eighteen," replied Mark without hesitation. He shrugged when I gaped at him. He was only fifteen, but he was physically mature for his age, so he might be able to pass.

"Uh huh. How 'bout you?"

Mark shot me an encouraging nod. I took in a breath and focused on deepening my tone.

"I'm, uh ... sixteen," I said, my pubescent vocal chords cracking on the number.

Straightened Hair threw back her head and laughed. Mark tried to fight it for a moment, then joined in. As they shared their mirth, the passenger door opened and Cornrow got in. She held a lidded drink cup in one hand and a thick pile of napkins in the other. She stashed the napkins into the console between the front seats.

"I miss something funny?" asked Cornrow.

Straightened Hair turned and smiled at what I knew was my beet-red face. "Li'l white boy sure cute when he blush. He got a frog in his throat."

Timber-laden barges drifted across the water below the suspension bridge as we crossed a wide river. No sign of alligators.

I leaned forward between the bucket seats. "Where you taking us, anyway?"

Cornrow ignored me as she sucked on the straw to draw vanilla milkshake up through it. I imagined a burst of creaminess flood into her mouth. I could almost taste it.

"Too many cops in KC," Straightened Hair answered as the Pacer descended the span toward land. "We got a good spot over here in KCK."

As if on cue, I saw the sign: *Welcome to Kansas*. I threw my full weight against the backseat. On our way to engage in prostitution that also qualified as statutory rape, we'd now crossed state lines.

Into *Kansas*, I thought, an idea dawning. I lifted my feet a few inches, tapped my heels together, and whispered, "There's no place like home." I repeated the action. When Mark raised an eyebrow at me, I smiled and lifted my feet once more.

My feet rested on the floor in front of the passenger seat, my jeans and tighty-whities bunched around my ankles. Straightened Hair squeezed lotion onto her brownish-pink palm. She reached over and smeared cream onto my genitals. She tugged on my penis, which had shriveled up to the size of a ChapStick. Even for me, that's *major* shrinkage.

"Li'l white boy gotta get hard. I don't wanna be flossing with no pubic hair."

At that moment, I was glad to even have pubic hair. My previously sparse patch of it had grown in that spring.

I stared out at the graffiti-covered wall of an abandoned warehouse in the dilapidated industrial district where we'd parked. What had I expected for thirty bucks, the Hilton?

She tugged more vigorously, as if my dick were a balloon she was stretching to blow up.

I slid a hand down the front of her spaghetti-strap dress. I cupped her bare breast, surprised by its weight. *It* felt like a balloon, a water-filled one.

She extracted my hand from the site of its exploration and returned it to my side. She bent across the console and took me into her warm, wet mouth.

I stole a glance into the backseat. Mark was breathing heavily, eyes closed, as Cornrow's head bobbed up and down in his lap. My gaze lingered there. I sensed myself grow hard.

"That's it, baby," purred Straightened Hair as she climbed over the console, hiking her dress and lowering herself onto me in one smooth motion.

I turned to face the back of her head. As she rocked her pelvis against mine, I reached a hand around and slid it down the front of her dress, cupping her bare breast. My fingers traced the edge of her nipple.

She put a hand around my wrist and returned my hand to my side. She held both my wrists against the outsides of my legs as she bounced up and down in my lap. With each bounce, my butt pressed into the clammy vinyl and her straightened hair brushed against my face.

I tried to turn away, but I couldn't escape contact. I closed my eyes and took a series of deep breaths. After a

9

couple dozen bounces, I felt my erection fade.

She stopped bouncing and howled, "Li'l white boy blew his load already!"

I gazed out at where a graffiti phallus ejaculated a globular splotch between the first two letters of "KCK" to misspell cock.

"... Yeah," I said.

"Still a virgin if you didn't cum?" I wondered aloud on that Cape Cod beach four years later. I'd had close encounters—of the third-base kind—since then, but nothing I could claim as legitimate sex.

One time early in our senior year, when my stepdad was away at a conference, I hosted a small party for strategic pairings of boys from my class and sophomore girls. In the middle of a make-out session preceded by a few beers and a couple vodka shots, my "intended" surprised me by sliding her hand down the front of my jeans. Moments later we were upstairs in my Persian foster brother's bed—since my room was already in use— her naked body straddling mine as she squeezed my hard-on and rubbed it against her silky opening. That's when things got fuzzy.

She called me the next day, upset I'd "deflowered" her. But she was the one who initiated—and controlled— our genital relations. I had no recollection of penetrating her at all. Besides, Babak would've said something if she'd bled on his sheets.

Still a virgin if you don't remember—or necessarily believe—it happened? Even if it had, I presumably once again hadn't cum. I didn't keep a condom in my wallet, and she hadn't expressed concern she might be pregnant.

Either way, it certainly wasn't anything to brag about. And I wasn't about to tell anyone about my adventure in Kansas City, at least not the whole truth of it. I'd disclosed to my older brother Adam, Peter, and other select male friends that I'd gotten a pro blowjob—

and for free, no less. But that was the end of the story.

I sipped from my beer, then set it down in the sand. I stood and wandered toward the vast ocean in front of me. With foamy water cascading over my feet, I reached my arms outward and looked up at the starry sky. Infinity beckoned, quietly but insistently, from all around me.

"Who the fuck am I?"

"Drew!" Peter called. He hustled my way from the dunes. "She's all ready for you."

"She doesn't want me," I replied, sidestepping the issue of what *I* wanted, or didn't.

"I came before I could get her off. You gotta finish the job," said Peter as if it were the only polite—and maybe a truly gallant—thing to do. But even if it were outright heroic, it wasn't at all romantic. The two penetrating experiences I'd just recalled hadn't been exactly satisfying.

Was this how I wanted to remember having legitimate sex for the first time?

"You definitely want protection," said Peter, holding out a condom. With his other hand, he made a pinching motion. "And be sure to watch out for crabs." As I stared at the condom, Peter slipped it into my pocket and gave me a pat on the ass. "Time you became a real man."

I knelt between her legs, my shorts and tighty-whities bunched around my ankles. I slid her sundress up her thighs, which fell open, and glanced up at her eyes, which remained closed.

"What's your name?"

"Flora," she murmured so inaudibly I might've misheard what was actually Laura.

"I'm Drew," I said. I spit into my palm and rubbed saliva onto my genitals. I started to tug—gently—on my limp penis. "Is this ... what you want?"

Flora-Laura took my free hand and brought it to her breast. I caressed it, then squeezed it, through the cotton

11

of her dress. I slid the strap off her shoulder, exposing her flesh. She grabbed my shirt and pulled me down onto her, our faces practically joined. When her lips parted slightly, I kissed her on the mouth. She pressed her palm against my cheek and pushed my head away.

"Sorry. I thought ..."

She guided me to her bare breast, and I understood. I flicked her nipple with my tongue, then suckled it. She moaned. She reached for my rising manhood. I reached for the condom I'd removed from its packaging and set on the rose-print panties lying nearby.

Protective sheath in place, I spread the pink petals of Flora-Laura's skin and—seeing no thorns—plunged into the wild.

Finally, I thought. Legitimate sex!

"Attaboy!" ejaculated Peter, after I affirmed with a stone-faced nod I'd done the deed—and to completion this time. Once I plopped down in the sand beside him, he raised a hand for a high-five. "What?" he asked when I left him hanging.

"It's just ... She's pretty drunk. Did she even know who I was?"

"She got drunk *on purpose*. To abandon her inhibitions. She could care less who it was."

"Abandon her inhibitions?"

"Drop all the shit that keeps her from doing what she really wants."

"I know what it means."

"And I know what you need," he said as he stood up. "We're going to town to celebrate."

"We can't leave her there. I think she passed out. Right afterward."

"What do you suggest we do? Take her with us? In that condition? It'd be kidnapping." Peter crouched down and clasped my face. "She found her way out here. When she comes to, she can find her way home. She's probably staying in one of those cottages down the beach. Nobody's gonna mess with her in there."

He started up the slope, pausing at the crest long enough to jingle his keys in the air before disappearing down the other side. I either went with him or walked several miles along deserted country roads in the middle of the night.

I imagined Flora-Laura lying unconscious in the little valley between mounds. My mind's eye traveled the length of her now familiar body from the scratchy remnants of glitter-paint on her toenails to the constellation of freckles across her chest right below her collarbone. When I got to where her face should be, I could picture only a featureless blur of skin and hair.

I snapped back to reality and punched the sand several times. I leapt to my feet. I bent over to scoop up the drained beer cans and the ruptured six-pack yoke.

And then I followed Peter.

CHAPTER TWO

JACK AND COKE, ON THE ROCKS

I followed Peter, like a shadow, with the phantom faceless image of the unconscious girl following me like a shadow inside my head. We crossed the crowded floor to an opening along the bar. I floated behind as he claimed the spot. In doing so, he bumped into a tall, twenty-something dude with a crew cut. Crew Cut scowled at Peter, who was focused on attracting the attention of the bartender, then went back to watching rodeo calf-roping on an overhead TV.

"Two shots of Jack and two drafts," Peter called out to a middle-aged man who'd glanced over at us on his way to deliver a pair of drinks.

That task completed, the bartender returned. "IDs?"

Peter slapped a laminated card, already in hand, onto the lacquered wood.

As the barkeep picked it up and scrutinized it, I turned away, dug my wallet from my pocket, and brushed off the grainy evidence of our recent exploit on the beach. I flipped through plastic sleeves containing my driver's license, my now invalid high school ID, the AmEx card my stepdad had co-signed so I could build credit, my library and gym cards, and a few miscellaneous photos. At last I got to the item I wanted. I slid it out and turned back to find a pair of wary eyes trained on me. I smiled as I handed over ironclad proof of identity: an authentic driver's license with my picture and my older brother's information.

A friend of Adam's who worked in the UMass ID office had forged a card with my photo and Adam's name that I took, along with Adam's birth certificate, to the state DMV, where I explained I'd lost my original. Making that felonious claim and posing for the "mug shot" had been nerve-wracking, but now I could walk into any bar with complete confidence—about getting served at least. I even had the UMass ID as backup. If I'd been thinking clearly on the ride into town, I would've moved them forward in my wallet.

"Another duplicate," said the bartender, insinuating but not outright accusing.

"Make it *four* shots of Jack and two drafts," replied Peter, tossing a twenty onto the bar before turning to survey the room. He smiled at something.

I looked in that direction. A familiar skinny dude in a Van Halen t-shirt—fitting, since "Runnin' with the Devil" was blasting from the jukebox—glanced up from playing pool. Peter nodded at him. He tipped his stick at us.

"That's what you meant by celebrate? I dunno, man. I can't afford—"

"Relax," Peter said. "Tonight's on me." He lifted a shot glass from the cluster that had appeared. "To you, my friend. Proud of you."

I clinked a shot glass against his and tossed back the whiskey, doing my best to minimize the involuntary display of my distaste for it. I knew I'd like the effects of it. Before long, the specter of remorse would fade into oblivion.

Peter guided me into his spot at the bar and set off through the crowd. When he reached the pool table, Skinny Van Eight-Ball greeted him with a slap-turned-clasp of hands. They stepped into a corner, where several members of Van's entourage shielded them from view.

"Another mudslide, Tina?" asked the bartender of the woman next to me. Surprised I hadn't already noticed her—a petite redhead with curves combining the bloom of youth and adult ripeness—I gazed at her delicate face for a moment or three after she nodded her response.

"Didn't your mother teach you it's not polite to stare?"

"Huh? Oh. Sorry," I stammered. "Lost in my thoughts."

"Must be some deep ones. Don't drown."

I nodded and sipped my draft, pretending to choke in an attempt at humor that elicited a genuine smile from Tina.

The bartender set a fresh drink in front of her. She tilted it toward him as she nodded thanks, then tilted it toward her mouth. I watched an ice cube press against her lips. She set down the glass and gaped at me. This time I had no alibi.

I slammed back one of the remaining shots, then slammed down the empty glass—far harder than I intended. As I chased the whiskey with gulps of beer, I heard a giggle from Tina and felt a sneer from Crew Cut.

"Couldn't wait, huh?" asked Peter when he returned, mercifully soon. "Fair enough." He raised the remaining shot and pounded it, then pounded the empty glass—with deliberate force—onto the bar. I felt an outright glare from Crew Cut and heard a hearty laugh from Tina.

"Oh, you boys. Bar babies. I have to admit ... it's kinda cute."

"In that case," Peter said as he leaned in close to her, "maybe you'll babysit our brewskis while we visit the potty? Beer is like mother's milk to us."

Tina nodded her acquiescence, and Peter plucked the stirrer from her drink and licked the clinging droplets from the end. He rolled the swizzle stick across his tongue and bit down on it like a toothpick as he gestured for me to follow.

17

Peter poked the dry end of the black plastic spear into a gold paper packet and scooped white powder onto its wide, flat head. He extended it toward me. "Man of the Night goes first." He chuckled. "This time anyway."

I accepted his offering and lifted the piled-high end into one nostril, plugged the other, and sniffed. I winced from another unpleasant sensation I knew would pack a potent punch soon enough.

Peter wasted no time taking his turn and passing me the re-loaded spoon. I snorted the contents up my other nostril.

"Speaking of first times," said Peter as he prepped his second bump. "Remember?"

I remembered. I remembered the first time he meant: the time we'd been introduced to the "hard" drug of cocaine. I also remembered the time I'd been introduced to what authorities called the "gateway" drug of marijuana. Oddly, I couldn't remember my introduction to alcohol. I had a vague notion that someone—an uncle or family friend—had given me a sip of beer when I'd been five or so. But I had no memory of the first time I'd imbibed to the point of intoxication.

Pot, yes. I recalled that rainy fall afternoon in vivid detail.

I was in my room playing with my Star Wars action figures. Ever since the original movie had come out in the summer of the previous year, I'd been collecting them on every possible occasion—as gifts on holidays and my birthday, most recently number eleven at that point, and as my own purchases whenever I'd saved enough allowance money to add to my, by then, nearly full set. I was presently reenacting the scene on the Death Star when Leia kisses Luke—"for luck"—right before they swing across a chasm by grappling hook. Years and two sequels later, the world would learn of their status as siblings, turning a modestly romantic interaction into a borderline illicit one.

"Hey, Shithead," said my own—adopted—sister from the doorway, where she remained long enough to add, "Come here."

I dropped Luke and Leia cold and followed Diana to her adjacent room. After all, she'd addressed me with her favorite term of endearment.

She rarely spoke to me at all those days. She'd drifted in a haze of depression since we'd moved to Massachusetts a few months earlier. Right before we'd left the Minneapolis suburbs in July, she'd run away from home, making it all the way to our dad's place in Southern Wisconsin, hoping to find asylum there. We'd reclaimed her on our way to New England. Now she sat on the ledge of an open window, gazing out at the surrounding woods. From her perspective, the tall thin trees must've seemed like prison bars.

"Close the door," she commanded.

I complied, curious about her impulse to include me in something so alluringly secretive. She held up a foil packet and asked if I wanted to get high.

"Sure," I said. I watched in fascination as she folded another piece of foil into a makeshift pipe and packed it with weed.

The dope had arrived that day, courtesy of the U.S. Postal Service, mailed from the Twin Cities by my fifteen-year-old sister's twenty-year-old boyfriend. A few months later he would put a gun in his mouth and pull the trigger. Diana was devastated by his death and even more so by his suicide note. He couldn't live without her, he wrote, alluding not to their geographical separation but to her recent rejection of his marriage proposal.

Nearly seven years later, I still remembered my first time feeling the harshness of the smoke against my throat. And I remembered dashing up and down the aisles of the local A&P roaring with delight an hour or so afterward, Diana in chase, worried our mom would see me and catch on.

19

She's so paranoid, I'd thought, confident I seemed like any normal sugar-fed kid.

By ninth grade, I was sparking up regularly. My pal "Peter Piper" had become the main supplier—with my occasional assistance—to our junior high. Looking back, I wonder if "Pied Piper" would have been a more fitting nickname, and not just because he sometimes wore one of those multicolored Rastafarian hats (with fake dreadlocks attached). In any case, between the dime bags we bought for ourselves in the UMass dorms and what we skimmed from the orders we filled for our classmates, we procured a sufficient supply of grass to toke up while waiting for the bus each morning, again during lunch period, and again after school.

Our favorite bake sessions took place on camping trips. We'd often wake to find our tent filled with smoke from the night before. For me, that was by far the biggest draw of being a Boy Scout. And, to come full circle, it had been one of our troop leaders—a college student volunteer—who introduced us to the chemical substance now permeating our blood-brain barriers.

"Wade Sugarman," Peter said. "Name like that he was born to be a dealer."

"I doubt that's quite what his parents had in mind," I replied, thinking the same was true of ours when they permitted us to attend the regional scout jamboree in the spring of our freshman year.

After the closing bonfire, we'd downed the two-liter bottle of pre-mixed rum and coke we smuggled into camp and then breached the gates of the Tri-County Fairgrounds to rendezvous with our sugar man, who'd arranged with Peter to transport us to his apartment for an all-night party featuring "new" coke, as it were—to us at least.

Peter closed the golden packet, then pocketed it and the stir stick. He faced the mirror and checked his nostrils for powder residue. "You feeling it?"

I looked at my reflection, then back at his, and

shouted, à la Ric Flair, "WOOOO!"

He grabbed me by the shoulders and turned me toward him, answering me with a shout of his own: "WOOOOOO!"

We stared intently at each other and simultaneously shouted, "WOOOOOOOO!"

As we approached our spot at the bar, which Tina appeared to have watched over well, Crew Cut tapped the shoulder of the beefy guy next to him and turned in our direction.

"Funny," he remarked, more to Beefy Guy than to us. "I'd swear I saw you go into the men's room."

"What's funny about that?" queried Peter, stepping right up to him as I observed the exchange with a strangely detached alertness. All lingering feelings from our earlier outing had slipped below the level of my conscious conscience.

"Usually when people go in pairs it's to the ladies'."

"Yeah," said Peter. "Ha." He turned his back to the would-be comedian and sipped his beer.

I half-noticed Peter wink at Tina as I continued to size up Crew Cut. My object of study glanced at Beefy Guy, who looked on with a dumb grin I imagined was more or less permanent.

"You hear screaming when they were in there?" Crew Cut asked, adding without waiting for a response, "I definitely heard screaming. Like bitches in heat. Or maybe even gettin' off."

I dimly perceived Peter sniff back and swallow cocaine drip as he fought to keep his cool.

"Aww, don't cry," said Crew Cut. He noticed me. "Whatchu looking at, little faggot?"

"Care to step outside?" asked Peter once he'd spun back around.

I heard Tina chuckle, presumably a response to his clichéd line. In other circumstances, I might've laughed

21

myself.

"Come on, man. Back off," I said, reluctantly taking my eyes away from Crew Cut as I slid between him and Peter and faced my friend. "It's cool. Let me handle this."

"I'll give you something to handle, all right, little fag—"

I whirled and landed a hard punch in the middle of Crew Cut's face, surprising myself as much as anyone.

He staggered back several steps and brought his fingers to the bottom of his nose, wiping at the blood oozing from his flaring orifice. He shook his head as he glowered at me and cracked his knuckles. "Now you've done it."

I felt and heard a ferocious roar explode from deep within me as I charged him, acting at once on animalistic impulse and with the presence of mind to realize my only chance at survival was to prevent him from swinging on me. I hooked my arms over his and rammed headfirst into his midsection, driving him back through the parting sea of patrons and into the wall. I felt and heard an agonized breath rush out of him. I continued to roar as I rammed into him repeatedly and with far more vigor than I'd brought to my earlier thrusting.

Then I felt cold steel press against my windpipe. I grew quiet and ceased my ramming.

"You finished?" asked the bartender.

"... Yeah," I said.

I unhooked the double whizzer. If only Coach had been there to see me throw that clinch! He'd surely have been proud of my performance, although he'd likely have wondered aloud why I so rarely managed to execute moves like that against my opponents on the mat. I raised my arms in the air, straightened up, and backed away as the bartender held the baton to my throat.

Tina appeared in front of me. She locked eyes with the bartender as she wrapped her fingers around the metal rod and gave me some breathing room. The bartender sighed and released me into her custody. She put an arm around me and walked me toward the door.

I saw Beefy Guy laid out on the floor nearby. Peter broke free from the pair of patrons restraining him and hurried to join us.

"Don't come around here no more," called the bartender, presumably not actually *trying* to imitate Tom Petty as the music video Mad Hatter. "Or you'll have a lot more to worry about than getting away with fake ID."

Yeah, I thought, like the wrath of "decency" crusader and self-appointed First Parent of the United States Tipper Gore.

And then we were in the parking lot. Late-night fog made it feel like we'd stepped from one strange dream world into another. Maybe I really had fallen down a rabbit hole?

"That's us," said Peter, pointing Tina toward the '67 Camaro his dad had restored and given to him for his eighteenth birthday-slash-graduation.

"Leave it. I'll drive you home."

"Look, lady, we appreciate the offer and all," he replied, separating me from her. "But I've got it under control."

"Oh you think so?" she asked. "That's what you call punching off-duty policemen?"

Peter let out a whoop and patted me on the back.

"I don't know what you're swimming in," Tina said as I stood beside the car while Peter circled around the front end. "But if someone throws you a lifeline, you better grab it, 'cause you are sinking fast."

I sank into the passenger seat as soon as Peter reached over and opened the door.

He grinned at me. "Motherfucker! You totally took it to that prick. Can you believe that douche was a cop?"

I nodded. I *had* totally taken it to that prick. And, come to think of it, I *could* believe that douche was a cop.

Peter held up the paper packet and plastic stirrer. "This calls for another bump." He dipped the spear into the powder. "You are truly the Man of the Night."

I nodded. "Just go ask Alice," I said, receiving a puzzled look along with the loaded spoon. I grinned at him like the Cheshire Cat.

I clutched the metal rung with one hand and pulled myself toward it as my toes searched for the next step. Slightly dizzy already, I didn't dare look down. Once I found a safe home for my arch, I brought my other leg up and planted that foot on the same step. I took in a breath, then released my grip and grasped at the next rung, catching it before the shingles dangling below me upset my equilibrium.

My hauling arm ached from the weight of the bundle. I'd shouldered it before mounting the ladder, but it'd slipped off a few rungs back. I'd been lucky not to drop it, and even luckier not to plummet two stories to the ground with it. A couple more repetitions of my cautious—but still precarious—approach to ascension, and I'd arrive at my destination.

As I grabbed the first rung above the eave, I heard Peter skid down the slope of the roof. His hands wrapped around my forearm and held it. I stepped up, bringing my face level with his.

"Jesus, dude," he uttered. "You look like shit."

No shit, I thought. And no thanks to you. I climbed two steps up the ladder so that my hips were nearly even with the uppermost rung.

"On three," he said. I swung the bundle below me, building momentum, as he counted: "One ... two ... three!"

I summoned every ounce of strength I could muster to heft my load toward him. Peter caught the package, which soon rested on the freshly laid shingles along the lower part of the roof. Discharging the weight I'd been carrying brought me tremendous relief.

"I told you to go easy this morning," sounded a raspy voice.

I glanced higher up the slope at my boss, a sinewy and leathery-skinned man of about forty. "Thanks, Mister

Fullman. I'll take a break now."

"It's Mike. I told you that, too." He winked at me. "Especially now you're a real man."

I gaped at Peter, who shrugged it off. "It's cool. He's my dad."

As I made my way back down to earth, descending the ladder as warily as I scaled it, I considered what it would be like to have Mike for a father. Peter's mother had left them—for another man, I gathered—years before. The entire time I'd known the Fullman family, since the start of sixth grade, it'd been only the two of them. Aside from Mike's occasional short-term live-in girlfriends, that was.

My own parents divorced when I was still in diapers. In my early years we all lived in Janesville, but my mom moved us to Minnesota when I was seven, and then out east after my new stepdad got a job there. I'd seen my real dad, on average, less than twice a year over the last ten. It wasn't easy to develop much closeness—especially not the kind of camaraderie shared by Peter and Mike—under those conditions.

"You're a neat kid," my dad once wrote to me on stationery I'd made him in a graphic arts class. I still had the letter in my chest of keepsakes.

My relationship with my stepdad started out great. When he and my mom began dating, he was a carefree bachelor who usually had a gin and tonic in hand. Diana, Adam, and I relished every opportunity to accompany our mother to his penthouse condo with a balcony overlooking the downtown skyline. He let us run wild, and he often joined us in playing Marco Polo, or dive-and-catch with one of those miniature hard plastic footballs, or even rowdier games in the pool.

All that changed quickly once we moved to Massachusetts as one family. I suspect it was a combination of the stress of his new job (in academia), the stress of his new parental role (for two teenagers and one pre-teen), and the stress of his new marriage to my mother (no comment).

I suddenly remembered an incident during our first year together. We'd taken a weekend trip to the Cape that, it dawned on me, had been my only previous visit to the peninsula. Our first night in a little cottage, Bruce felt indignation at something I said—a complaint about his literally sticking his finger into the family pie—and went off on a verbally abusive tirade. My siblings and I fled to the beach, where we huddled under a pier to stay out of a cold spring rain.

Once the storm let up, Diana ventured back to the cottage to check on our mother, whom she found loading the car with our bags after what had been a major blow-up by Bruce, in which he'd held the bedroom door shut from the outside to keep our mom trapped within. We drove the three hours back to Amherst in a steady downpour matched by the flow of our collective tears, leaving the new head of our household to find his own way home.

For some reason, our mother gave him another chance, and he didn't squander it. He quit drinking, and they went to counseling and started attending Bahá'í gatherings. Over the next several years, he underwent a transformation nothing short of miraculous. By the time our mom asked for a trial separation, during which she moved back to her native North Carolina—with me in tow—to attend graduate school, he'd become a new man.

Like our mom, I failed to appreciate the change until later. In fact, one time in tenth grade, believing he'd come into the family room to eavesdrop on my phone conversation—a few days after I'd been caught smoking pot—I unleashed some rage of my own, whipping the heavy rotary model at his head, missing my target by mere inches and penetrating the plaster wall beside him.

Even so, he was there for me when I needed him most. Several months into residing in Chapel Hill—living alone with my mom for the first time—I tried to kill myself by overdosing on antihistamines. After much soul-searching by both of us, my mother and I agreed it would

26

be best for me to return to the home, the school, and the friends I'd left behind in Massachusetts. For reasons I couldn't fathom given our rocky past, Bruce opened his doors to me.

He'd already taken in Babak, who'd fled his homeland to escape the persecution faced by Bahá'ís in Iran, leaving behind his parents and younger brother. (His story of being smuggled across the border and imprisoned in Turkey deserves its own telling.) Babak's older brother had managed to catch a flight out of Tehran the one day the airport was open between the fall of the Shah and the rise of Ayatollah Khomeini, subsequently becoming a member of the Amherst Bahá'í community while attending UMass. As a favor to Mehrdad, Bruce agreed to act as the new immigrant's legal guardian, so Babak could attend my high school. That's how I ended up "batch'ing it"—as Bruce called it—with a Persian foster brother and my soon-to-be-ex-stepfather.

As I tramped across the job site toward the trailer, it occurred to me I'd never adequately thanked Bruce for effectively saving my life. So what if he didn't buy beer for me to drink at the house like Mike did for Peter?

That's when I felt something foul rise up inside me. I bent over and expelled toxic bile from my system. I wiped my mouth and looked up at the roof. Peter and Mike hammered away without any sign of having witnessed my pathetic display. I kicked sandy dirt onto the puddle.

Minutes later, as I gazed at my ashen reflection in the trailer bathroom's grimy mirror, an old Bill Cosby comedy routine popped into my head. In it, the biblical Noah resists taking steps to prepare for the flood. The thunderous voice of God delivers one knockout punch line:

"How long can you tread water?"

CHAPTER THREE

SEA BREEZE

Even if you've never been to Cape Cod, you probably know it has a lot of beachfront. Fullman Construction operated that summer out of Chatham, where Peter and I were staying in a rental cottage with Mike. Our stargazing spot—and the site of our tag-team match with Flora-Laura—was on Hardings Beach, along the outer (Atlantic Ocean) shore of the peninsula, close to where it curves north. The roadside bar where we held the second round of our evening's double-bill was just outside town on Route 28, which, if you continue northward for roughly twenty minutes—more like thirty by bus, my mode of transportation that summer when I wasn't chauffeured by Peter—leads to Orleans. About a week after that eventful night, I found myself on Skaket Beach, in the bend of the inner (Cape Cod Bay) shore near Orleans.

"Why do you care?" I asked, then wished I'd been less blunt. We'd sat at the concession stand patio table without exchanging a word since our arrival, and I couldn't bear the silence for another moment. I took a deep breath and dove in all the way. "About what happens to me. Some *baby* you caught staring at you—or, you know, in your general direction."

Dimples formed in Tina's cheeks as she pursed her

lips and stared out toward the water. "You remind me of someone," she said. "Someone I loved. Someone I wish I could've saved from himself. Someone I *might've* saved, if I'd handled it differently." A single tear rolled out from behind her sunglasses and down her cheek, leaving a glistening trail.

I sensed a flash of insight into her psyche. "A younger brother? Is he ... dead?"

"He's not dead. But there are days I sure wish he was," she replied, adding with a shrug, "It's my husband."

So much for my powers of intuition, I thought, as we slid back into silence. When she rotated the straw of her Diet Coke between the thumb and fingers of her left hand, I noticed she wasn't wearing a ring.

"We're separated," she answered my question before I could ask it. "Going on a year. It's definitely over. Just a matter of finishing the paperwork."

I nodded, as though dissolving a marriage could be so uncomplicated. My mother and Bruce had completed their divorce not long before this, and I'd seen the emotional impact even a comparatively amicable severing of the nuptial bond had on the parties involved.

I suppose I should explain how Tina and I came to be at the Skaket Beach concession stand at all, much less in the midst of such an awkward and weighty conversation.

I'd shown up late that afternoon—after Mike let us go for the day and I made my way to Orleans—at the dentist office where she worked as a hygienist. She was understandably surprised to see me in the waiting room when she appeared there to greet the last patient on her schedule. I told her how, after literally taking a good, hard look in the mirror, I'd decided to ignore the bartender's warning—and considerable ridicule from Peter—and return to the tavern in search of her, which I'd done every night since.

"You don't get out much, do you?" I'd asked.

"Nope," she'd replied.

I'd gone on to tell her how the bartender—who, it

30

turns out, was also her uncle—finally gave me the name and location of her employer, apparently won over by my resolve.

"Or maybe he decided to let me be your problem instead of his," I'd said.

"He was looking out for you," she'd replied. "If Billy and Billy had seen you there ..."

"Wait. You mean both those asshole cops are named Billy? As in hillbilly?"

"Or billy club."

"Point made," I'd said.

"Likewise," she'd replied, with a wry smile.

A similar smile now appeared as she changed the subject of our concession stand conversation from her life circumstances to mine. "Let me guess. College student from Boston?"

"I start this fall. In Seattle. I just graduated from Amherst Regional High."

"Seattle," she repeated. "Goodness. And you really are a baby. What, eighteen?"

"Almost. My birthday's next month. The twenty-fifth. And, yes, that makes me a Virgo. Please, no jokes about—"

"But close to the cusp with Leo," she interjected. "Do you know your rising sign? What about your moon sign?"

"I thought your sign was your sign."

"Not exactly," she said. She raised her drink. "Anyway ... to your looming adulthood."

"To your impending divorce," I replied.

Another silence followed the "clink"—or, more accurately, soft thud—of Styrofoam cups as we sipped our sodas and reflected on our futures.

"You up for a walk?" she asked. "I want to show you something. Down the beach a bit."

"Sure," I said.

With the tide out, the flats stretched quite a ways from the dunes. We walked barefoot on the damp sand near the water's edge, long and distorted shadows following us. The low sun cast an amber glow on Tina's face.

"What will you study?" she asked. "Must be some special subject to go all that way."

"English," I answered, prompting her to raise an eyebrow. "It's a really good program, for both lit and creative writing." I gazed out at the bay. "And about as far away as I can get."

"*That*," she said, "I understand."

We walked in an easier silence. Tina pointed to a bird, which she identified as a tern, hovering offshore. It dove into the water and resurfaced with a fish in its beak. As it flew up and over land, another bird, which I recognized as a seagull, swooped in and pecked at the tern in midair. Tina charged in the direction of the birds, yelling and waving her arms. The tern dropped the fish onto the sand and jabbed its bill into the gull, which immediately broke off the attack, snatched up the fish, and soared away.

"Gulls are big bullies," Tina told me with a frown.

"Only so many fish in the sea," I said. "Sometimes you gotta fight to get yours."

"Hmm," she replied. She gazed across the flats toward the dunes, then grabbed my hand. "Come on."

I dug my feet into the sand, remembering my last foray beyond the ridge.

"Relax," she said. "I'm not going to jump you. You're still underage, and technically I'm still married."

I took in a breath and followed Tina into the tall grass sprouting up from the soft mounds. She led me to a clearing. We crouched at its edge. She held a finger to her lips initiating another silence, this one filled with curious anticipation.

After some time I heard a sound: *peep-peep*. Tina scanned the grass across the clearing. Another *peep-peep* sounded. Tina's eyes locked on the source. A small, sand-colored bird hopped from the grass into the clearing.

Peep-peep, it chirped.

After a moment, several similar birds emerged. We watched the members of the little flock dart across the sand in short bursts, stopping every now and then to peck at the ground. As Tina smiled at the sight, I felt my own mouth mirror—and inch closer to—hers.

She took my hand again and led me back through the grass and over the ridge.

"It was a signal," I said once we returned to the flats. "That birdcall. Telling the others it was safe to come out." I wondered if I was safe enough with Tina to tell her about Flora-Laura, whose corpse-like figure continued to haunt me with its indistinct visage.

"Piping plovers," she said. "I could watch them all day. You have to be careful or you'll disrupt their feeding. It's a threatened species. In part from the overpopulation of gulls." She broke away from me to pick up a discarded potato chip bag. "People make it easier for gulls to eat, and that gives them an unnatural advantage over their competitors." She crumpled and pocketed the bag and took my hand yet again.

I spread my fingers so that hers slipped between them. The fit felt perfect. Whatever you do, I thought to my anxious self, don't screw this up.

As we strolled back along the shore, Tina told me about her volunteer work with wildlife conservation organizations, which extended to turtles as well as birds. Growing up on the Cape, she'd dreamed of becoming a marine biologist. But she gave up on that after getting married right out of high school. Her husband was the front man for a popular local rock band. While Joe and the other members of Shark Bait smoked weed and jammed in a garage, certain they'd soon emerge as the next Aerosmith, she went to work as a receptionist in a dental office. While her husband and his chums played gigs in Boston bars, drinking up their share of the cover charge in the form of whiskey and tequila shots, she went to night school and, after several years of study, passed the licensing exams required to be a hygienist. She didn't mind being their sole source of financial support. She believed in him—maybe more than he believed in himself.

In hindsight, she blamed herself for not recognizing the toll his frustrated aspirations were taking on him in time to help him turn things around. He grew increasingly moody and distant from her and his band mates alike, eventually blaming the group's failure to break out on a lack of commitment from the drummer, who'd never missed a rehearsal—much less a show—but who'd managed to establish a career as an electronics technician on the side.

Joe's downward spiral culminated in a series of ugly blowups. One prompted the drummer to quit, which the lead singer took as proof he'd been right about him all along. Another saw Joe total the band's van—and nearly kill himself—in a drunk-driving accident.

I wondered—but didn't ask—if she suspected him of ever cheating on her. Everyone knew musicians get all the pussy they want.

By the time Tina finished telling me her story, we'd made it back to the concession stand near the parking lot and ordered burger baskets, which we ate in relaxed silence as we watched the sun descend across the bay.

"What about me reminds you of him?" I asked once we finished our meals, as the fiery orb began to drop out of sight. "Besides my totally losing it the other night."

"You have a spark in your eye," she said. "It's faint. But it's there. It's what makes you want more out of life. Makes you want to be a writer. Makes you want to change the world."

She was right that I felt a compulsion to force myself upon the world, to exert a positive impact on it, and that I imagined I'd do so through my writing. But the only "more" I wanted out of life—right then, in that particular moment—had nothing to do with those grand plans.

"What you said before, about me being underage and you being married. Does that apply to kissing?" I asked.

34

"Because I'd really like to kiss you now."

She turned away with a sigh, and I waited for what I trusted would be a delicate attempt to avoid breaking my heart. I waited and watched the other folks gathered on the beach: mostly couples coupling.

"I suppose a kiss would be okay," Tina said, then proceeded to initiate one.

We kissed, softly, and probably not as briefly as it seemed. The sound of applause—which for a fleeting moment I mistook to be for us—caused us to part lips and look out across the flats.

The sun had set, but its refracted rays painted the sky and the few clouds above the horizon vivid shades of red, orange, and yellow before giving way to a crystal blue expanse.

"Okay then. Goodnight," said Tina from behind the wheel.

I nodded at her, opened the passenger door, and stepped onto the curb in front of Mike's rented cottage. "Listen," I said as I leaned back into the car over the vacant seat. "I'm here for six more weeks. Maybe we could see each other every week?"

"You only want to see me once a week?"

"What? No! I meant *at least* once."

She pushed me away and reached for the door handle. "I'll pick you up Friday at seven," she said before pulling the door closed and driving off. I couldn't fault her for wanting to get back to Orleans. We both had early mornings ahead of us.

Once Tina's no-frills compact—an early '80s Dodge Omni—disappeared into the dark, I turned to face the cottage. The blue glow of the TV flickered through the large front window. I padded across the grass toward the entrance, trying to anticipate what might await me inside.

I stepped through the door into the living room and saw—and heard—Mike seated on the sofa with his head tilted over the back edge as he snored. Peter sat at the opposite end, watching a baseball game with the volume way down, a tallboy beer in hand, barely visible in the dimly lit room. I switched on a table lamp to its low setting, illuminating an impressive collection of pizza and Chinese takeout boxes and empty cans and bottles. Peter's attention remained on the screen.

"Sox winning?" I asked. I waited for a response until Peter nodded, still without looking my way.

The team was in the midst of a mediocre season and would end up finishing in fifth place in the American League East with an even won-loss record. That didn't matter to members of the Fenway Faithful like the Fullmans. They watched every game possible—in person when Mike could land tickets and get to Boston for an evening. I'd been fortunate enough to be invited to tag along on occasion over the years, including twice already that summer. My loyalties were superficial in comparison to theirs but still fairly obsessive by normal standards.

"You missed over half the game," Peter said, after I'd stepped into the adjoining kitchen area. "Pair of doubles for Boggs. He and Billy Buck each have a couple ribbies." I followed the team closely enough to know that meant Boggs had extended his hitting streak to twenty-five games. (It ended at twenty-eight a few days later.)

Wade Boggs deserves special mention, and not only because he's a Hall-of-Famer who won the AL batting title five times in a six-year stretch—including that very season with his career-high .368 average. He deserves special mention because of the unlikely way in which he accomplished his success. He was the rare slow runner who hit few home runs. He managed to offset that lack of natural athleticism through incredible discipline. Due to his refusal to swing at bad pitches, he drew a tremendous number of walks to go along with all the singles and doubles he sliced and poked into gaps. For Boggs, discipline also meant adhering rigorously to routine. He left home for the ballpark, sat down at his clubhouse locker, entered the dugout, took batting practice, and ran

36

wind sprints at exactly the same time and fielded exactly the same number of ground balls before each game. Although he isn't Jewish, he drew the Hebrew symbol for *chai*—or "life"—in the batter's box before every plate appearance. He ate chicken for every pre-game meal. (His long-time mistress claimed he showed a similar affinity for eating something else.) Even typically superstitious fellow professional ballplayers considered him extreme in all this. According to former teammates, he demonstrated another remarkable capacity for extremes by regularly consuming sixty or more beers during a single cross-country travel day. Wade Boggs, man of prodigious and mysterious powers.

Most people now remember the other player Peter mentioned, Bill Buckner, for the ground ball that would roll between his legs in the tenth inning of Game Six of the 1986 World Series, perhaps costing the team a championship. That's totally unfair to a guy who had a solid twenty-year major league career, including terrific seasons for Boston in '85 and '86. Maybe I'm more forgiving than some folks because my introduction to Red Sox fandom had prepared me for heartbreak. The year we moved to Massachusetts, the Sox and Yankees ended the regular season deadlocked atop the division and played a tiebreaker at Fenway Park. New York won the game—and went on to win the World Series—thanks in large part to a three-run blast over the Green Monster by light-hitting Bucky ("Fucking") Dent. Although I was devastated to see my new home team lose that way, part of me couldn't help but marvel at the underdog's heroics.

"Guess where I was, and who with," I said as I plopped into an armchair and cracked the beer I'd taken from the fridge.

Peter finally turned his gaze away from the game and toward me. "You found her?"

"We had a drink. Went to the beach."

"Are you shitting me? She's, like, a grown-up. A real woman."

"She's twenty-five," I said. "And married."

"Dude," he said. "She's another man's woman."

"They're not together. Like you said, she's a grown-up. She can do what she chooses."

"And what did you and Little Miss Grown Up—excuse me, Little *Missus* Grown Up—choose to do at the beach?"

"Oh, you know," I said. "Watched the sunset. But first we took a walk. Along the water." I paused for dramatic effect. "Up into the dunes."

Peter sprang from the couch, his hand raised for a high-five as he charged across the room. This time, I did not leave him hanging.

"Dude! You are a total stud!" he exclaimed, as though to the entire world. "And I'm like some kind of mad scientist who creates a monster."

Mike leapt to his feet and yelled something incomprehensible. He looked around the room groggily. "What's up? Sox winning?" he asked, adding before we could answer, "Ah, fuck it." He staggered down the hallway toward his bedroom.

Peter and I exchanged an amused snort. "Put a six-pack in the old man after working in the sun all day and he's all done," said Peter, shaking his head. He sat on the arm of my chair. "All right. Let's go. Details."

"A gentleman doesn't kiss and tell."

"Good thing you're no gentleman. How'd it compare? You know, to the other night."

I reflected on both his assertion and his question as I took a long, slow sip from my beer. I looked Peter right in the eyes. I swallowed the contents of my mouth, then smiled and zipped my lips.

CHAPTER FOUR

CHAMPAGNE PUNCH

"I've been thinking," Peter said. He paused long enough to drive a screw into the panel of drywall I held in place against the framing. "About how to celebrate your official entry into adulthood."

The grin on my face faded.

I grinned a lot those days. My two and sometimes three dates with Tina each of the last five weeks had filled me with a buoyancy I'd never known. I couldn't help but grin. I'd fallen in love for the first time.

Grinning was also a way to kiss and not tell. At least not explicitly. Or quite truthfully.

Our dates had ended with progressively intense make-out sessions, recently including fairly heavy petting through our clothes. We'd even migrated to the backseat of Tina's car to eliminate the gap between us and avoid the inconveniently placed—for our purposes—emergency brake. The closest we'd come to actual sex was when I'd once taken off her shirt and, after overcoming the challenge presented by an unfamiliar front clasp, opened her bra, glimpsing her perky breasts for the first time. As I caressed and then suckled them, she'd unbuttoned my shorts and started to unzip them before abruptly putting on her own emergency brake and separating herself from me.

If Peter and the pair of other youngish guys from the construction crew were inclined to misinterpret my frequent grinning, or my sudden lack of interest in other and especially younger women, or the newfound swagger in the way I smoked cigarettes and undertook various other routine activities, as an indication I was getting laid on a regular basis, so be it. Man of the Night? Make it Man of the Month.

I knew what I was about to tell Peter wouldn't win me his vote for Man of the Year. "I've been meaning to talk to you about that," I said. "Tina and I are—"

"You gotta be kidding me!" he replied. He drove a screw nearly through the drywall.

"It's our last weekend together," I said.

"It's *our* last weekend together," he replied. He stepped away from me to the next stud and drove screws into the drywall panel.

"I'll be back on Sunday night. That's still my birthday. Just you and me."

"Back from where?"

"Some swanky inn. Provincetown. She couldn't believe I've never been."

"Watch out for pirates, matey," said Peter.

"Pirates?"

"You know, butt pirates. P-town's full of 'em." He bumped his crotch against me, nudging me back until he stood where I'd held the panel, which no longer needed my support. He drove screws into the drywall and the stud behind. "She's not a fag hag, is she?" He lowered the screw gun. "Holy shit! Is that why she ditched her hubby? Is he a closet homo?"

"No," I replied. "I mean, I don't think so. How should I know?"

"You could ask her."

"She doesn't like to talk about him. Or their marriage. But that's not why she left him."

"What the hell *does* she like to talk about?" He faced

40

me. "Seriously. I wanna know."

"All kinds of things. The movies we go to. Books we've read. She loved *The World According to Garp* as much as I did. Both versions."

"I saw that flick," said Peter. "Good message. You should take heed. Don't let a married woman blow you in a parked car. She might bite off your dick when her husband rear ends you."

"Uh huh. We talk about other stuff, too. Society. Life. What we want to do with ours."

Peter shrugged. He moved to the far end of the drywall panel and drove screws into it and the last stud on that side.

"So what should I expect for Sunday?" I asked.

"I'm gonna have to rethink things after this curveball you threw me," he replied. "Expect the unexpected."

Commercial Street in Provincetown consisted of about what I expected from its name and location in a quiet fishing village turned artsy tourist mecca: an array of rustic to fancy shops, restaurants, bars, and hotels lining a narrow road traversed by throngs of pedestrians, bicyclists, skateboarders, and roller-skaters. (This was before rollerblades became popular.) There were even a few cars, with drivers either brave or ignorant enough to contend with all the other traffic.

Despite Peter's warning, I hadn't expected so many pairs of men to display affection for each other in public. I noticed a higher than usual number of female pairs as well, but most were more discreet in their interactions and could've been nothing more than friends.

"You've seen gay people before, right?" asked Tina. She'd noticed me staring at two handsome, muscular, shirtless men holding hands. One's chest was hairy; the other's was completely smooth. With their tanned skin, they looked like golden gods.

"Not ones I knew for sure were gay," I replied. "Some

kids at school, a few teachers. People call them fags behind their backs, and sometimes even to their faces. But nobody's ever admitted it." I could only imagine what people would've said—or done—to them if they had.

I also hadn't expected so many celebrities, much less one particular celebrity impersonator. As we approached a glitzy tavern, I spotted a group of tall, big-haired individuals in feminine attire congregated outside the door. One bore a remarkable likeness to Cher.

The real-life star's film *Mask* had come out that spring. But this was not drug-addict-biker-mom Cher. This was skimpy-sequin-dress Cher. I couldn't take my eyes off ... *her*?

"Whatchu lookin' at, little fan-man?" Not-Cher called out, prompting me to avert my gaze. "You're cute when you blush. Pussy—I mean cat—got your tongue? Wanna ditch the bitch and come get to know a *real* woman?" Not-Cher smiled at Tina. "No offense, darlin'."

"None taken," Tina replied through a laugh as we strolled by Not-Cher and friends.

I resisted the impulse to turn my head for another look once we passed. When Tina stopped to peer into the window of an art gallery down the block, I couldn't help sneaking a glance back.

Not-Cher blew me a kiss.

"That's a guy," I said. I'd definitely never seen a real, live crossdresser before.

"Yep," Tina replied. "You like that?"

"*What?*" I asked. I saw she was pointing at a watercolor on display in the window. "Oh." The image depicted a beachscape. "Sure," I said, then took a closer look. Piping plovers dotted the sand while gulls circled overhead. "Yeah, I really do."

Tina nodded and stepped inside. As I waited for her to return, Not-Cher and her backup queens exited their streetcorner stage into the establishment without even a wave.

"It's a gift," said Tina, after emerging from the store

42

and handing me a small matted print of the painting. "As a reminder."

"I'm never going to forget you," I said. I'd expected this moment to come at some point over the weekend. "No matter how far apart we are."

"Not of me," she said. "A reminder that there's more than one way to be a bird."

Oh-kay, I thought.

"Oh!" she exclaimed, taking my hand. "Come on."

She led me across the street to a tiny doorway barely visible between two upscale shops. According to the hand-painted, weathered sign, we were venturing into the mystic realm of a fortune teller: Tarot cards, crystal balls, and palmistry were all on offer; for a mere five dollars per reading, our destinies would be revealed.

Tina chose to have her fate determined by the tarot deck. I have no idea what cards she was dealt. Madame Cherie—who resembled the female impersonator from the nightclub across the street in more than name—insisted her readings were private affairs, to be witnessed only by the subject, and never to be shared. I passed on the cards and crystal ball, preferring to learn what the alleged seer could divine about me from my own body. By disclosing her findings, I now risk incurring Madame Cherie's everlasting curse. If you believe in that sort of thing.

"Your hands are soft for a man," she said, holding mine lightly in her own. Before I could tell her I did construction work, she let go of one and scrutinized the other.

"I'm right-handed," I told her.

"No matter," she replied. "On all young men, we read the left, for it shows your potential. Come back when you're older, and we'll read the right to see how you've fulfilled that promise." She felt the palm pad at the base of my pinkie. "A well-defined Mercury mount. You're a good communicator, with keen insight into others."

Favorable traits for a writer. Maybe there's some

truth to this stuff, I thought.

She pressed softly on the pads below each of the other fingers, then more firmly on the fleshy mound at the base of my thumb. "A somewhat elevated Venus mount. This predisposes you to promiscuity."

Or maybe, I thought, *it's all a bunch of malarkey.*

"Now we shall read the lines," she said. "That is, I will read the lines, and you can read between them." She squeezed my fingers together and bent them back, spreading my palm open. "Your heart line is deep and red. You are ruled by temperament."

"Does it say anything else?"

"About your love life?" asked Madame Cherie with a smile. "The line is long with quite a few small breaks. The possibility exists for a satisfying and lasting romantic relationship. But it's likely you will undergo a number of traumatic experiences along the way."

Great, I thought. As I wondered where Tina fit into that scenario, Madame Cherie said something about cross marks on my head line and my facing a series of inner crises.

"Ah! See how your fate line forks?" she asked. She pointed to a comparatively faint crease beginning at the bottom middle of my palm and soon branching apart. "That means your life could go in either of two quite different directions."

"Can I pick which one?"

"Your decisions in key moments most certainly will influence your destiny. But you won't necessarily be able to predict where the choices will lead."

So much for the big revelation, I thought.

"Your life line is deep," she said. "But not particularly long. Rather short, in fact."

"You mean I'm going to die young?"

"For your longevity we must look elsewhere." She rocked my hand back and forth as she eyed the base of my wrist. "Good news! You have *four* rascette lines. And strong ones. These here, like bracelets. Three is far more

44

common. You could live to be a hundred years old."

That might be a bit much, I thought, albeit with some relief.

"Because it's also deep, the shortness of your life line is more good news. You can overcome any physical problems you may develop." She took another look. "Hmm."

"What?" I asked.

"You have a second life line. This often reflects extra vitality. Initially I thought it was just that. It would go hand in hand—get it?—with your propensity for longevity and health."

"But ..."

"It's perfectly parallel to the first."

"And ..."

"This might be interpreted as a sign you'll lead a double life. Maybe you already are."

Hours later I was still trying to get my mind around what Madame Cherie had said. Not the double life part so much. That simply didn't make any sense. What, like being a secret agent? Or having a wife and kids in two different cities? But several other parts seemed like they might add up to something. I couldn't shake the feeling that my ability to influence my destiny, my chance at a satisfying and lasting romantic relationship, and my divergent fates were related. I stared at the lower half of my palm. The split occurred early in the line. Did that mean the decisive moment would occur early in my life?

"Whatcha thinking?" asked Tina.

"Sorry," I said, looking up and across the table at her. I reached for her hand and pressed my palm against hers. "I know we're not supposed to share any details. But didn't your reading give you a lot to contemplate?"

"Oh," she said. "I guess so. If you believe in that sort of thing." She withdrew her hand in order to lift her fork and stab at her salad. "How's your soup?"

45

I brought a spoonful to my mouth to find out. "Cold."

"It's Vichyssoise," she replied. "It's supposed to be."

With the mood lightened, we fell into casual conversation for the rest of our dinner, managing more or less effortlessly to avoid the three topics no doubt weighing most heavily on our minds: the confidential "fortunes" we'd been told; my imminent departure from the Cape; and what would happen that night when we shared a room—and bed—for the first time. In fact, until the moment our tuxedo-clad waiter strutted over to our table bearing a slice of chocolate cheesecake with a lit candle on it, there'd been no explicit acknowledgement of the occasion.

"You're not going to sing, are you?" I asked as he set the plate before me with a flourish.

"We don't do that here," he replied before sashaying away.

I gazed at the candle, trying to settle on the best possible—but still realistic—wish.

As soon as I'd blown out the flame, Tina slid a gift-wrapped package across the table. "Happy birthday!" She raised her champagne flute and emptied the contents.

"You already gave me something."

"That was just a whim. This is your real present. Well, one of them."

I tried—with moderate success—to disregard the suggestive implications of her remark as I picked up the small rectangular package and worked the ribbon off one end. I removed the tissue paper covering the box. The top was stamped with a familiar logo: a stylized letter P with an arrow jutting from it and the word Parker below.

What a crazy coincidence! "They make these in the town where I was born," I said as I opened the container. Inside rested a stainless steel ballpoint. I'd never owned a legitimate "fine writing instrument" before.

"This model, *The Classic*, was introduced in 1967," said Tina, with a wry smile I knew well by then.

I realized the pen's place of origin—like the year—

was no coincidence. Of course she'd known. She'd chosen it for that reason.

"Read the inscription," she said.

I rotated the shaft until I saw the words engraved on one side: *Mightier than any sword.*

"This is totally awesome," I said. "Thank you."

"Now eat your cheesecake," she replied. "I want to be in the room by midnight."

The bedside clock radio read 12:01. Smooth jazz emanated from the speakers. I sat on the edge of the bed, facing the closed bathroom door, from under which a wide, thin band of light spilled into the mostly darkened room. The only other illumination came from a lamp in the far corner on its dimmest setting. My often restless right leg bounced up and down of its own accord until I put a hand on my knee and pressed my foot into the carpet.

I waited for what seemed like an eternity before glancing back at the clock: 12:01.

The bathroom door opened and Tina appeared in the doorway, backlit. She wore a short chemise with, I soon discovered, nothing under it. I stood without taking my eyes off her.

She put out the bathroom light and glided across the floor to me. We kissed. I was caught off guard by the level of her ardor, which topped even our hottest backseat make-out sessions. Whatever self-restraint she'd utilized to control her passions had been shed in the bathroom with her classy dinner attire.

She lifted my arms and pulled my shirt up and over my head. She flung aside the short-sleeved polo—the dressiest top I had with me that summer—and ran her fingers across my chest. As her hands explored my upper body, caressing and groping, mine did the same to hers, first on top of the satiny garment, then beneath it. Her hands found their way to the front of my khakis.

Moments later I was lying on my back, naked, with Tina—still in her lingerie—pressed against me. She sat upright astride my midsection and looked me in the eyes.

"Are you ready?" she asked.

I nodded.

She reached under the pillow and extracted a condom.

Now *that's* maid service, I thought.

Tina tore open the wrapper and slid out the condom. She reached both hands behind her. I felt the latex ring press against me as she unrolled it to the base of my penis. She planted a hand on my shoulder and shifted her weight up and back, guiding me inside her with her other hand.

I was nearly overwhelmed by the intensity of feeling—the physical sensation *and* my emotional response. My eyes started to close, but I forced them to stay open, my gaze connecting with hers. As she rocked her pelvis against mine, I thrust upward, matching her rhythm. Our breathing fell into sync. The tempo of our movements increased, and our joined breath kept pace. We maintained eye contact right until the climactic fireworks blinded us.

Tina collapsed onto the bed beside me. I wrapped my arm around her and pulled her close. I finally understood what it meant to make love.

I had no idea how long it had lasted, but I was sure the bond would endure forever.

I glanced over at the clock: 12:08.

The ride back to Chatham the next day, like the hours we passed in Provincetown after awakening, transpired mostly in silence. The grin I'd worn with increasing frequency over recent weeks now felt etched into my face. I imagined it stretching from ear to ear like a cartoon character's. I assumed Tina was basking in a similar glow. Every so often we traded sighs.

As we neared our destination, I emerged from my

blissful reverie when it dawned on me that my time with my first genuine lover was on the verge of coming to an end. Peter would be waiting with something wild planned. Tina and I had to work all week. And I was scheduled to leave the Cape the next Saturday. How would we possibly maintain our connection from afar?

That worry vanished from my mind—momentarily at least—when I spotted a red VW Rabbit parked in the driveway of Mike's cottage. Two figures lurked in the front seats.

"Wait here a minute," I said to Tina, swinging open the passenger door before the Omni came to a complete stop along the curb, then hopping out as soon as it did. As I approached the Rabbit from behind, I confirmed my suspicion—and fear—with a glance at the motto on the license plate: *First in Flight*. But I had nowhere to run.

The driver's door opened, and my mother stepped out. "It's about time," she said, before noticing—and proceeding to stare at—her counterpart in the other vehicle. "Who's that?"

"What are you doing here?" I asked.

"Well," she said, returning her attention to me, "we've spent the last hour sitting in the car, wondering why—and where—you ran off without us."

"How could I run off without you when I wasn't expecting you?"

I didn't even know she was in the state. She'd finished her master's degree in public health education in June and gotten hired to work with Native American tribes in Nevada beginning that fall. I'd been under the impression she'd drive up from North Carolina later that week. We'd spend Labor Day weekend together in Amherst and then head toward our respective westward destinations. At least that was the plan.

"Peter wanted it to be a surprise," she said, explaining more than she realized. "Where is he, anyway?"

"That motherfucker!" I shouted as my hands balled

49

into fists.

"Andrew Lovell!" she shouted back. Then she fake smiled and tilted her head to one side as she looked over my shoulder. "Hello. I'm Bonnie. Drew's mother."

"Tina," replied my lover as she approached. "Drew's ... friend."

"It's okay," I said, reaching for her hand right as she folded her arms across her waist and clutched her sides. "I told her I'd met someone special."

"You told me you had a girlfriend. You neglected to mention she's not exactly a girl." She fake smiled at Tina again. "Is Drew *special* to you as well? Or do you always date minors?"

"Mom! I'm not a minor anymore."

"You were when she met you."

I stepped away and tried to calm myself. I saw that Bruce had gotten out of the car and was watching us, with obvious concern, across its roof.

"I never should've let you come out here without better supervision," said my mother, directing the comment toward her ex-husband as though he were to blame for the entire situation. "I looked in the window. There's trash all over the place! What kind of man houses two teenage boys in that environment?"

Certainly not Bruce, I thought.

"Go get your things together," she said.

"What? Why? I'm not leaving today. I have another week of work."

"Oh, you're leaving all right."

"I'm an adult now. You don't get to tell me what to do."

"If you expect me to help you pay for college, then you sure better believe—"

"I don't! I don't expect that," I said. I set my jaw. "I'm not going to college."

"What?" the two women asked in unison.

I strode over to Tina and took her hands. "I'm not going to Seattle. I'm not going anywhere. I want to be with you."

"Drew ..." said Tina.

"Not quite what you had in mind when you seduced my son, is it?"

"Drew," Tina repeated, ignoring my mother. "I can't let you do that. I can't let you give up your dream."

"I can write anywhere. I can learn what I need to learn to be a writer anywhere. You'll be my muse. My inspiration."

"No," she said. "That's not who I am for you."

"What do you ...? Why are you ...?" My confusion gave way to something else, and I felt tears well up. I tried to blink them away before gazing into her eyes. "I love you."

"No," she said again. "You don't. You're *in love* with me, but you don't love me."

"What does that even mean? There's no difference!"

"You barely know me."

"I do. I do know you. And you know me. You *see* me. Like no one else ever has."

"I'll always hold you in my heart," she said, blinking away tears of her own.

"I'm not. Going. Anywhere." I gripped her hands more tightly.

"Would you excuse us for a moment?" she asked our rapt audience, already leading me toward her car by the time my mother waved a hand in the air. "I have to tell you something," she said once we were partly shielded from my parents by the Omni. She took in a breath. "I had an appointment with my lawyer on Friday. To sign the papers."

"About time," I said. "I thought they'd never be ready."

Frankly, I hadn't been at all sure we'd make love in P-town, given that my turning eighteen removed only one of the two ethical barriers she'd felt in regard to our sexual contact. But if she'd signed the papers ...

"They've been ready," she said, after sighing out the

51

breath. "For weeks now. I've had three appointments to sign them. I cancelled the first two. On Friday I didn't cancel. But I still didn't sign the papers."

"I don't understand," I said.

"The papers are ready, but I'm not. I don't know when—or if—I will be." She shrugged.

I turned away and tried to process what was happening.

"That spark in your eye?" she said. "The one like my husband's. It's also what makes him do things that end up hurting him. And others. Because he can't accept the world as it is, and he doesn't know how to change it. If you let it, that'll drive you to destruction."

I yanked the car door open, grabbed my overnight bag, and slammed the door shut. "I guess this is goodbye then," I said, looking at her with spark-free eyes.

Tina kissed the tips of her fingers and extended them toward my cheek.

I ducked under her arm and marched toward the house. As I stomped across the yard, I heard my mother's relieved—and vindicated—sigh, and I felt Bruce's compassionate and sorrowful gaze.

By the time my mother appeared in the doorway to my room in the cottage—maybe a minute later—I'd already started cramming the rest of my clothing into my larger duffel bag.

"My baby," she said, opening her arms. "My poor baby."

I lurched into the embrace, my body convulsing in a sudden fit of sobbing as her upper limbs enfolded me against her trunk.

And that's how my "Summer of Love" concluded, just like the original had eighteen years earlier, with me cradled in my mother's arms, crying.

Peter returned in time to watch me load my bags into the hatchback of the Rabbit. I glanced over at his Camaro, parked where the Omni had been a short while before, and pantomimed tipping my cap at him as he looked on through the windshield with a satisfied smirk. He'd thrown me one nasty curveball all right, intensifying if not actually changing what had been the inevitable outcome to that day.

We've crossed paths a handful of times since then, on trips I've made to Amherst to visit family or attend high school reunions. Our interactions have reflected the different tracks we've followed since our friendship ended.

I never saw Tina again. She wrote to me once, though. It was a brief note, informing me she had indeed signed the divorce papers—the day after our tearful goodbye. She didn't say if she'd waited for my sake, or for her own. Perhaps she didn't know.

I knew something vital. I knew what I'd felt for her. What I'd felt *from* her. *With* her. I knew what was possible. Or at least I thought I did.

And I was resolved to settle for nothing less.

SECOND MOVEMENT
HOLY DAZE

CHAPTER FIVE

DEVIL'S NIGHT

The rap of knuckles on my apartment door jolted me from my spell.

I blinked several times, clearing the spectral image of yellow text on green background etched on my retinas from staring at my word processor monitor. I glanced at the dog-eared paperback amidst pages of notes on my desk. The book cover showed a frog-like creature—"the Under Toad"—along with the name John Irving and title *The World According to Garp*. My recent reverie, like many others overtaking me while I worked on that essay, had been prompted by recollections of connecting with Tina over our shared love for the story and the author's skillful telling of it.

Not that I was still hung up on Tina three years after our summer romance. Or that I remained inexperienced in the ways of love. By then I'd had sex with more women than I cared to—or could—remember. I'd fucked a faceless blur of white chicks, Black chicks, Latina chicks, Asian chicks, and at least one Native American chick. Welcome to Seattle! I'd fucked women of various ages—as old as forty—and assorted shapes and sizes. (I preferred petite ones. I liked how it felt to hold a woman smaller than me.) I'd even fucked a woman in a wheelchair. Well, I fucked her in a bed. But you get the point. Simply put, I did not discriminate.

The last was a particularly fascinating interaction of bodies. Wheelchair Girl was born with a spinal deformity that resulted in her having two vaginas. Only one worked in terms of reproduction. But both were "open for business" and "ribbed for her pleasure" with sensitive tissue. The divergence occurred inside a single set of labia. It took steady concentration, but if you got the angle and swivel right, you could slide from one vagina to the other with each thrust.

But none of those experiences satisfied me. I don't mean I never achieved orgasm. I mean the encounters left me unfulfilled. In the words of Bono, from a song released eighteen months earlier in the spring of my sophomore year, I still hadn't found what I was looking for.

The knuckles rapped on my door again, with a more insistent—and familiar—cadence.

I wasn't surprised to find my buddy Scott in the hallway when I opened the door. I *was* surprised to find him dressed in a pale blue '70s-style leisure suit with an open collar and a thick gold chain around his neck. The slicked back hair and vintage shades were more par for the course with him, as was the liter of whiskey in his hand.

"You weren't even gonna show," he said as he stepped past me, shaking his head. He strode across the living room and into the kitchen.

"What, for the trial run of your time machine? By the way, good to see you. Come in."

"You've got all day tomorrow to finish that paper," he said as he opened a cabinet. He took two tumblers from the shelf and poured several fingers of whiskey into each.

"This one's tricky," I replied. "I might use it as my writing sample for grad school."

"You can revise it later." He handed me a glass, then clinked his against it and sipped. "Hell, you will anyway. After it gets an A. And you know damn well you'll get in wherever you apply, Mister Perfect GPA." He sipped again. "But making *summa cum laude* is one thing, and making *someone cum loudly* is another."

"I don't even have a costume. That is what you're wearing, right? A costume?"

"Fuck you," he replied. He clinked his glass against mine, this time harder, then drained its contents. He slid the empty glass across the counter toward the sink and stepped past me, this time into the hallway leading to the rest of the apartment.

I raised the tumbler to my lips and sipped with a smile.

"Get in here!" he called.

"What, you need someone to hold it for you while you—" I cut myself short when I saw he'd gone into Becca's bedroom rather than the bathroom.

I hustled to join him before he did anything to earn me her ire. I found him standing in front of her open closet, inspecting items on hangers.

"She's got decent taste," he said. "And she's not exactly ugly. You bone her yet?"

"We're roommates. And she'd kill me if I spilled anything. It's all too small anyway."

I'd filled out nicely during college, adding a solid ten pounds of muscle through regular visits to the campus weight room. But I was still no Adonis.

Scott held up a black cocktail dress. "Short and tight, just right. If you wanna be this guy's date, that is."

"I'm jealous," said Kimmie, the much hotter—and slightly more vapid—of the two sorority girls leaning over me from opposite sides, as she applied lipstick to my puckered mouth.

"I know!" said Felicia, brushing my second eyelash with mascara. "Those cheekbones."

Scott's head appeared between the women's ample pairs of breasts, which were now positioned to stab him in

59

the ears with their seemingly ever-erect nipples. He looked at me for a moment. "Shit, bitch," he said. "You are kinda hot."

The three of them stepped back. Scott took a swig from the whiskey bottle.

I rose from the chair and peered at the reflection of me in the mirror. I had to admit they were right. The rouge accentuated my bone structure in dramatic manner. Between the cosmetics, the blond wig, and the stuffed bra under my roommate's dress, I made one sexy crossdresser.

I'm fucking insane, I thought, as I gestured for Scott to pass me the half-empty bottle.

I'm fucking drunk, I thought, as I guzzled the last swallows of whiskey from the bottle. At least I think I had that thought. When I woke up the next day, much of the night was a blur—in more ways than one, as you'll soon see. So my recollection of specific details can't be trusted as completely reliable. Some of my account comes from information provided later by Scott and others. Some comes from forensic evidence, like my bruised—and still rouged—face. And some comes from my own hazy impressions, formed in part, perhaps, by my imagining how the events *might* have unfolded based on how I saw myself as I sought to reconstruct the remembered fragments into a coherent narrative. Even if what follows isn't the objective truth, it's *my* truth.

I'm fucking drunk, I thought, gazing around the fraternity house social room. Costumed revelers packed the floor, drinking and laughing in pairs and small groups. My eyes landed on a solitary—and singular—figure: a petite she-devil in tattered red dress, pointed tail, and horns, with dark hair and eyes, olive skin, and beauty mark on her cheek.

As I soaked up her presence, an arm slid around my shoulders and a hand squeezed one of my fake breasts. I

60

swatted the groping paw away.

"Gimme that," said Scott.

I handed him the bottle, happy to be rid of the empty vessel.

"Dude. You finished it? Damn. Then I guess you're ready for action."

"I'm ready for her," I said, eyes still locked on She-Devil.

"Angie," he said. "Kirk's girlfriend. Our fraternity president."

"Ah."

"Absolutely off limits. What about Felicia? She likes your cheekbones."

"Eh."

"Her nickname among the guys is Fellatia. And she will."

"Oh. Okay."

I waded into the crowd with clear purpose. Sometime later, still searching for something I remembered being promised but unable to recall what that was, I encountered Scott again. More accurately, he hooked my arm with a crook as I wandered past, dragging me over to him and the shepherdess he was chatting up. He tugged on me right as I sipped from a beer I'd stood in line more than ten minutes to procure, sloshing the contents of the plastic cup onto my chin and hand. I whirled in the direction of the pull, truly ready for action now.

"Fucking jerk," I said, before realizing who was responsible for my sticky condition. "Oh. Hey. Cheers." I licked my hand, then tipped the cup at him and drank from it.

"Seems Little Bo Peep has lost her sheep," he said. "I told her I'd lend a hand, and soon find her woolly lamb." He slid his hand across his own crotch, in case I'd missed the innuendo of his lyrical imagery. "You cool flying solo?" he asked.

I waved him off, and he gestured with a chivalrous sweep of his arm for Little Bo to lead the way. Once she took a couple steps, he used the crook to lift her skirt and expose her lace panties. She restored her modesty by brushing away the crook and smoothing out the skirt. Not to be deterred, he turned the crook over and used the curved edge to prod her lower buttocks, prompting her to glance back with a *sheepish* smile. (Rimshot!)

"Aww. Did your boyfriend ditch you for some slut?" a voice asked.

I eyeballed the body, clad in tight black leather, of a woman with lines drawn on her face to represent whiskers. "You're one hot pussy," I said. "I wish I was a man so I could fuck you."

"Me-owww. Too bad you're not," she replied and walked away.

My gaze followed her until I noticed a pair of naughty cowgirls. *Giddyup*, I thought, and spurred my way toward them.

"Look at the drunk little floozy," said Felicia as I approached.

"Not too drunk to saddle up," I replied. "I may not be hung like a horse, but I'll give you one helluva *bucking* bronco ride."

"If you'll excuse me," said Kimmie, "I've got a craving for a Marlboro ... Man."

Fine, I thought, that leaves me alone with ... what's her name again? I squinted at her face. It blurred.

When she started to walk away, I grabbed her arm. *Got it*, I thought. "Come on, Fellatia. You know I—"

"What did you call me?"

"Fellatia," I repeated, hearing it this time. "I mean Felicia."

She yanked her arm free and stalked off after Kimmie.

Fuck me, I thought, knowing full well there was no chance of that happening—or even getting a blowjob from her—now. Oh well. Plenty of other options. I looked around the room and saw a sea of blurred faces, bodacious breasts, and bulging biceps.

62

Maybe I should go home, I thought. I took a wobbly step toward the exit and bumped into someone. I felt myself get shoved away and into several other people. I raised my hands in a silent apology as I fought to maintain my balance.

A tiny hand came to rest on my shoulder, steadying me and guiding me to a nearby wall. I leaned against it and gathered my wits.

"Are you okay?" asked She-Devil, also known as Angie, or, more formally and far less frequently, Angela. At least I assumed it was the same she-devil as I tilted my gaze from the unrecognizable blur of her face along the svelte but curvy form filling out the costume.

"Perfect," I said, straightening up. "But I wish I was a man so I could fuck you."

"What did you say to her?" a voice boomed as a much larger hand grabbed my shoulder and spun me around, then slammed me back against the wall.

"Stop it, Kirk," said my guardian she-devil. "He's harmless."

Kirk, his face hidden behind a Michael Myers mask—extra popular that year due to the release of the fourth *Halloween* movie—pressed a rubber butcher knife to my throat.

I shook off the last bit of dizziness from my recent whirlwind of activity and stared into his eyeholes. "You know why the killers in horror flicks use such big knives?" I asked. "They're symbols. Wish fulfillment. For ... inadequacies."

She-Devil laughed, and I glanced over at her. The beauty mark on Angie's cheek appeared as the lower half of her face came into focus.

"She knows what I'm talking about."

"Whip it out and stick it in!" she shouted.

"Sometimes it's so big," I added, "the creepy dude has to carry it around in his hand the whole time." I ran my tongue along the blade.

Angie laughed harder as Kirk pulled the knife away

in disgust. The rest of her face came into focus. Her dark eyes enchanted mine.

Kirk ripped off his mask. His blurred face looked around at the handful of frat brothers who'd stepped over to monitor the situation. "Show him the back door," he said.

Two of the frat brothers held my arms behind me while a third, costumed as Randy "Macho Man" Savage, delivered a series of blows—real ones—to my midsection. One landed squarely on my solar plexus, dropping me to my knees.

I looked up at Macho Man's raised fist. "What, no folding chair?" I asked, getting not even a snicker in response.

The punch connected with one of the cheekbones Felicia had so admired, snapping my head to the side and knocking me out of the grasp of Macho Man's tag-team partners and onto the ground.

I climbed onto my hands and knees. Stay down, I thought. I looked back as Macho Man flipped up the bottom of my dress.

He grabbed my hips and pounded his crotch against my ass. "You like that, bitch?" he asked. "Show up here again and you'll really be fucked."

He shoved me forward, and I sprawled face first into the damp grass. I heard laughter and high-fives as Macho Man and friends left me to rejoin the party.

I rolled onto my side and curled into a ball.

I awakened still lying on my side in a ball but no longer on the fraternity house lawn. Apparently I'd managed to find my way home. I peered over the edge of my bed at the wig and lumps of padding on the floor, and it all—well, parts of it—came flooding back.

Becca appeared in the doorway. She sat beside me

and pressed a baggie filled with ice to my upper cheek.

I flinched from the sting of cold and tenderness as she held the cubes against the sore spot, which soon went as numb as I felt inside.

"Sorry about your dress," I said. I could only imagine the stains I'd picked up: grass, mud, beer, and perhaps even blood.

"Let me guess," she replied. "Scott had something to do with this. Not the dress." She indicated my general condition. "This."

"He would've had my back," I said.

She rolled her eyes, shook her head, and sighed. "I'm surprised he didn't convince you to go as the Statue of Liberty," she said. "Since you're already carrying a torch for him."

That's clever, I thought. But also ridiculous. And he totally would've had my back.

"You would've had my back, right?" I asked as Scott prepared to knock.

He lowered his fist. "You're my bud," he answered.

Exactly, I thought.

"But they're my brothers," he added. He touched the fading bruise on my cheek. "And I told you she was off limits."

I brushed his hand away from my face. "... Yeah. I definitely had it coming."

"I definitely had it coming," I repeated moments later, having moved from the hallway into the room on the other side of the door.

Kirk stared at us from his perch across the floor.

"Completely out of line," I continued. "Way too much to drink. Couldn't see straight."

"He had no clue who he—" Scott said before being cut off.

"I get it. It happens," said Kirk. "Hell, I've been there. Once or twice."

"That's not who I am," I said. "I need you, and her, to know that."

"Yeah, well, I may have overreacted myself," he replied. "It's just ... when you've got a girlfriend as hot as Angie ..."

"No doubt!" chimed in Scott.

"She says I have trust issues. I should've known you were no threat."

"This guy? Fuck no. He totally respects the Guy Code. Right, dude?"

"Totally," I said. "Another man's woman."

Kirk rose from his seat on the desk and approached where we sat beside each other on the bed. Scott stood to meet him, and I followed suit. "It says a lot," he told Scott, "that you were willing to come in here and vouch for him." He looked at me. "I respect this man's judgment. If Scotty has your back, you must be cool." He extended his hand. "No hard feelings on my part."

"Likewise," I said, clasping his hand for a couple vigorous pumps.

"We could probably find a place for you. Here at Sigma Chi."

"I'm a senior," I said.

"The benefits of brotherhood extend long after you graduate," he replied, then smiled and winked at me. "At least that's what the brochure says."

I chuckled and looked at Scott. He shrugged.

"Think it over," Kirk continued. "It'd be a chance to prove what kind of man you are."

"I'll give that careful consideration," I said, then led Scott toward the door.

"Oh, hey," Kirk said before we'd quite made it there. "You around for Thanksgiving?"

Scott turned to face him. I did the same.

"Angie wants to have some kind of orphan dinner thing. At her place. You should come. Her sister Dina will be there. So will this exchange student from France they've been hanging out with. Both hotties."

"Sounds good to me," Scott replied.

"What do you say, Drew?" Kirk asked. "You in?"

This could be trouble, I thought.

"Sure," I said.

CHAPTER SIX

HORN O' PLENTY

I felt the back of Scott's hand brush against my scrotum as he reached between my legs.

"Hut hut hike!" he barked.

I thrust the ball into his waiting palms and sprinted forward as Kirk, lined up facing me, backpedaled, then turned and ran alongside me. I glanced over my shoulder and saw Scott motion to the right as he cocked his arm. I stutter-stepped left and then broke hard on a diagonal in the other direction, wrong-footing Kirk for a moment and creating enough space between us to give Scott a clear target. I caught his pass in stride and raced downfield, lifting the ball overhead with one hand as I neared the end zone in what was almost a premature celebration. Right after I crossed the goal line, Kirk tackled me, sending the ball flying from my grasp.

I scrambled to my feet, retrieved the ball, and spiked it close to where Kirk remained on the ground.

"Easy there!" he said.

"That's two-hand touch?" I replied.

Scott arrived, out of breath, before Kirk and I could engage in further unsportsmanlike conduct. My scoring mate and I exchanged a high-five.

"Okay! All tied up. Drew's back on D," said our

designated QB. He'd played baseball in high school and had a far more accurate arm than either of us. He offered Kirk a hand. "Come on then, Captain," he said in a vaguely British—Irish?—accent I'd never heard him use, "let's be winning it for the United Federation of Brothers."

Sigma Chi, I thought, is apparently a fraternity *and* labor union.

"Crap," said Kirk after glancing at his wristwatch as he reached to accept Scott's boost. "Angie wants to eat at two. We better get over there."

"That's cool," Scott replied. "I can catch the end of the Cowboys game." He picked up the ball and flipped it to me. "The inaugural Turkey Bowl MVP goes to Lightning Lovell for his late-game heroics."

"Sorry about that takedown," said Kirk, patting me on the shoulder as we started toward the parking lot. "And nice move."

Damn straight, I thought, then considered he might be sincere. I acknowledged his gesture with a nod. Maybe he's not so bad.

Once we got to our cars, Kirk took another look at his watch. "You know," he said with a grin as he reached through his open passenger window and into the glove compartment. "We probably do have time for a quick bone." He held up a fat doobie.

"Oh yeah!" said Scott.

Nope, I thought, he's not so bad at all. And the weed proved to be fantastic.

"Hey," said Kirk after we'd burned the joint to ashes and sat on the hood of his car for a silence of indeterminate length. "You know what they say about ties, right? Well ..."

"How long have you and Angie been sisters?" I asked.

"All our lives," replied Dina. "That's how it works."

"Ohhhh. You're *sister* sisters."

Kirk's pot-inspired plan to cajole them into making

70

out no longer seemed so appealing. With any luck, he'd forgotten all about it by now.

"I look like a sorority girl to you?" she asked.

No, I thought, *you most certainly do not*. Between her frizzy blonde shock of hair, the star tattoo on her neck, and her eyebrow piercing, she appeared more streetwise than stuck-up.

"For that matter," she added, "does *she*?"

"Not exactly," I said, although in Angie's case I could imagine the possibility, even if she didn't quite fit the classic type.

"Cheers to that," she replied, leaning in from her seat on the armrest of the chair I'd occupied, still fairly stoned, for some time. She tapped her wine glass against my beer bottle.

"What're we toasting?" asked Johnny, raising his bottle.

Those were the first words he'd spoken in my direction since the cursory greetings we exchanged upon our arrival. Not that I blamed him for focusing his attention on the two young women on either side of him on the sofa.

Now they all looked our way, and we theirs. They made quite the multicultural threesome—if stereotypically so—with his muscular Black body and headful of dreads between the lithesome and pale French exchange student Sabine, who wore her hair in a stylish bob, and Melissa, a Latina whose waist-length, super-fine black tresses provided a linear contrast to her thick feminine curves. Between them, the sofa overflowed like a cornucopia of sexiness.

"To individuality," said Dina, capturing the essence of the entire sequence.

Everyone lifted their drinks and sipped. Except for Scott. He stood in the center of the room, transfixed by the images on the television, which emanated football sounds at a volume unnecessarily loud for the short distance between him and the TV.

71

"So, Sabine," I said, seizing an opportunity to pose a question I'd formulated soon after our introduction. "Has anyone ever kidnapped you and tried to entice you into conjugal union?"

She looked at me blankly. Could she really be unaware of the origins of her name?

"You know," I added, "like in the legend. From ancient Rome."

"The Rape of the Sabine Women," said Dina.

"You want to know if someone tried to rape me?" asked the visitor from modern France.

"No!" I replied. "It wasn't that kind of rape. Not a sexual assault. More like an appeal. A heroic rescue even. The men persuaded the women to marry them. Voluntarily. By promising them rights. Rights they didn't have at home under their oppressive fathers."

"And did the men keep those promises?" asked Melissa.

Not exactly. I sighed and shrugged.

"Uh huh," she said. "So it was a rape after all."

"That's one fucked-up story," said Johnny.

"Not everyone thinks so," I replied. "Hollywood made a film based on it. A hit musical. *Seven Brides for Seven Brothers.*"

"I watch this movie," said Sabine. "I like it very much. All the dancing."

"See," I said to Johnny, but intending it for Melissa as well.

"Wasn't that the name of a TV show?" asked Dina. "From when we were, like, in middle school. With that guy who plays MacGyver now. And one of the kids from *Stand by Me.*"

"River Phoenix," I said, relieved to discuss a new topic. "He's also young Indiana Jones in the next movie. Keep your eye on him."

I meant that as a prediction of career success, not as a warning about the dangers of drug use, which would end his life five years later, or in regard to his commitment to political and social activism, about which I knew nothing at the time.

Dina took it another way altogether. "Oh, I will," she said. "He's hunky."

"Speaking of hunky," said Johnny, "check out that gorgeous mound of flesh."

I looked over and saw Kirk place a platter of carved turkey at the head of a buffet line of traditional items. My eyes soon locked on even more alluring flesh, as Angie made her first appearance of the day, emerging from the kitchen with a basket of rolls, which she set on the other end of the table. I watched her remove, fold, and set aside her apron.

"You're kind of obvious," Dina whispered in my ear.

I glanced at her, then at the sofa. Johnny and Sabine peered at the spread, but Melissa smirked in my direction. I turned my best poker face toward the table, where Angie and Kirk stood waiting to address the room.

"Hey, Scott. Mute that for a sec," said Kirk. After getting no response, he waved at him. "Scotty!"

Another moment passed, then Scott casually turned to Kirk with an inquisitive gaze.

"Kill the sound."

"Aye aye, Captain," Scott replied with a lilt, then aimed a remote control at the screen and lowered the volume, accompanying each press of the button with a laser-gun sound effect.

This time I got it, recognizing the accent as Scottish and now understanding his earlier reference to the Federation. Watch out for Klingons circling Uranus, I thought, amusing my half-baked self to no end. I wondered if I'd been recruited to play the role of Spock or Bones.

"Okay, people," said Kirk, "let the feasting begin!"

As we rose in unison, Angie raised a hand. "Before we start ..."

"Please don't make us all say what we're thankful for," interjected her boyfriend.

"No one else has to say anything. But I would like to say I'm thankful to be sharing my favorite holiday with each of you. Today, this group is my family."

"To family," added Dina, "old and new, permanent or temporary."

"Now can we eat?" asked Kirk.

"Sabine," said Angie, "since this is your first Thanksgiving, please do the honors."

"It will be my pleasure," replied the foreigner. She pranced across the floor and picked up a plate. "I love the turkey leg!" she said as she lifted a drumstick from the platter. She gaped at it.

Angie grabbed the other drumstick and traded with Sabine, then thrust the half-eaten one at Kirk. "Munchies much?" she asked.

Kirk bugged out his eyes, growled, and bit down on the bone held in her hand, eliciting a chorus of laughs.

"Who's ready for dessert?" asked Angie, eliciting a chorus of groans.

If the game plan had been to introduce Sabine to a true American spectacle of overeating, we'd all earned MVP awards.

"I know what we need," said Johnny. He nodded at Kirk, who nodded back.

Kirk moved his plate from his lap to the floor and climbed out of the recliner he'd taken for the meal. He extracted a small mirror and razor blade from the drawer of a nearby end table and brought them to Johnny, who dug a small paper packet out of his pants pocket.

Illogical, I thought. Everyone knows cocaine suppresses appetite.

"I never get hungry on coke," said Angie.

Vulcan mind-meld, I thought. And no-handed, no less.

"Weird," replied Johnny. "I totally crave sweet things when I do it. I eat a ton of that shit. But I never seem to get fat." He lifted his shirt to showcase a ripped set of abdominals.

"I feel my appetite getting *whet* already," said Dina.

"Even if it doesn't boost our appetites, it'll offset the tryptophan and boost our energy," Johnny added. "So we don't sit here like slugs all night."

As you may know, it's not actually the tryptophan in turkey—which contains levels of the substance comparable to other meats—but rather the heavy dose of carbohydrates that causes the drowsiness common after holiday meals. As you probably don't know, scientific studies have found evidence that cocaine has a more complex relationship to metabolic function than long believed, increasing appetite for fatty foods but inhibiting fat storage. So Johnny's claim—his intuition anyway, if not his reasoning—was more on the mark than any of us realized.

Before long, Johnny had arranged eight thin rows of powder on the mirror. While he parceled out the coke, Kirk rolled up a dollar bill. They nodded at each other, then passed the items to Sabine.

"*Merci*," she said, and snorted a line.

I watched the mirror and tooter make their way from Sabine to Melissa to Dina, both of whom partook without pause, then to Angie, who shrugged before ingesting a line. She handed the paraphernalia to Kirk, who took his turn and sent the kit along to Scott. He sniffed a line, then held out the mirror toward me.

"I'll pass," I said. I hadn't done coke in over three years, since the night I'd gotten into a barroom brawl with an off-duty cop. "I don't like the way it makes me feel. Or act."

"That's cool," said Johnny. "I'll do mine and yours. But when we pair off for sex, I get two women, and you're gonna have to jerk it."

"*What?*" I asked.

"The family that plays together stays together," said Dina.

75

Kirk grinned and nodded.

"We're just fucking with you, Drew," said Angie.

Kirk's face and shoulders fell.

"I wasn't," said Johnny, reaching for the mirror. "At least not about this part." He snorted a row of powder.

"One line isn't gonna kill you," said Scott.

Probably not, I thought. I looked at Angie, who shrugged.

Johnny glanced up at me as he moved the tooter from one nostril to the other.

"Wait," I said.

"I can't wait," I said to Angie as I set a pile of dirty plates in the sink, "to taste your pie." Go bold or go home, I thought. Amazing the effect a single line of cocaine can have on one's courage—and, as you'll soon see, on other psychological and physiological functioning.

"Well," she replied. "First it needs cream."

Damn, I thought, I really like this girl.

"Care to whip some up for me?" She handed me a carton of heavy cream and metal bowl she'd just removed from the refrigerator.

"I can't think of anything that would give me more pleasure," I told her, and meant it. I raised an eyebrow when I noticed a whisk in the bowl.

"Not used to beating it by hand?" she asked.

Correction, I thought, I *love* this girl. At least I *could* love her, once I get to know her better.

"Sugar's on the counter," she said, then bent to retrieve something from a low shelf in the fridge, giving me a direct—and breathtaking—view of her rear end. I stood there, admiring its perfection, until she straightened and turned around with a pie in each hand. I averted my gaze. "Something wrong?" she asked.

"I'm sorry," I stammered. "About the party. What I said to you there." That actually was what I'd come into the kitchen to tell her.

76

"Don't ever apologize," she replied. "Not to me anyway." She slid the pies onto the counter, keeping her back to me. "Nothing you or anyone else says—or does—can really hurt me."

"What are you, Wonder Woman? I'm trying to take responsibility for—"

"That's important," she said, turning to face me. "Being responsible for your actions. Accountable. But only to yourself. You're the only person you owe an apology. Or forgiveness."

"Why did you have Kirk invite me here today?"

"I didn't. I simply told him he needs to prove he trusts me. He did the rest." She smirked. "I bet it's killing him we're in here alone right now. But he doesn't dare come check up on me."

Kirk *had* looked rather flummoxed when I got up to follow her.

"You," I said, "are a mischievous one."

"So are you," she replied. "I see it in your eyes. Yours is a good mischievousness."

"And yours?"

"I wasn't costumed as Wonder Woman." She took a step toward me so that our chests nearly touched.

This can't happen, I thought. Not here. Not now. I tried to swallow the lump in my throat, which only made it worse. I felt my airway constrict.

"Are you okay?" asked Angie.

No, I suddenly wanted to scream, I'm *not* okay. *I'm suffocating*, I yearned to cry from the mysterious depths of my soul. My field of vision narrowed to the astonishing creature before me. Reflected light—its source unknown—formed a halo over her head.

Angel of what? I wondered, as darkness closed in on me.

I looked up at the smiling face of my savior.

"Dude," said Scott. "We thought you were dead."

"If it weren't for Scotty, you probably would be," Kirk added.

"You most definitely would be," said Dina.

"What happened?" I asked, trying to see past the three figures crowded over me. *Where'd she go?*

"You fainted," a comforting voice answered from beyond my view. Scott, Kirk, and Dina withdrew, and Angie crouched beside me. "You stopped breathing."

The cocaine, I thought. No, I *knew*. And I knew as surely I'd never do that drug again. (I still haven't.)

"Would you like to sit up?" she asked.

I nodded.

Scott crouched on my other side. The two of them supported me as I raised my upper body and slid back against the refrigerator. From my new vantage point, I saw Melissa, Sabine, and Johnny looking on from across the room. Kirk and Dina stood closer.

"Scotty gave you mouth to mouth," the former informed me.

"It was kinda hot," added the latter.

"Much appreciated," I said to Scott, half-wishing I was giving those thanks to Angie.

"I've got your back," he replied. "When it really counts." And I believed him.

"Now that the excitement's over," said Johnny, "how 'bout dessert?"

"Is that all you think about?" asked Melissa. "Food and sex."

"No. I think just as much about getting high. And catching the perfect wave. Oh, and particle physics, Renaissance humanism, and the destruction of the Amazon rainforest."

"Everyone can go wait in the living room, and I'll bring out the pies in a few minutes," said Angie as she stood.

That's right, I thought. She and I had unfinished business. "I still owe you that cream."

"Maybe another time," she replied. "We need to chill.

78

I mean, the stuff does. It's been sitting out too long." She collected the carton and bowl and stretched above me to put them in the overhead freezer compartment.

Do not so much as glance up, I thought, picturing how her breasts would look from that angle, and then from every angle I could imagine.

"And you're in no condition for that sort of activity," she said.

She crouched down and took hold of one of my arms. Scott gripped the other. They lifted, and I planted my feet beneath me and straightened my legs. I nodded, and they released me. I wobbled for a moment, then regained my equilibrium. Angie flashed me a polite smile, then turned to a cabinet and opened it.

"You good?" asked Scott.

I watched Angie reach into the cabinet for a stack of dessert plates. Kirk slid his arms around her waist and pressed his hips against her from behind. She arched her back, and he nuzzled his face against her neck.

Another man's woman, I thought.

"... Yeah," I said.

CHAPTER SEVEN

FIRST NOEL

"Need a minute?" my brother asked.

I nodded.

"Sure brings back memories, huh?"

I nodded.

Looking up at the house from Adam's car, I couldn't help but travel back in time—in my mind, that is—to childhood summers the two of us and our sister spent visiting our father, his second wife, and our two stepbrothers and one half-brother. This Christmas reunion would be the first gathering of us all in many years.

"We were kinda shitty to you," said Adam.

My wrists burned from the rough rope binding them. My eyes burned from gravel dust in the air along the unpaved driveway. Neither compared to the burning in my gut from my hatred for the bullies I called brothers. I looked at my opponent and felt my anger shift from its rightful source in his direction.

You've brought this on yourself, my friend, I thought, justifying what I was about to do. It was stupid of me to claim I could beat him up with my hands tied behind my back. But he was the one who'd accepted the offer from my older brothers to make me prove it.

He charged at me, his own eyes burning with a fire I'd never seen in them. We'd been playmates for years, me—age twelve—and this ten-year-old who lived next door to my dad in the Wisconsin countryside. Earlier that summer we'd spent a night camping under the stars down by the creek dividing our families' lands and ended up in the same sleeping bag, comparing my changing body to his prepubescent one and exploring possible interactions based on my rather limited understanding of what I'd heard some "deviant" men did together.

Since then, I'd allowed my shame to express itself as abusive behavior. I even coerced him to get down on all fours and let our male dog, drawn by the scent of his family's bitch in heat, hump him from behind, while I roared at the sight. So I wasn't surprised he jumped at the chance to fight me with a handicap designed to offset the considerable difference in our physical maturity. He had an opportunity for payback. And he was set on exacting it.

Except my claim, while stupid in the sense I should've known it would be put to the test, turned out to be correct. I really could—and did—beat him up with my hands tied behind my back. I simply sidestepped his attack and tripped him to the ground, where I kicked and kneed him in the ribs and gut until he was bawling like a little girl.

As my brothers pulled me off my victim, I recalled the last time they'd compelled me to take part in so horrifying an event. Two summers earlier, when I was ten, Adam and Ken—both thirteen at the time—held my arms behind my back and forced me onto my knees, while Bob—nearly fifteen—duct-taped my favorite G.I. Joe to a stake he then planted in the sandpit behind the house.

"See how we treat our POWs around here?" asked Ken, who later graduated from the U.S. Air Force Academy.

His elder brother doused the action figure with

gasoline and put a match to it, engulfing Joe's entire body, including his 1970s "life-like" hair, in flames.

Even in their early teens, Bob and Ken, of Norwegian stock, were built like lumberjacks. Both went on to become state champion wrestlers and all-conference linebackers. They made Adam, whom my parents adopted and who was already more muscular and athletic than I would ever be, seem almost puny.

Maybe that explains why Adam went along with their bullying even though it meant inflicting harm on me. Under most circumstances, he was my ally and protector. His betrayal of me in these situations may have hurt more than anything else.

I now realize all three of them were doing the best they could under the influence of deep insecurities, conditioned beliefs, and internal pressures of their own. But all I could see at the time was malicious behavior.

"Look at the baby cry!" exclaimed Bob.

Tears indeed streamed down my face, due to irritation by black smoke and noxious fumes from melting plastic as well as the emotional trauma. Before long, my cherished man-doll was reduced to a charred mass.

"Now let's get Shim into the garage and take care of those girly locks," said Bob, using their gender-splicing nickname for me and my shoulder-length hair.

All three of them had buzz cuts. Soon enough, so would I.

The passenger door flew open and a pair of sturdy hands grabbed me and dragged me from the car—and back to the present from my not-so-nostalgic trip down memory lane. Bob, a mountain of a man at age twenty-five, clutched me against his broad, hard chest.

"How you been, kid?" he asked, releasing me from the bone-crushing embrace. He passed me to the waiting Ken, who applied a brawny arm to my head like a vise grip and used the knuckles of his fist to grind "noogies" into the top of my skull.

"Welcome home, Wonder Boy," said the younger of my stepbrothers through his half-clenched and completely square jaw. Now in the first year of his post-academy military service, he still wore the same crew cut he'd borne since his early teens.

"Where you stationed these days?" I asked, once he liberated me from the headlock.

"Dad didn't tell you? First of the year, I'm headed to Fairchild. In Spokane. You can visit me on the base."

"Yeah, maybe," I said. I wondered if he understood just how far that was from Seattle. Not that I'd consider setting foot on a military base in any case.

"They'll have a good barber there, right?" asked Bob, tugging on my shaggy hair.

A floodlight illuminated the yard. Bob and Ken stepped aside as our father descended the sole step from the front porch and crossed the grass. I started to open my arms for a hug but caught myself in time to avoid an awkward moment when I saw him extend a hand. We shook.

"Good to see you, son," he said.

"Yeah, Dad. You, too."

"Well, come on inside. Your brothers will get your bags. Right, boys?"

"You betcha!" exclaimed Bob and Ken in unison. They stampeded to the open trunk and more or less elbowed Adam out of the way to grab my duffel bag and knapsack. They followed Dad into the house, leaving Adam and me on the lawn.

"*Step*brothers," I said. "You're my real brother."

Adam slid an arm around my shoulders.

"How's it been going here so far?" I asked.

"Oh, you know," he replied. "Long, uncomfortable silences interrupted by brief moments of extreme tension."

The scent of bacon and coffee finally lured me out of my quarters in the midmorning. I'd retreated to the den, or "animal room"—so-called for the images of lions, zebras, and other big game on the wallpaper—soon after my arrival the night before and hidden out there since. As I stepped into the kitchen, the aromas that enticed me gave way to the odor of cigarette smoke.

"Frankly, I'm glad she didn't come," said my fiftyish stepmother Betty between puffs. "She's dumb, ugly, and a bitch."

The three twentysomethings making up her audience—Diana, Bob's fiancée Karen, and Ken's girlfriend Barbie (yes, believe it or not, all-American male Ken dated a blonde bombshell named Barbie)—nodded their agreement, which I deduced to be in regard to Adam's new, much older wife Pamela (not Eve but perhaps with shades of Lilith), who'd stayed in Massachussetts to spend the holiday with her adult son and his family while my brother joined our sister and our young niece and nephew on the trip. I wondered if Diana really felt that way about our sister-in-law. Pam could be a bit abrasive at times, but I got along fine with her.

"Morning, Uncle Drew!" five-year-old Stephanie called from where she was stretched out in the middle of the linoleum floor. "Wanna color?"

"Morning, sweetheart. Maybe after breakfast." I nodded toward the circle of faces now staring in my direction. "Morning, ladies. Where's everybody else?"

"Your father and the boys are going hunting," Betty replied. "Christmas Eve tradition."

With precision timing, Dad stepped in from the hallway, dressed in bright flannel and carrying a rifle pointed down through the crook of his other arm. Bob and Ken, in similar attire and stance, trailed closely behind. The two of them went to the table and kissed their significant others. Then Adam walked in, likewise outfitted for the hunt.

I gaped at him, and he shrugged. I understood. "Why

85

didn't anyone wake me?" I asked.

"And cut short your beauty sleep?" replied Ken.

"Bet you're excited to have someone to play with," Bob said to Stephanie as he tussled her hair, "while the men are outside."

Stephanie looked up at me with a smile.

"I'd like to come along," I said, with a nod to Adam before turning to my father. "You got an extra one of those?"

Stephanie sighed and resumed coloring.

"You ever fire a gun?" asked Dad.

"I won a prize for marksmanship at Boy Scout camp."

It was my biggest accomplishment in terms of the organization's mission. If they awarded merit badges for drug and alcohol consumption, I'd have been highly decorated.

"I did not know that about you," replied my father, nearly smiling.

There's *a lot* you don't know about me, I thought. And vice versa. Maybe it's not too late to change that.

Suddenly a shot rang out! (I've always wanted to write that.) The blast came from an enormous brush pile where Dad had sent Bob and Ken to flush out any varmints holed up inside, near the sandpit where they once incinerated G.I. Joe.

Meanwhile, at the bottom of a steep hillside, lying in wait for the frightened prey, stood the family patriarch and his three "less-experienced"—i.e. presumed incompetent—hunter sons. The other member of our coalition was my sixteen-year-old half-brother Billy. His participation in this rite of male bonding surprised me, considering only three years earlier he'd sat on our father's lap and tearfully announced he wanted a sex-change operation. In response, his parents withdrew him from the local public school, where he'd undergone severe bullying, and enrolled him in a fancy private school upstate. The new environment seemed to have straightened him out—although perhaps not quite to his mother's full satisfaction.

"There!" said Dad, pointing at a rabbit darting along the hilltop.

We three Mouseketeers shouldered our guns.

"This is no rifle range. Quarry's moving fast. Remember to lead him."

I glanced over at Adam. His gun barrel dropped a couple inches right before he fired. Dirt flew into the air partway up the slope.

Dad shook his head. I resolved not to let him down.

I peered through the scope and locked my sights on the blur of fur, tracking it a few seconds to gauge its speed, then panned the rifle slightly ahead as I squeezed the trigger.

The critter went tumbling head over heels right before I felt a powerful recoil and heard a loud retort.

"Way to go, Eagle Eye!" my father shouted, clapping me on the back.

Billy lowered his unfired gun with a frown.

Wait, I thought. I did it?

Did I ever. Once we joined the others atop the hill, we discovered I'd hit my target right in the neck. In Dad's words, it was a "perfect kill."

"Nice shootin', big man," said Bob, tussling my hair much like he'd done to Stephanie.

"You sure you don't wanna join the service?" asked Ken.

We started toward the house, with Dad carrying the carcass by its hind legs. Approaching the back deck, where the two of us would dress my kill—my perfect kill—while the others continued the hunt in the woods across the road, I saw Stephanie standing in the yard with Diana.

"Uncle Drew," she said, "why'd you shoot the bunny rabbit?"

Fuck. Why had her mother let her watch that? In the absence of Stephanie's father, who abandoned my sister for another woman after impregnating Diana with my now three-year-old nephew Calvin, I'd become one of the little girl's primary father figures. I'd spent each summer of my college years living with them in Amherst, exchanging assistance with childcare for room and board.

"Well, honey," I replied, crouching to look into her innocent eyes as I tried to think of a reasonable response. I remembered something my father had told me when I was around her age. "Rabbits are pests. They get into Grandpa's garden and eat the vegetables he grows for us."

"You're a mean person," she said, then ran into the house. Diana shrugged and followed.

I peered into the faces of the men around me, hoping one would offer a word or two of wisdom—or at least understanding. Blank expressions met my gaze until I reached Adam, who averted his eyes. Maybe aiming into the hillside had been a smarter move than I'd realized.

"Bah," said Bob, gesturing for my other brothers to get moving, which they did. "She's gotta learn some time." He turned and took a few steps toward the driveway.

As I watched him walk away, I had to curb an impulse to bring my rifle to my shoulder one more time. From this distance, I thought, it would be so easy to make another *perfect kill.*

"Ready to skin the beast?" asked Dad. He held a buck knife with a curved, pointy blade and serrated back edge above the dead animal.

"Not enough Thumper for everyone," Dad said as he set the platter of meat on the table. "Since Drew's the only one to bring home any game today, he gets his fill first. Then I get my share for cleaning and cooking it. We'll see what's left after that. Pass your plate, son."

"I think I'll stick with Betty's ham," I replied, handing the dish the other way. "Smells awesome." I'd eaten rabbit before. Prepared well, its flavor really does resemble chicken. But feasting on a creature I'd killed for the approval of my distant father and in doing so earned the revulsion of my beloved niece would no doubt leave a taste in my mouth more foul than fowl.

"Suit yourself." He heaped several pieces of the flesh I'd watched him cut from bones onto his plate. "Boys?"

Bob and Ken eagerly extended their plates toward him. Once they and the rest of us had been served their meat of choice and various side dishes had made their way around the extended oval, we all bowed our heads while Betty offered thanks to the good Lord and asked Him to bless the meal.

"How's your mother?" Betty asked after she secured heavenly favor for our digestion. "Must be tough living alone in middle age. I guess that's why she left the country at Christmas."

"Our family—our *side* of the family—doesn't really celebrate Christmas," I replied. "Mom and Bruce are Bahá'ís. She's in the Holy Land on pilgrimage now."

"Her absence is our gain," the woman known to her stepchildren as "Wicked"—only half-ironically—said with a smile. "It's nice to have you here for the holiday, for a change."

"What's a Ba-ha-hi?" asked Barbie.

"It's kinda like a sect of Islam," answered Ken.

"I thought it was some Jewish thing," said Karen.

"It's an independent faith," I explained. "From Persia. As religions go, it's actually—"

"What's wrong with Christianity?" asked Barbie.

"I never said there's anything— ... Can we talk about something else?"

"I heard a good joke the other day," said Bob. "What's the hardest part of having AIDS?" He grinned. "Convincing your parents you're Haitian."

Betty, Ken, and Karen laughed heartily. Adam, Diana, Billy, and I chuckled. Offensiveness aside, it *was* clever. (In case you're too young or otherwise don't remember, early reports about HIV infection emphasized three main populations: gay men, intravenous drug users, and Haitians—the last of which would seem preferable

89

from a certain perspective but wasn't something your parents could be expected to believe.) Not everyone found the witticism amusing. Dad forced a half-smile. Barbie looked as befuddled as Stephanie. Calvin paid us no heed from his high chair as he squished mashed potatoes between his fingers.

"What's AIDS?" asked Stephanie. "And what's Haitian?"

"Never mind that," said Bob. "It's grown-up humor."

"She's gotta learn some time," muttered Dad, mostly under his breath but loud and clear enough for me to hear.

I excused myself and stepped into the adjacent kitchen to refill my water glass, and to process. Maybe the old man's more sensitive than he lets on, I thought.

"You know, right?" whispered Adam as he joined me at the sink. "About Uncle Jim."

"No. What happened?"

"He left Aunt Charlotte and moved in with his lover, who happens to be a man." Adam nudged my glass aside with his, as I'd failed to notice the water overflowing the rim of my glass onto my hand while the astonishing news—and its implications—soaked into my consciousness.

"Dad's brother is gay," I said.

"Dad's *twin* brother," noted my adopted one but near-twin in spirit.

"That joke. Does Bob know?"

"Well, I mean, he's definitely a dick. But I sure hope he's not *that* big a dick."

"Who's got a big dick?" asked our half-brother as he crowded between us to slide his glass under the stream.

Good ole buddy Billy, I thought. He entered the world several weeks early, but since then had an unfortunate habit of being a bit too late, and not only when it came to shooting rabbits.

"Who do you think, Billy Budd?" I replied. "Weren't your ears burning?"

He smiled with satisfaction as he shut off the faucet.

90

We turned and started toward the dining room together.

"Ohhh! I get it now!" Barbie's voice sounded from the table.

I paused in the doorway to the family room. As I expected, the sole occupant, sitting in his favorite recliner, was my father. I didn't expect him to be in the dark, or semi-dark. The only illumination came from colored Christmas tree lights flashing on and off in a sequence designed to seem random.

"Hey, Dad. Don't mean to disturb you."

"Not at all. Come in, come in."

I did so, taking a seat in the matching recliner most often filled by my stepmother.

"Cleanup finished already?" he asked after a considerable silence.

"They kicked me out. Too much 'blood on my hands' to be any help."

He sniggered at the sort of wordplay we both enjoy. Another lengthy silence ensued.

"Can I ask you something?" I finally inquired.

"I'd rather you didn't."

"Oh. Okay." I waited until the next silence became unbearable, then rose from the chair. "I'll...I'll let you—"

"Wait," he said. He looked at me for the first time since I entered the room. "What did you want to ask me?"

Oh boy, I thought. *So many things.* Why did you and my mom split up? I had some good guesses about that. Are you happy with your life? His answer to that, too, seemed easy enough to predict: "Beats the alternative." Mostly I wanted him to talk. About anything that mattered. About how something—anything—made him feel. In particular, about how it felt to know his genetic double was gay. How did that impact his own sense of self?

"Just wanted to see if I could borrow your car," I said. "Go into town for a drink."

91

"Keys are on the hook. Be safe." He turned his gaze back to the colored lights.

Be safe, I thought. That could be his life's motto.

I sat alone in the low-lit room, gazing at the string of colored lights hanging—but not flashing on and off—above the bottles behind the bar. Bells jingled as the front door opened.

I peered over my shoulder at a tall, heavyset man of about thirty. If his beard had been long and white, I would've asked where he parked his sleigh. But it was dark and quite short—glorified stubble, really.

He glided to the bar and slid onto a stool not too far from me. His way of carrying himself made him seem like a gentle giant. He nodded in my direction. I reciprocated.

"You got time for one drink," said the middle-aged woman who poured mine fifteen minutes earlier, as she emerged from the back room where she'd gone right after.

Gentle Giant glanced up at the clock on the wall: 9:45. He and I exchanged a look. Christmas Eve.

"What's this young gentleman having?" he asked the bartender.

"Kentucky's finest," she answered. "Bourbon."

"Well, in honor of the Restoration of the House of Bourbon after the defeat of Napoleon, I'll have the same. A double, please, since they had to beat him twice. And one for my ally there, if he wants it, on me."

She stared at him for a moment, then shook her head and reached for the bottle. After pouring his drink, she looked toward me. Once I'd shrugged and nodded, she topped me off.

I raised my glass toward Gentle Giant. He reciprocated.

"Merry fucking Christmas," he exclaimed with an overabundance of seasonal gaiety.

"Gonna have to suck it down faster than that, fellas," said the bartender after we sipped. "You may not have families you wanna go home to, but I do. As soon as I finish wrapping these presents for my grandkids, it's closing time." She then disappeared into the back room.

"Grandkids," said my new drinking buddy. "Another unfortunate consequence of being a breeder. I'm perfectly content being the favorite uncle."

I know what you mean, I thought. At least I *used to be* the favorite.

"Breeders," I said. I'd never heard it as a term for people with children. "You make them sound like animals."

"Aren't they?" he asked. "Aren't we all? Granted, some of us exercise better control than others over our more bestial impulses."

Good point, I thought.

"But what fun is that?" he added with a smile, then drained the contents of his glass.

Excellent question, I thought.

"Listen, I don't suppose you ..." He mimed taking a drag from a joint.

"You got some?"

"Back at the hotel."

Oh, I thought.

"Given that having another drink here isn't an option, I'm heading there now. Care to join me for a nightcap?"

Be safe, I heard my father's voice say inside my head.

Be *realistic*, I thought in reply. This man isn't dangerous.

"Sure," I said.

"You starting to relax a bit?" asked Gentle Giant. He set a glass of water on the desk beside an ashtray in which the remains of the joint smoldered.

I nodded from the swivel chair as he moved behind me. I flinched when I felt his hands land on my shoulders near my neck.

93

"This okay?" he asked, massaging my trapezius muscles with surprising strength.

Between leaving the bar and arriving at the hotel, I realized he might have more in mind than merely getting high. As I followed his car from one place to the other, I noticed a bumper sticker—*Dancers Do It To Music*—that somehow made all the other clues, obvious in hindsight, come together. (I'd since learned he taught ballroom technique in Chicago.) The idea of being alone—and stoned—with a gay man in his hotel room filled me with a mix of fear and fascination. There's nothing to worry about, I'd told myself. *It takes two to tango.*

I now nodded consent as he continued to knead my skin and the tissue below it. I let my chin drop to my chest and closed my eyes. As I took a few slow, steady breaths, I felt the knots—and my inhibitions—loosen. At the same time, my curiosity—among other things—was on the rise.

His hands floated to the outsides of my shoulders and he turned me, and the chair, one hundred and eighty degrees. I opened my eyes and gazed up into his as he guided me to my feet. He took my face in his meaty but oh-so-gentle hands. I reached my arms up and around his neck. Our bodies, and our lips, pressed together.

I'm kissing a *man*, I thought.

"Beard scratching you?" he asked after I pulled away to catch my breath.

"I like it," I answered, touching the softer than expected scruff on his cheek.

He raised my arms and removed my shirt. "You're gorgeous," he said, gazing at my lean-muscled form. He removed his own shirt, revealing chest hair even thicker than mine and a torso more stocky than portly.

He's *substantial*, I thought.

I drew myself against him and kissed his hot, salty mouth.

I splashed cold, crisp water onto my face and gazed at the

94

reflection in the mirror.

You just had sex with a *man*, I thought.

"Indeed I did," the figure looking back replied aloud.

Would you do it again? I asked silently as I reached for a towel.

"Maybe," said the figure before blotting up the wetness on his skin.

I had to admit it wouldn't be fair to judge something by a single experience. And this one had certainly been better than my first, second, or third time with a woman. Better than most, I thought, recalling the tingling I felt as he cupped my testicles in one hand and caressed my erection with the other, the charge that surged through me when he took me into his mouth.

I came almost immediately, which didn't seem to bother him a bit. He smiled and rolled onto his back, inviting me to reciprocate. Stroking and sucking his cock and balls as he'd demonstrated on me—albeit more clumsily and without the same results—had given me an even bigger thrill.

Best of all, he seemed to really enjoy fucking me. And I enjoyed his enjoyment of it.

His initial entry hadn't been as painful as I anticipated. He pushed his swollen head against my virgin anus with steady but gentle-as-ever pressure until my sphincter relaxed and allowed him access to my rectum. The mild discomfort I felt during his most spirited pounding seemed well worth it when I saw the blissful expression on his face as he orgasmed.

The only weird moment occurred after he fingered my asshole with lube. He started to rub the gel all over his hard dick, as if intending to slip it inside me without a condom.

"Gotta be safe," I'd said.

He sighed and rolled his eyes. Then he got up to get one, waving it in the air as he returned to the bed. He made sure I saw him unroll it along his shaft before he lifted my legs and pressed them toward my midsection, blocking my view of the actual penetration.

There's the evidence he complied with my wishes, I thought, as I stepped over to the toilet to pee and saw the used rubber at the bottom of the otherwise empty wastebasket. I felt a double sense of relief as my bladder discharged a heavy stream of urine and my brain discharged a slight trace of concern.

Then I spotted something unexpected: The condom had a sizable tear.

I suddenly remembered another vaguely weird moment from our interaction. As he intensified the pace, depth, and force of his thrusting, at one point he pulled all the way out, seemingly by accident. He paused, presumably to secure the protective sheath in its proper position, and then resumed fucking me. Had he noticed it was broken and continued anyway?

Once I finished pissing, I crouched over the trashcan and inspected the condom. The rupture was near the nipple-like tip—which had not fulfilled its function as a reservoir—and about the width of his erection.

It hadn't taken long after he made the adjustment for him to finish.

Did he actually ...? Maybe he even cut it with something. Maybe he's HIV-positive and mad about it and wants to infect others!

I gaped at the figure in the mirror. *What have you done?*

"If you ever find yourself in Chi-town, get in touch," said Gentle Giant, handing me his card as I zipped up my jeans. "We can have ourselves more good times."

I took the card without comment, not wanting to delay my exit any longer than necessary, lest I act on a bestial impulse far less pleasurable than the one we'd indulged. A blow to the nose or mouth might draw blood, and I didn't want to risk getting more of his potentially tainted fluids on me. Before slipping the card into my pocket, I glanced at the printed text: Noel Gray, Belle of the Ball Dance Studio.

"When it's a man's name, it's pronounced Nole," he said.

Yeah, I thought, *as in Coward.*

"See ya," I said, once I laced up my boots. I snatched my coat from where he'd hung it in the closet and escaped into the hallway without looking back.

CHAPTER EIGHT
COUNTDOWNS AND RESOLUTIONS

I strode down the hallway looking forward to what lay ahead. I'd survived the rest of my stay in Wisconsin without experiencing a complete breakdown, but on several occasions I had to make a hasty departure from a room, lest I lose control of my emotions in front of my "less-than-kind" kin. Exactly a week after waltzing into virgin territory with Noel the Gentle and Cowardly Giant—a mistake I *hoped* to live to regret a long time—I was eager to purge my psyche.

Even if I didn't remember the apartment number from my one previous visit, I would've known I was in the right place by the alternative rock music audible through the door. Not long after knocking, I was greeted by the angelic face I'd been imagining all day.

Angie touched the corner of her lips to each of my cheeks—a salutation no doubt learned from Sabine. I hesitated to reciprocate, fearful of the possible consequences. She pulled me into the room by my hands.

"Let's get this party started!" exclaimed my host, putting some original—and spicy—seasoning in the Salt-N-Pepa reference.

It seems to be well underway already, I thought, as I took in the collection of familiar bodies swaying and grinding to the music.

"Beam me up, Scotty!" said Kirk, holding out his empty glass.

Watch out for Klingons circling Uranus, I thought, no longer quite as amused by that play on words, which took on new dimensions now that I'd been blasted by a photon torpedo. But I enjoyed Kirk's pun on the brand of whiskey in the bottle Scott poured from. I realized I might actually be starting to like the guy.

Kirk looked at his watch. "Crap! Ten 'til. We really better beam ourselves up there."

A frantic scramble to gather essential items and a mad dash to the building roof followed.

Emerging from the stairwell I was struck by cool night air—unusually, and thankfully, dry for the season— and by the view. Angie lived near the summit of Queen Anne Hill, which gave its name to a neighborhood slightly north, and a hair west, of downtown. From our vantage point, the illuminated city skyline provided a radiant backdrop for the Space Needle below the slope in the cultural area known as Seattle Center. I zipped up my leather jacket as I stood with Scott near the edge of the low-rise building's top.

Kirk popped the cork from a bottle of champagne and poured bubbly into plastic cups, which Angie distributed. The group consisted of the same new—and likely temporary—family members with whom I'd celebrated Thanksgiving. She got the cups handed out just in time.

The lights of the Space Needle pulsed.

"Ten!" we shouted together after the first blast of fireworks shot out from the Needle. We counted down to one, as one, as additional rounds fired into the air from higher up the shaft each time.

At the stroke of midnight, a pyrotechnic barrage exploded from the crown of the Needle.

"Happy New Year!" we all cheered before swallowing fizzy fluid.

Then, in keeping with tradition, people kissed. Angie and Kirk got it started. Johnny and Sabine went next. Dina looked from Scott to me, then turned and laid one on Melissa, who did not shy away. With a shrug, Scott grabbed my face and planted his lips directly on mine.

My mouth started to open before my head snapped back in recoil. I stared at him.

"Love ya, bud!" he told me, wrapping an arm around my shoulders and giving me a squeeze. "It's gonna be a great year for us. Graduation, here we come!"

"That's months from now," said Angie, sliding between us and linking an arm with each. "Tonight we're gonna party like it's 1999!"

A few hours into 1989, the party reached its climax and faded into a state of repose. I sat on the living room floor, my back to the sofa on which Dina, Melissa, and Scott had passed out, fully clothed, in a three-way cuddle. Sabine was curled up in Johnny's lap in the armchair, where they alternated between making out and zoning out.

"We're heading to bed," said Kirk as he picked up stray cups from the tables.

Angie approached with a sheet, pillow, and blanket. She opened the recliner and spread the sheet over the cushions, then set the pillow and blanket on top. "For you," she said.

"Thanks."

As they started toward the hallway, she put a hand on his shoulder and stretched up to whisper in his ear. He shook his head. She pouted at him.

"Come on, Angie," he said.

"Ever try ecstasy?" she asked me.

"No," I replied. I'd never heard of it. I presumed it was a drug. "What's it like?"

"*Ex*-actly how it sounds," she answered. "Pure bliss.

You feel nothing but goodness."

"I sure could use some of that," I said.

"It's too late to drop tonight," replied Kirk.

"Why is everyone being such party poopers? No resolutions, no all-night diner, no fun! Drew, are you with me?"

Oh yes, I thought. In every way.

I looked at Kirk. His eyes pleaded.

"No," I said. "He's right. I'm beat."

"Fine," said Angie. "But you have to promise to do it with us soon. With everyone. *That* can be your New Year's resolution."

"There's a rave next weekend," Kirk noted.

"What's a rave?" I asked.

Even if you've never attended one, you probably have a decent idea about what goes on at a rave, as mainstream as they've become over the years. At the time, the underground, drug-fueled dance parties had just started to pop up along the West Coast, mostly in the San Francisco area, but occasionally in Seattle.

"Don't try to *ex*-plain," said Angie. "Let him *ex*-perience it for himself. Saturday. Deal?"

"Deal," I said. I am resolved to be someone you can count on.

"Thanks, Drew-Drew," said Angie, enhancing my identity in a way no one else ever had. "This is *so* much better."

You can count on me, I thought.

I gazed at her with what I suspect were highly dilated pupils. My vision was soft, as if I were looking through the special camera lens used to film Cybill Shepherd on *Moonlighting*. Angie and Kirk, her co-star in this fantasy episode—and in what seemed like a potentially long-running series—snuggled in one corner of the Jacuzzi-style bathtub, wearing their swimsuits. I sat on the opposite edge, shirtless and with my slacks rolled up to avoid the warm water in which my lower legs soaked.

The rave hadn't quite lived up to Angie's *ex*-pectations. Everything was great at first. We procured eight hits of ecstasy, from a young man costumed as the Mad Hatter—a less creepy one than Tom Petty's music video version—and then joined the throngs of other ravers grooving to ear-splitting techno-pop music around a gigantic, glowing mushroom in the center of the warehouse floor, while colored laser lights flashed to the beat.

Right as I started to really feel the effects of the drug, Kirk tapped me on the shoulder. "We've gotta get her home," he said, gesturing to where Angie leaned against the wall near three pieces of abstract art, her arms pinned across her body, which I could see tremble. "Crowds sometimes freak her out when she's high."

I nodded.

"Can you drive?"

I considered the question, then nodded.

"Stay with her while I tell the others, okay?"

Nod.

As Kirk waded into the sea of dancers, I meandered in Angie's direction, pretending to admire the bizarre combinations of shapes and spirals on the nearby panels. They truly were fascinating, but my real interest was in getting her to focus on something other than the hordes of *ex*-plorers invading her sense of personal space. And it worked. My attention to the images drew hers to them and distracted her from herself until Kirk returned and guided us to her car.

"Can I tell you something?" Kirk now asked from the other side of the tub, after we heard the sound of the apartment door open and close. "Before they come in." In response to my nod, he continued. "I want you to know ... if it ever seems like I don't ... trust you ... it's not you. It's me. My own insecurity." He climbed to his feet and spread his arms. "Can I have a hug?"

I stood and stepped into a fierce embrace. I felt untainted affection from—and for—Kirk.

103

A moment later, I felt an even bigger wave of that, as Angie hinged us apart and joined us in a triptych of pure love.

I heard the bathroom door open. Without separating, we shifted our gazes toward the newcomers, who wasted no time stripping to their underwear and stepping into the tub. The five of them surrounded the three of us and added another layer to the group embrace.

After a while, Kirk released his hold on Angie and me. Following his lead, the others moved back.

"Take off your pants," said the captain of our enterprise.

"Huh?" I asked.

"The man said take off your pants," Scott replied.

I shrugged and peeled off my slacks, already wet in spots from contact with Kirk and Angie. I tossed them aside.

"Everyone sit in the water and hold your knees against your chest," Kirk told us. Once we'd complied, bunching together inside the rim, he leaned out of the tub to swing the bathroom door shut. "Get ready to take ten deep breaths." He reached for the light switch. "And ... go!" He flipped the switch, plunging us into darkness.

I lost count as we breathed in and out in unison. We all stopped at the same time, though, so if I guessed wrong, so did the rest of the group.

When the lights came back on after our final *ex*-halation, images seemed crisper, colors appeared brighter, and palpable energy pervaded the air.

Nothing but goodness, I thought, echoing Angie's description. *Pure bliss.*

I don't recall much about how I passed the—eight?—hours between the onset of the drug's peak effects and the break of day. I have vague recollections of drinking orange juice or taking a toke of pot every now and then to reactivate the high. And a lot of dancing.

I know this much for sure: Unlike the bodies intertwined with mine on the living room floor when I first noticed a ray of light striking the carpet below the window curtains, I didn't sleep. I never crashed the way I had whenever I snorted more than a line or two of cocaine. I certainly didn't experience an adverse reaction like I had from a single bump on Thanksgiving. The state of euphoria simply diminished—so gradually as to be imperceptible—until it was gone. Or was it gone? I still felt so good.

As I gazed at the peaceful sleeping faces around me, numbering only five, I remembered Angie and Kirk had retired to her bedroom at one point, presumably to act on the erotic impulses they'd been *ex*-hibiting for some time by then. So I was surprised when she soon appeared from the hallway dressed in jeans, sweatshirt, and sneakers.

"I'm going to church," whispered Angie, keys in hand. "Care to join me?"

"Sure," I said. "Is Kirk coming?"

She shook her head as she knelt near me and supported Dina's head while I slid my shoulder out from under from its weight. "He wouldn't appreciate it."

I nodded, not convinced I would either. I extracted a stiff leg from where it intersected ones belonging to Scott and Sabine. Free of those entanglements, I rose and went to put on my Sunday best—in this case, my funky rave attire.

Aside from sharing our recurring impressions of how amazing it was to be out in this new world, Angie and I didn't speak much during the drive through Queen Anne and Magnolia and into Discovery Park.

"I didn't know there was a church out here," I said once she'd parked in a visitor lot and we'd gotten out of the car. I'd ventured into the five hundred acres of urban wilderness a mere handful of times before this. "Do you mean that chapel?"

105

"No, silly," she replied as she skipped along the start of a trail. "The park *is* my church."

Now *that* makes much more sense, I thought, and skipped into the woods after her.

"In Nature, 'I become a transparent eye-ball. I am nothing; I see all,'" I quoted Emerson.

"'Currents of the Universal Being circulate through me; I am part or particle of God,'" she responded, reciting the essay's next lines. "See. You've read my bible without knowing it."

"But I never really *got it* until now," I said.

The view from our perch on Magnolia Bluff, overlooking Puget Sound toward Bainbridge Island and the mountains of the Olympic Peninsula in the distance, was beyond majestic. I felt like I was atop the original Mount Olympus itself. Like I could transform myself into my pick of the classical elements or states of matter.

"If I tell you something, will you promise to keep it a secret?" asked Angie.

"Of course," I answered.

"When I was fifteen, I got pregnant."

"Oh. Wow. I'm sorry you had to—"

"Don't be," she interrupted. "I'm not. I'm grateful. I didn't have an abortion. I gave birth to him. Danny. He's six now." She turned her face away from me and gazed out into the ether. "I had to give him up. But I know we'll be together again someday."

"I hope you're right," I said. For a long time, I said nothing else. How do you follow something like that? And then I knew. "My turn. Secret for secret." I felt as grounded as the earth. "When I was home for Christmas ... No. Forget it."

"You can trust me," said Angie, taking my hand. And I believed her.

I relied on that faith to stoke the fire of my resolve. "I had sex with a man." I felt cleansed by the admission, as pure as crystal water.

"Well," she replied after a beat, "did you like it?"

"I guess so. But I'm not gay."

"Okay."

"And it's not something I'll be trying again any time soon."

"Why not?" she asked.

I told her about the condom and my fears he'd infected me with the deadly virus.

"Did you get tested?" she asked.

I told her my doctor said I would need to wait some months to be sure about a negative result.

"Scary," she said. "But—and I don't mean to sound flip—we all die some time."

"So ... what? *Carpe diem*?"

"Pretty much." With that, she sprang to her feet and galloped along the bluff toward a path descending to the beach.

I scrambled to mine, filled up with air, and chased after her.

"We're creatures from another world," said Angie, gazing at our reflections in the mirror. The clay-like sand we'd scooped up from the shore and smeared all over each other's faces—leaving only our eyes uncovered—had dried onto our skin during the ride back to her apartment.

Kirk knocked on the bathroom door as he pushed it the rest of the way open. With barely a glance in our direction, he plodded to the toilet and peed into it.

"Look, honey. Drew gave me a facial." Angie suppressed a laugh. "After I gave him one." She snorted.

I covered my mouth with a hand to keep from laughing, worried my terracotta shell would crack and crumble.

Kirk peered over his shoulder at us. "Oh, right," he said. "I heard those mud mask things are good for your complexion." He flushed the toilet and stepped between us to wash his hands. "I'm glad you two are making the most of the day."

Damn straight, I thought. Seizing it like there's no tomorrow.

CHAPTER NINE

LSV-DAY

Gravity brought us back to Earth. I planted my feet on either side of the plank to cushion my landing. Beside me, Angie did the same. Sabine, who presumably had less experience with solo seesawing, and apparently less awareness that what goes up must come down or that for every action—in this case deliberate upward propulsion—there's an equal and opposite reaction, failed to slow her descent and crashed into the ground, hardened by freezing temperatures and a recent lack of precipitation, provoking a startled cry from her and pot-enhanced giggles from us.

"It's funny to you I break my tail?" asked our French companion, her pronunciation of the first word as "eats" prompting an additional outburst from us.

"No, honey," Angie replied, after her fit subsided. "Of course not. Want me to kiss it and make it all better?"

Sabine answered with a pouty nod. She stood and lowered the back of her pants and panties as she bent forward. Angie crawled over and kissed her bare buttocks.

"Umm ..." I said. "In public. Broad daylight. Kid zone."

"It's not like I'm rimming her. Maybe you want me to?" She flicked her tongue in the air.

Sabine yanked her clothes back up. She wrinkled her nose and pinched her mouth at Angie. "*Eats* not--"

"What the hell was that about?" Kirk interrupted as he approached with the other members of his away team.

I realize that term wasn't used on the original series. But *The Next Generation* had started to air about a year and a half before this, so that's how I thought of it.

"Looks like we got here just in time," Scott said.

Johnny raised an eyebrow at Sabine, who shrugged, then poked the tip of her tongue through her lips and wiggled it back and forth.

Before long, we were seesawing in earnest and the way it's meant to be done, in pairs. Johnny had taken up position opposite Sabine, and Kirk had assumed his place across from Angie, leaving Scott as my default partner.

"*Eats* for sure she will get it?" asked Sabine.

"Let's hope so," Angie answered. "Since the boys couldn't deliver."

"Don't worry," said Kirk. "Dina will do whatever it takes."

"Are you calling my sister a slut?"

"No. But if the condom fits ..."

As Kirk let the phrase hang, Angie rolled onto her back off her end of the seesaw as it brushed the ground, sending his end plummeting like a stone. It slammed into the dirt.

"Fuck!" he screamed, collapsing onto his side and clutching *his* stones.

Angie laughed so hard she expelled air from her vagina.

"Did you just queef?" asked Scott.

Angie nodded and laughed harder. She queefed again.

"Damn," Johnny said. "I'm gonna start calling you Queen LaQueefah."

"Who is this?" asked Sabine. "Queen, how you say ...?"

The rest of us—other than Kirk, who remained curled

in the fetal position—shook our heads and shrugged.

"White people, I swear," said Johnny. "Don't you watch *Yo! MTV Raps*? Queen Latifah! She's got a bitchin' single out. Five years from now, she really will be the Queen of Hip Hop."

"Sorry," said Angie as she went to check on Kirk. When she crouched beside him, she queefed once more. "*I am* Queen LaQueefah!"

This time, everyone—even Kirk—joined Johnny in an expression of merriment.

"They're here!" exclaimed Sabine, pointing toward the street, where Dina and Melissa got out of the latter's parked car.

Dina waved us over as she marched to the playground carousel. Moments later, our gang of eight was assembled in a circle near the center of the platform.

"Unusual color," I said, looking at the capsule of powder in my hand. "So dark."

"Suddenly you're an *ex*-pert?" asked Dina. "It all depends on the batch."

Fair enough, I thought.

This *was* merely the third batch I'd seen. In the five weeks since our original *ex*-cellent adventure (the *Bill & Ted* movie was due for release the following Friday), Sigma Chi functions obligated Kirk and Scott to at some point absent themselves from almost all our regular weekend gatherings at Angie's apartment. We'd all pledged to take the drug only if everyone could participate. Otherwise we'd limit ourselves to weed and booze. And, for some, a line or two of cocaine now and then. Angie had joined me in strict abstinence.

The one other time we'd rolled—three weeks after the first time—had featured more of the same behavior as my introductory *ex*-perience. (Sorry. That's a hard habit to kick.) But two of the highlights were new activities: the men crawling around the living room with the women riding our backs—all of us having stripped down to our underwear, of course—while the Cure's "Just Like

111

Heaven" blasted; and the telepathic conversation I had with Angie.

Yes, that's right. We engaged in mutual mindreading. If you believe in that sort of thing. I didn't myself initially.

When it happened, we'd again found ourselves the only two awake. Our eyes had met and locked from opposite corners of her bed, with the rest of the group crammed between and around us. Kirk's head rested in her lap, while Dina and Melissa pinned me in place.

"Here we are," I heard her voice say even though her mouth hadn't moved.

Not quite the view from Magnolia Bluff, I thought, directing the words her way as though it would be the most natural thing in the world for her to comprehend them.

"It's all a matter of perspective," her disembodied voice replied.

So it is, I thought. *Shall we trade more secrets?*

"Do you have another?" her raised eyebrow asked.

Oh yes.

"Hmm," her sparkling eyes conveyed. "I bet I can guess this one."

I bet you're right, I thought.

"Let's leave it to the imagination," her playful smile communicated. "For now."

That's probably for the best, I thought.

"I have something for you," a new intensity in her eyes said. "I'll get it later."

Okay, I thought.

Another part of my brain pointed out that everything she "said" before then was something I might have expected, or hoped. But not this latest statement. Its originality—and its promise—made it seem less likely for me to make up inside my own head, which I realized was how my rational mind interpreted the exchange all along.

I looked into her eyes again. She smiled, but the connection was lost.

Oh well. Fun while it lasted. Even if I'd imagined it.

As I got ready to leave some hours later, after the two of us had finally joined the others in a bit of peaceful slumber, Angie disappeared for a moment before returning with a book, which she handed to me after our goodbye hug.

"It's a gift," she said. "Or a loan. It's one of my all-time favorites, so I'd like to get it back once you've finished. It's what I said I'd get for you."

"Wait. That was real?"

"I know. Freaky, right? But in a cool way."

"... Yeah."

I read the title on the worn book cover: *Siddhartha*.

"I can't wait to talk about it with you," she'd said as I stepped through the door.

"Let's drop and get back to Angie's," Kirk now said to the assembly, snapping me out of the memory and back to the playground.

"Let's go on an outing!" Angie replied. "It's such a nice day."

I gazed at the sky. After the typically rainy January and record cold we'd had earlier in February, the sunny and mild weather—in the mid-forties—did seem rather pleasant.

"To seeing the light!" Dina exclaimed.

She dry-swallowed her capsule, and the rest of us followed suit. Dina hopped off the roundabout, grabbed one of the bars at its perimeter, and ran in a circle, rotating the platform disc.

"Hang on," she said. "This ride on the merry-go-round's about to get wild."

"Sometimes I wish I could peel it off. I wish we all could," said Johnny, gazing across his exposed torso and along his arms. "And just be the me—the we—beneath the flesh."

Sabine nodded as she stared at the skin on her hands.

113

"Other times I want it to shine like a dark diamond dug up from deep within the earth," Johnny continued. "You know?"

Melissa got up from where she'd been cuddling with Dina on the sofa and stood before him with her palms on his cheeks. "*El mundo es un misterio*," she said. "*Nuestras vidas están llenas de maravilla. Actuar siempre con amor. Todas las diferencias se desvanecerán.*"

"You have the most beautiful spirit," he replied.

"You speak Spanish?"

"Not a word of it." He flashed an ivory smile. "Not a word."

I did speak it. At least I understood it. I studied the language all through junior high and high school, and although I tested out of the university's requirement I took a refresher course my sophomore year.

Here's how I heard her words: The world is a mystery. Our lives are filled with wonder. Always act with love. All our differences will disappear.

"*Bésame*," she said, and brought her lips to his for what she requested.

"*Embrasse-moi*," Sabine said to Dina, who complied.

As the two pairs kissed, both in the French style regardless of the participants' individual native tongues, I rose from the armchair. Part of me wanted to observe more of this lovely scene. But I knew exactly where I needed to be.

"I feel an urge to spend some time with *my self*," I announced, mostly *to* myself.

My bare soles left trace impressions in the soft carpet as I padded across the living room.

Moments—or was it longer?—later, I faced myself in the bathroom mirror, staring at my own shirtless chest and shoulders. The dense hair between my collar bone and nipples blended into a smooth coat of fur. I shifted my gaze upward. My irises lightened and brightened. My chin and nose extended into a snout. When I opened my jaws wide, my teeth grew long and pointed. My shoulder-

114

length tresses metamorphosed into a full-fledged mane.

I recognized what I was seeing as a physical reflection of some deep level of my psyche. *I'd discovered my Inner Lion!*

I emitted a silent roar. The vibrations took visible form, hovering in the air in front of me. My ears perked up at a distant sound.

I heard Kirk's hushed voice from the hallway: "You were totally right. He doesn't want to be her boyfriend. He's happy being her *girl*friend."

I understood why he'd say that. He saw us in our mud masks. She no doubt told him about the time I accompanied her to Nordstrom's and helped her pick out two new outfits from the dozen or more combinations she tried on. But he clearly knew nothing about our exchange of secrets in Discovery Park. Or our unspoken exchange in her bedroom.

"You may enter," I said as I sensed him about to knock.

After a brief pause, the door swung inward and Kirk and Scott materialized in the opening. My reflection reverted to normal.

"Angie's freaking out," said Kirk. "This shit's part acid or something."

"I noticed."

"Scotty and I are gonna try to find some pure X. To soften the vibe."

"Be careful," I said. "It's a jungle out there."

Standing on the threshold of her bedroom, I watched Angie stare at the ceiling from the center of the king-size mattress. I smiled when her face morphed into half-woman, half-lioness.

"Hey, dude," she said without ever so much as glancing at me. Her countenance reverted to normal.

I approached the bed. "Kirk said you were in a bad way."

115

"I was. Got better after he left. He was annoying the shit out of me."

We settled into silence. I lay on my side near the edge of the mattress and gazed at her profile. I wanted a distanced perspective.

"Did you read the book?" she asked.

I nodded. I'd finished it the day before, hopeful we'd have this opportunity.

"And?"

"It's remarkable. I'm trying to digest it all. I'm sure there's a lot I don't understand. Yet."

"What *did* you understand? Or what did you find most compelling? Applicable. To you."

"The part near the end, when Siddhartha encounters Govinda again, and he explains the difference between seeking and finding. That the seeker finds nothing, because his eyes see only what he seeks. I think I'm mostly open to what comes my way. But I feel like on some deep level I'm seeking something but don't know exactly what. So I might not find it even if I *do* see it."

"I hear you," she said. "You wanna know my favorite part?"

Not long after I nodded, she closed her eyes and took several slow breaths. Right as I wondered if she'd fallen asleep, her eyes opened and she began to recite.

"*Tenderly he gazed at the streaming water, at the transparent green, at the crystalline lines of its mysterious patterns.*"

As she spoke, her visage became a vision, her features no longer recognizable as themselves. Instead of her actual physical presence, I saw a form I could identify only as pure beauty.

"*He saw bright beads rising from the depths, silent bubbles drifting on the surface, sky blue reflected there.*"

With each slight movement of her face—what I presume to have been the flutter of an eyelid, the flare of a nostril, the quiver of a lip—for me the essence of beauty was redefined.

116

Continue, I thought. Continue for eternity and let me ever cherish this perpetual redefining of beauty.

"The river gazed at him with a thousand eyes, with green, with white, with crystalline, with sky blue eyes."

"How he loved the water, how it delighted him, how grateful he was to it!" I exclaimed in sudden, effortless memory of something I'd read a single time. And then, with a shudder, I fell backwards off the bed.

"You okay" she asked when I failed to make a sound after landing with a thud.

"You okay?" asked the black stallion seconds later as he bolted into sight—upside down from my viewpoint—in the doorway, with three wild mares herding up behind him.

"Lady and gentlemen," said Dina, standing in front of Johnny, who was flanked by Sabine and Melissa. "I present to you ... Flavor Unit!" She darted over to the armchair and climbed into it, facing the trio as they made rhythmic sounds and moved to the beat.

Johnny started to rap Queen Latifah's "Wrath of My Madness"—changing all mentions of the artist's name to the one he bestowed on Angie that afternoon. As he proceeded to rule the mic, he promised to throw a lifeline to our minds.

Please, I thought.

Johnny pulled Angie to her feet from her seat on Kirk's lap in the recliner. They danced together as he intoned rhyming patter about diving into his (her) madness and its wrath, with references to spirit and water that reminded me of the *Siddhartha* passage Angie and I recited earlier that night. Behind them, Sabine and Melissa sang as a "rasta" chorus, with quasi-Caribbean accents over their own, as Johnny must have instructed them in a private rehearsal.

Angie leapt onto one end of the sofa and danced across the cushions, planting her feet beside and between

117

our legs when she got to me and Scott. She paused in front of his face and thrust her hips forward as though threatening to queef at him. He mock screamed and covered his head with his arms.

"Queen LaQueefah *is* getting higher!" Angie exclaimed, echoing a line from the chorus. We'd dropped our second hit—this time of unadulterated ecstasy—maybe an hour before. "Dive into the wrath of my madness!" she cried.

In that spirit, Angie leapt from the sofa in the general direction of Johnny, who managed to catch her without getting knocked over. He hooked her under her arms, their chests touching, and rotated in place so her legs spun around in a circle, forcing Sabine and Melissa to retreat. Dina scrambled to her feet and reached for Angie's as they whirled past, catching them and bringing an end to the spectacle when Johnny stopped rotating in response to the resistance.

"Let's put our hands together for Flavor Unit," said Dina, fulfilling her role as emcee and helping her sister onto her feet.

Angie joined Johnny, Sabine, and Melissa as they took a bow. Kirk, Scott, and I clapped, hooted, and whistled.

Dina gestured for us to quiet down. "For our next act ..." she said, in an unforeseen continuation of the show. She looked expectantly at us, moving her eyes from Kirk to me to Scott.

"I'll go," said Scott as he stood up, eliciting cheers from all sides. He paced around the room, hitting his fists together as if preparing for a championship fight, while Angie and Dina reclaimed their previous seats and Johnny, Sabine, and Melissa squeezed onto the sofa beside me. Scott assumed a wide stance in the middle of the floor and directed his gaze at me. "Once upon a time, there were two freshmen."

I smiled in anticipation of hearing his version of how our friendship developed.

118

Our first meeting had been on dormitory move-in day. Rather than waiting for the busy elevator, I chose to climb the stairs to my third-floor room, overloaded each time in a typically stubborn attempt to minimize trips. For my third—and what I was determined to make my final— ascent, I managed to figure out how to carry everything remaining in the new-to-me Toyota Corolla SR5 I'd driven across the country. (I'll spare you an account of my stop in Wisconsin to visit—and bond with—my dad. You can imagine for yourself how that went.) What I hadn't figured out was how to open the door from the stairwell to my hallway without dropping it all.

"I took one look at you and said to myself, 'I'm gonna make a man out of him,'" Scott told his audience.

Interesting. So that's why he'd come to my aid. I was a *damsel in distress* to him.

"And over the last four years that's exactly what I did."

"Thanks," I said.

"You're welcome. You truly came into your own this year." He proceeded to recount some of his fondest memories from his successful enhancement of my masculinity.

I wasn't really listening anymore, but I suspect he mentioned my learning, from him, how to hold my liquor. He possessed a remarkable capacity—if still an amateur compared to Wade Boggs—for drinking massive quantities of booze without losing control or blacking out or exhibiting signs of a hangover the next day. And I'd guess he took credit—to some extent deserved—for building up both my physique and my confidence about approaching women, as well as my skills in that regard. The Sigma Chi Halloween party offered a fine illustration of the combined impact of his tutelage on my success.

Apparently I was feeling the lingering effects of the acid more than the others were at that point, as they seemed to be enraptured by the fabulist in front of them, while I was constructing my own mental narrative in an

119

attempt to answer the suddenly urgent and profound question of why we *were* friends. Among other things, I thought about conversations we'd had about death. When I was eight, my closest friend since nursery school was discovered in his rocking chair one morning, dead of unidentifiable causes. When Scott was ten, his teenage brother was killed in a bizarre—and blameless—cycling accident. So we shared some level of awareness that not just old people die, and that this life can end without warning or explanation.

Scott reclaimed my attention as he brought his tale to an end. He described how we'd been mistaken, more than once, for a same-sex couple when dining out together. He said he knew this from subtle looks and comments by servers and other restaurant staff.

I hadn't noticed that. I doubted I would've missed anything overtly homophobic. And Seattle was fairly gay-friendly. Now that I thought about it, we did often share a dessert.

"I don't even care what they think," he concluded. "That's how much I love you, bud."

"And they lived happily ever after," said Dina, rising from the chair and joining Scott. "Let's hear it for Scotty's dude-felt valentine to Drew."

I led the room in applauding, perhaps with more—sarcastic—vigor than appropriate, judging by the hand Melissa placed on my leg.

"That's right," Angie said. "Valentine's Day is next week. That's our year anniversary."

She and Kirk kissed.

Only a year. And I'd known them for a quarter of it.

"Hell yeah," said Kirk in response to something she whispered in his ear. He stood up, lifting her with him. "We're next."

"Wait. We should ask them first."

"Ask us what?" inquired the mistress of ceremonies.

"We wanna have sex in front of you," answered Kirk, setting Angie onto her feet.

120

"We want to share our lovemaking with you," she corrected him.

"What, right here? Now?" I asked.

"Only if everyone wants us to," she replied.

"I'm totally in," Johnny said without pause.

Scott echoed him. Dina and Melissa nodded with different levels of enthusiasm.

"You mean we can, eh, participate?" asked Sabine.

"You wanna have an orgy later, that's up to you," replied Kirk. "We're not into that."

"What do *you* say?" Angie asked.

I felt a dozen other eyes join hers on me. I tried to seem nonchalant as I shrugged.

Once the main act of our showcase got underway, I alternated between forcing myself to watch and taking in the reactions of my fellow voyeurs. Kirk sat upright in the middle of the floor, his legs extended and knees slightly bent, his hands planted behind him for balance. Angie straddled his pelvis, facing him as she rocked hers back and forth, her breasts brushing against his chest. Johnny bobbed his head in rhythm with Angie's movements. Sabine caressed her own body—all over. Scott gawked like a little boy witnessing a magic show for the first time. Melissa observed with seemingly dispassionate attention. Dina stared across the circle at me.

"You liking this, Drew?" she asked.

"It's certainly not *titillating* me." I hadn't meant it to sound so snappish.

Angie ceased rocking and twisted her torso toward me. "Of course not. That's not at all why we're doing it. It's an expression of—" she stopped in midsentence when Kirk tried to turn her back by her breast. "Please don't pull on me."

"What are you looking at him for? I'm the one you're fucking."

"Fucking? That's what this is for you? A cheap thrill? A hot fuck? Then why don't you jerk yourself off while Sabine and whoever else is into that watches?" She rolled

121

off him, sprang to her feet, and dashed down the hallway. A door slammed.

Kirk crawled out of the ring and grabbed a throw pillow. He held it in front of his crotch as he stood and hurried after her.

"That brings our *ex*-hibition of love to a close," said Dina. "Thank you and good night."

CHAPTER TEN

EGGSHELLS

The view from Magnolia Bluff, even with Angie beside me again, didn't thrill me quite the same way this time. That was partly due to the rain falling from the hazy skies. But we weren't about to let the precipitation—a light mist, really—deter us from meeting at the park on the first sixty-degree day of the year, which coincided with the vernal equinox *and* the first day of spring break. It was also Holy Monday. If you believe in that sort of thing.

Angie and I had hardly seen each other in the last five weeks, caught up in schoolwork and other aspects of our "real" lives. That's why I was so underwhelmed to be sitting there now, just the *three* of us. For some reason, which I had yet to fathom, she brought Scott along.

Much had changed between him and me since I heard his "fairy" tale version of our friendship. We continued to spend time together, studying at adjacent library carrels, going to movies, etcetera. But our interaction lost its vitality. The only truly exciting activity we shared was auditioning for *Jeopardy!*, which had come to town to recruit contestants for its first-ever college tournament. Even that became tinged with disappointment, when I advanced from the written test to play a mock game against other finalists and he didn't.

Exactly how was I supposed to tell Angie my big news with him present?

"We need to do something special in honor of Drew's big news," she said, as if reading my mind. Then I realized she must be talking about my *other* big news.

"Oh?" asked Scott. "Did he do something notable?"

"He didn't tell you?"

"I was waiting for the right time."

"He got into grad school," said Angie. "His first choice. In Florida."

"Wow," Scott replied. "That's about as far from here as you can get. Well, congrats."

"What's really cool about it," I explained, "is that the doctoral program at FSU allows a creative dissertation. So I'll be fully qualified to teach both literature and fiction writing. If I stayed here I'd have to choose between them and get either an MFA or a scholarly PhD."

"Makes sense," said Scott.

"I have some big news of my own," Angie announced.

I put my more delicate matter aside as I pondered what hers might be. Had she made contact with Danny? Did Scott even know she had a son?

"I broke up with Kirk."

"What?" Scott and I asked.

"When?" he followed up.

"Right before I picked you up."

"Why?" I asked.

"He's a total buzzkill. And now he says he can't even get high while he's interviewing."

"Yeah," said Scott, who, like Kirk, was on course for a career in Corporate America. "Failed drug test. Game over."

"I wanna go wild this weekend. To celebrate my freedom. You boys in?"

"I'm not looking for jobs yet," Scott replied.

So much for fraternal loyalty, I thought.

"I passed that test," I blurted out. "The one I'd been so anxious about."

"When were you ever worried about a test?" asked Scott.

"This one was different," I said, looking at Angie.

She nodded her understanding. "In that case," she said, "we need to have ourselves a real *ex*-travaganza."

"Just the three of us?" I asked. "What about our pledge?"

"Let's keep it *intimate*," she answered.

Whatever you say, I thought, abandoning my own familial loyalty.

"But maybe we should invite my sister. Or Sabine. I like even numbers."

"I don't trust Dina," I said. "No offense. But not after our 'accidental' acid trip."

I considered suggesting Melissa, but "going wild" didn't seem to be in character for her. Besides, I'd never noticed much attraction between her and Scott. And that was the point, right?

"If we're the Four Musketeers," said Angie, "at least one of us should be French."

"Un pour tous, tous pour un," said Sabine, as we stood in a tight circle with our clenched fists touching knuckles in the center.

"One for all, and all for one," the three of us replied. We turned our hands over, opened them, and swallowed the capsules resting on our palms. We'd now taken two within an hour.

Good thing that's the last of them, I thought. The night should prove a real *ex*-travaganza all right.

Our evening had already proven quite an adventure. If I were recounting it as an episode from the Dumas novel, I'd tell you how D'Artagnan (I) visited London (raves got their start in England) to receive the diamonds (duh) from the Duke (our dealer, aptly—for the historical context of the original story and the setting of my version on Easter weekend—named Christian), narrowly escaping

125

the clutches of the Comte de Rochefort (Kirk) and Milady de Winter (Dina).

If you're familiar with the nineteenth-century book—or the '70s film adaptations—you may be following the same train of thought I started to travel in my mind at the time, namely that Angie would have made a better Constance—and a fine Raquel Welch to my Michael York. But that would mean she died in the end—by her sister's hand!—and I wasn't about to even imagine that possibility.

Incidentally, the epilogue to this story will not reveal that Kirk and I settled our differences and became friends. After eluding him at the rave that night, I never saw him again. As for what he was doing there, my guess is he decided to take one final ecstatic ride before curtailing his drug use, perhaps to console himself over the breakup.

By the time the second hit kicked in we'd doffed our clothes, including our underwear, and ventured into the hallway, propping the door ajar with the security latch in case we needed to make a fast retreat into our room. We had no business being in a hotel that nice—which, although not *that* nice, we could afford only through a promotion from AmEx. We had little concern—but plenty of awareness—about what behavior was appropriate for the situation.

We first took turns shuttling each other down the hall in the wheeled desk chair. Angie and Sabine now somersaulted along the carpet. They reached the end of the corridor and flopped onto their backs in laughter. Scott ran toward them, arms raised overhead as if racing to victory. They pointed at his bouncing genitals and laughed harder. He dove onto the floor between them.

I sprinted in their direction, determined to outperform my counterpart despite knowing I had less "bounce" in my step. When I got about fifteen feet from them, I twisted and planted my hands for a cartwheel. My momentum carried my legs over my head faster than I expected. I lost control and landed hard on my back near

126

the others, who erupted in hysterics.

"I hope the sword is not broken," said Sabine, flipping my penis from side to side.

More like a *dagger*, I thought, especially in its current drug-shrunken state. If it's not one thing …

"It's two in the morning!" called a voice from behind a door that had opened a crack. "Take it outside."

The door slammed shut. We exchanged exaggerated expressions of alarm.

"That's actually a great idea," said Angie in an excited whisper.

As the first light of day broke, we stepped through the tree line into someone's back yard. We'd waited a few hours to follow through on Angie's proposal, mainly because Sabine needed convincing she wouldn't get arrested and be sent home on the next plane. Also because Scott and I wanted to formulate a plan of action. Where would we go and what would we do? Shopping and dining, the two things most Seattleites did on forays to the eastside suburb of Bellevue, were clearly not options. Angie finally convinced us to embrace the unknown—*carpe diem*—and we laced up our sneakers, into one of which I tucked our keycard, and shrouded ourselves in the top sheet from the king bed, which we threw off as soon as we made it across the parking lot into the surrounding woods that, we'd just discovered, separated the hotel property from a nearby—and affluent—residential neighborhood.

We headed straight for the hot tub in a pavilion on the deck. After a pleasant soak in the warm, still water—not wanting to risk alerting the homeowners of our trespass by turning on the heated jets—we climbed out, put back on our shoes, into one of which I again secured the keycard, and made our way to the front lawn, shaking our naked bodies at the house in a combination of spirited dance of rebellion and ineffective attempt to dry ourselves.

127

"Perfect!" cried Angie, after she spotted a child's bike lying on its side in the driveway.

She rushed over, righted the bike, and hopped onto the seat. She gained considerable speed as she rolled down the steep street from the hilltop home. Near the bottom of the slope she careened into the curb at a bend in the road and flew over the handlebars onto the grass.

"That stunt could've killed you," I said, once we made a mad dash down the hill.

She had already risen, apparently unhurt, and picked up the bike from where it tumbled and skidded to a stop on the pavement and was now wheeling it on its bent front rim toward us. (If the owner of that bike reads this, please contact the publisher, and I'll make restitution out of my royalties.)

"Listen," she replied. "I'm really glad you're not dying. Let *me* worry about *my* life." She broke into a jog, pushing the bike ahead of her up the hill. "Come on, or we'll miss the sunrise!"

"What did she mean?" asked Scott, after Sabine scurried after Angie. "About dying."

"Well, neither are you," I said after a brief pause. "Right?" I knew I hadn't satisfied him, but that would have to suffice.

I hurried up the hill, with Scott right behind me, and we joined the women as they were about to round the corner of the house. The four of us soon sat spread across the back slope of the roof, facing east, where color streaked the sky over the woods.

"You say this town it's called Bellevue?" asked Sabine. "In French, this means 'beautiful view.'"

Indeed, I thought, gazing at Angie's nude form, appreciating it for its aesthetic value far more than its erotic quality.

She caught me looking, then scooted over and laid her head on my shoulder. I slid an arm around her waist. Scott crept over to Sabine and cuddled her. We sat like that, in silence, until we heard a dormer window slide open.

"Is someone out there?" a voice called.

We exchanged looks of alarm—genuine ones this time—and scampered down the slope away from the attic window and toward the hot tub pavilion that provided convenient access to the roof. Getting down was a bit trickier than getting up, but the urgency of the scenario didn't allow me to dwell on my fear of falling.

We fled across the yard and into the woods. Amazingly, Angie led us right back to where we left the sheet. As she and Sabine shook it out, I knelt down to tie a shoelace and glanced at the outside of my foot, where I'd tucked the keycard into my sneaker.

Uh-oh.

We couldn't help but giggle as we shuffled across the lobby toward the reception desk. Hotel guests in line for the breakfast buffet—Easter Sunday edition—gaped at us wrapped up together in the sheet, with Scott and I bunched against Sabine and Angie from behind.

We'd conducted a quick search for the lost keycard before concluding it was most likely lying in the grass where I landed after leaping from the hot tub pavilion. Going back there didn't seem prudent, given that Cardinal Richelieu might well have called out the palace guard.

"Room number?" asked the clerk, with a smirk, before we said a thing.

I told him, and he produced a new keycard, which Angie accepted through a slit where she and Sabine held the sheet closed in front of them.

"Thank you so much," she said. "Also, can we please get a late checkout?"

We'd changed the nightstand clock radio from the alternative rock station we blasted in the midnight hours to one better suited to our mellow morning energy. At the moment, Belinda Carlisle's "Heaven Is a Place on Earth" was playing, and I couldn't imagine a more appropriate song. The four of us remained naked under the sheet, now draped over our lower halves as we lazed on the bed. Angie's head rested on my chest, with her breasts pressing against my ribcage and her fingers tracing circles around my navel.

Scott and Sabine, who lay beside us in a similar position, started making out. Before long, he rolled her onto her back and disappeared under the sheet. His head moved between her legs. She closed her eyes and moaned.

As I watched them, I felt Angie's hand slide beneath the sheet and down along the inside of my thigh, then back up to the crease where my leg meets my pelvis. My entire body trembled in response to her touch.

"This okay?" she asked.

I nodded.

Sabine's breathing deepened. Angie's caresses spread.

"Ohhhhh yessss," said Sabine, seemingly unaware she was speaking at all, much less for both of us.

I felt Angie's hand wrap around my penis, which was no longer shrunken, or flaccid. She stroked me.

Sabine screamed in pleasure as she climaxed.

Scott emerged from beneath the sheet and reached toward the floor beside the bed, where he'd placed his overnight bag. When his hand reappeared, it held a condom. As he tore open the wrapper, Angie released her grip on me and extended her hand toward Scott. He shrugged, set the condom on her palm, and stretched down to get another one.

"Are you sure?" I asked.

"If you can't fuck your friends," she answered, "who can you fuck?" She tossed back our side of the sheet, then unrolled the condom around my erection.

"Do you want me to ... warm you up?

She shook her head as she swung one leg over me and straddled my hips. "I'm already wet," she said,

130

unnecessarily, given that I slipped inside her without the least resistance. She rocked her pelvis back and forth on top of me, matching Scott's rhythm as he pushed his hips forward between Sabine's legs, penetrating her.

Before I recognized the significance of the sudden, rapid pulsations in my cock, I felt myself release into the condom. I sighed out a long exhalation, apparently having held my breath for some time.

"Already?" she asked. "We just got started."

"After months of anticipation," I replied.

Angie slid off me onto her side and laid her head on my chest, where she had a direct view of Scott thrusting over and over into Sabine.

I knew better than to hope for a resurrection.

CHAPTER ELEVEN

IN MEMORIAM

"Fuck the world!" I yelled from the rooftop of Angie's apartment building.

"Fuck the world!" Scott echoed me.

"Fuck life!" I shouted.

"Fuck life!" he repeated.

"Fuck death!"

"Fuck death!"

"Fuck everything!"

"Fuck everything!"

If you've ever ingested psychedelic—a.k.a. "magic"—mushrooms, perhaps you can relate. Either way, I should explain how I came to be, at nearly midnight on Memorial Day Eve, at that site in that state of mind.

"What is liberty?" said Alex, reading the words I'd written with the magnetic stylus on my podium screen. "That's the correct response. And how much did he risk? Everything!"

Go bold or go home.

To win I still needed the prodigy beside me—a sixteen-year-old college senior—to have either missed it or mis-wagered, the latter of which seemed unlikely given this juvenile genius was Asian, and thus an obvious math whiz. I'd struggled in this opening match until early in the Double Jeopardy round, when I got back in the game by sweeping a College Sports category—a feat not actually as impressive as it might sound, coming against a nerdy teenager and a bubbly Ivy League coed.

"Now we come to the young man who held a solid lead going into the Final Jeopardy round," continued the quiz show host. "What did he write?"

"*E pluribus unum*," said my opponent with a shake of his head, answering the rhetorical question in violation of the instructions we were given to remain silent until the visual reveal.

"Oh, too bad," replied Alex once the Latin phrase appeared on the front of the podium. "The clue, as you may recall, specified it was a single word. Your wager? Nothing! You might well still advance as a wildcard. In the meantime, congratulations to today's automatic semifinalist, Drew Lovell."

I pumped my fist for the camera. *Winner!*

I wish I could say I won the entire event. I *should* have at least made the finals. I led my semifinal from the start and, aided by a true Daily Double, built a nearly insurmountable advantage heading into Final Jeopardy. *Nearly* insurmountable. Still, all I had to do was get the question right or have my two rivals get it wrong.

By the time Weird Alex arrived at my podium, I knew I'd lost on *Jeopardy!*, as both other players had answered correctly, and I hadn't. After the deduction of what I bet— precisely enough to cover my closest competitor's maximum possible score—I was left in third place.

If I *had* gotten it right, there's no telling what might've happened in the two-day final. My "play-it-safe" quarterfinal opponent did indeed advance as a wildcard, won his semifinal, and finished as runner-up in a tight match. The future lawyer who edged him for the title—and $25,000—also went on to win the next Tournament of Champions—and its $100,000 prize.

Even so, I pocketed $5,000, which funded a trip to Europe that summer (recounted in the next chapter) and paid off a portion of the debt I incurred through my somewhat irresponsible college lifestyle. I'd earned a full scholarship, but I took out yearly loans to help with expenses. And I didn't hold back on spending, especially on college staples like booze.

When I'm persuaded to relate this story in person, everyone wants to know the question I choked on. And I *did* choke. It concerned early American literature, a favorable subject for an English major—or, in this case and to my downfall, three of them. In fairness, I'd never set eyes on that particular work. But I knew it existed and, had I not panicked under the pressure of the moment, I likely would've pieced together hints in the clue and come up with the title.

If you want the actual category, clue, and correct response, you'll have to find that information for yourself. Or ask my half-brother Billy. He'll be pleased to tell you how, playing along at home, he knew the answer instantly.

The phone call notifying me I was chosen as a contestant came the day after my failed coupling—the first one—with Angie. In the two weeks between then and my weekend trip to Los Angeles to participate in the competition, I did almost nothing but memorize questions and answers from the Trivial Pursuit game I'd long enjoyed playing. I once won a match-up with that same half-brother on my initial turn, before he even had a chance to roll the die.

In hindsight, all that studying didn't help much. But it was a convenient excuse to avoid interacting with Angie, lest we undertake another attempt at sexual union I feared would end in more disappointment for her—and humiliation for me. The pressure of *that* moment would've eclipsed even what I felt under the spotlight, in the camera eye, before a live studio audience, on that Hollywood stage. I needed time to prepare for the more intimate performance as well.

I didn't anticipate my temporary physical withdrawal would induce her to turn elsewhere for satisfaction so soon. *Talk about premature emasculation!* And, more crucial to the eventual outcome of the situation, I never imagined she'd turn where she did.

Before departing for sunny Southern California, I accepted Angie's offer to pick me up at Sea-Tac after my flight back. I figured I'd return home either triumphant and confident or defeated and in need of tender loving care, two scenarios I'd be thrilled to have her join.

"Hey, Drew-Drew!" she called as I stepped from the jetway into my arrival gate.

I stared at the young man beside her. Where did I know him from?

"Hey," he said as I approached.

"I'm so *ex*-cited to see you!" she *ex*-claimed as I reached them.

That's when I recognized her companion as Christian, organizer of raves and supplier of MDMA, LSD, and other drugs. Without his customary and deliberately strange party attire—which I'd seen range from the Mad Hatter to Cap'n Crunch to the Cat in the Hat—he appeared almost boy-next-doorish. But he would prove to be nothing like an archetypal boy next door. Unless that boy happened to be sociopathic serial killer and rapist— sometimes even in that order—Ted Bundy, who claimed to have committed his first murder right there in Seattle and whose death by execution in Florida's electric chair three months before this sparked a rave-like mass celebration outside the prison.

While I was aware of Christian's involvement in illicit business, as he and I walked through the concourse on either side of Angie, I still had no idea how deep that involvement ran, or how dangerous he—and his associates—actually were. Nor did I have any idea how *intimate* her dealings with him had become, much less where they were headed. But I could plainly see they were high at that moment, early on a Monday afternoon, and that caused me concern.

"How 'bout I drive?" I suggested once we located her car in the parking garage.

"Nonsense!" she answered.

Christian grabbed my duffel bag from my hands and tossed it into the open trunk, the first action by him I observed that was anything other than totally chill.

"You wanna roll with us?" he asked as the Honda Accord rolled along I-5 into the city. He and Angie had their windows down—it was a glorious day, the first seventy-degree one of the year—and they each extended an arm out parallel to the car, oscillating their hands up and down through the passing air as though gliding over invisible waves.

"Yeah, Drew-Drew," she said. "Come with us."

"Where you going?"

"Where else? I'm gonna show Christian the view from the bluff." My first real clue.

"I better pass. Lots of schoolwork to catch up on." No lie there. I'd hardly cracked a book. "Besides, I'm exhausted. A bunch of the contestants got drunk together after the taping."

"Right! How'd it go?"

I'd thought she'd never ask. "I'm not supposed to say. But I can tell you my *first* show will air on May eleventh."

"What's Alex like in person?" she asked, apparently missing my subtext.

To be fair, that's the other thing everyone wants to know. Figuring that in her present condition she'd soon grow distracted, I gave her a cursory account of my varied impressions of the quiz show host.

All I'll say about that now is I initially misjudged him over one of our interactions. After I let a spot in the finals slip through my fingers, I looked at him and said, in my best imitation of Marlon Brando in *On the Waterfront*, "I coulda been a contender."

"Instead you're just a bum," he replied.

I took offense at the remark and held a grudge about it for years, not realizing it was a clever rejoinder, a paraphrase of the next line from the movie, which I'd never seen. I knew the line I quoted only because of my sponge-like ability—conducive to *Jeopardy!* success—to absorb cultural references even out of context. Ironic, huh?

(Sorry, Alex. You put up a valiant fight against cancer. Rest in peace.)

Once the Accord came to a stop outside my apartment building in the U District, Angie turned behind the wheel and faced where I sat in the backseat. "Here we are," her expression seemed to say, reminding me of the start to our telepathic conversation.

I wondered if another exchange like that were possible without the benefit of chemical enhancement. On my part anyway.

I wish I could be alone with you, I thought, calling on every neuron I could summon.

"Well," she said with her embodied voice as her mouth opened and closed, "here we are."

"Right," I answered. So much for that. "Thanks for the ride. If one of you would be kind enough to let me out, I'll let you be on your merry way."

Christian nodded, swung open the passenger door, and stepped onto the curb. A moment later, he thumped on the back of the car.

Angie pulled the lever to release the trunk. I pulled the one to adjust the passenger seat.

"Maybe we could hang out this weekend," she said as I tilted the seat forward to clear my exit route. "Christian gave me some killer bud."

"Sure," I said. "Sounds awesome."

"Have fun hitting the books. The park won't be the same without you."

Then don't go without me. It's supposed to be *our* house of worship.

Her hand landed on mine where it gripped the side

138

of the passenger seat for leverage as I moved to climb out of the car. She gazed into my eyes. "Congrats on making it past the first round. I can't wait to see you shine on TV." She hadn't missed my subtext after all.

As I stepped onto the curb with a smile, I found Christian waiting there with my duffel bag, which he pressed against my chest.

"Welcome home," he said.

"I think about baseball," said Scott. "Or, if that doesn't work, punching a brick wall."

"Doesn't that ... I don't know, defeat the whole purpose?" I asked.

"Not if the purpose is to make her cum before you do."

"Yeah." Remembering the '86 World Series should do it, thought my Inner Red Sox Fan.

"And to put it in baseball terms, you're down to your last strike."

If you understand Scott's analogy, you must realize I'd had a second failed coupling with Angie by then. I'd gone to her apartment, at her invitation, the Saturday after she gave me the ride. It was my turn to give her one—once we smoked a bowl of Christian's killer bud.

As we undressed each other between kisses and caresses, the conditions seemed near perfect for a successful coming together. It was the middle of the afternoon, and I'd stayed home to read the night before, so I was well rested and energized. For me, marijuana has an aphrodisiac effect. It heightens my sensuality, reduces my anxiety, and, usually, increases my sexual stamina—without causing the difficulty achieving an erection I sometimes get from cocaine and other stimulants such as ecstasy.

I hadn't counted on Angie throwing me a curveball.

"Spank me," she said as she started rocking up and down on me.

139

I gave her ass a light slap.

"Harder, please."

I gave it a firm smack.

"Harder! I've been a naughty girl!" She pouted when I hesitated. "Come on! Spank me hard!"

I did so, twice in quick succession.

"Yes! Even harder! Hurt me!"

I really let her have it. She cried out in pained satisfaction, and I cried out in surprised pleasure as I felt myself release into the condom.

She stopped rocking. "Again?" she asked, reminding me of the hasty outcome of our earlier experience.

"Sorry," I said.

She collapsed onto the bed and rolled away. "Not quite the punishment I wanted."

Two weeks later, I still felt the sting of her comment. And confusion about her slight kink being such a turn-on. For *me*.

"Distracting myself won't do much good if I don't have any warning," I said to Scott.

"Can't help with that," he replied.

I gazed out across Red Square from where we sat on the plaza steps. A tiered walkway led to a fountain erupting into the air, with Mount Rainier—not erupting—visible in the distance on another gorgeous spring day.

"Have you talked to her lately?" he asked.

"Too busy. You know, with midterms."

I really had knuckled down on my studying, but as with my trivia training it was mostly a means of avoiding further awkwardness. It was also a way to avoid worrying about her. I'd heard from Melissa that Angie and Sabine, and sometimes Dina, were regular attendees of Christian's nightly private parties, which, according to Angie, as described to Melissa, were truly wild. And Angie had a high standard when it came to wildness.

"Bullshit," he said. "And you know it. What the fuck is happening to us?"

I turned and stared at the three red brick monoliths

rising from the plaza into the sky nearby. I liked to think of them as representing Lenin, Stalin, and Trotsky—the Three Moscowteers?—even though I knew the first one had been built to ventilate steam from the underground parking garage and the other two added for aesthetic reasons.

"Ever since we broke the pact, everything's gone to hell," Scott added.

"It started going bad before that. Like when Kirk got so uptight and controlling."

"Or even earlier. Like when you fell in love with another man's woman."

"You got me there," I said.

Scott put his arm around me. "In this case, I can't say I blame you."

My "fifteen minutes of fame" lasted five days, the amount of time between the airing of my *Jeopardy!* episodes. Actually, the fame lasted quite a bit longer, as people on campus and around the city continued to recognize me for weeks. The *glory* lasted five days. I went out each night that Thursday to Monday and never paid for a drink. I spent each day alone with Angie.

We initiated a reconciliation of sorts in time for her to attend the quarterfinal viewing party at my apartment. During the first commercial break, after she mentioned liking the UW sweatshirt I wore on the show, I retrieved it from my bedroom and gave it to her, "for luck." Apparently she was touched by the gesture. That led to a lot more touching between us. She accompanied me to a bar we liked on the south end of Lake Union, and we ended up stumbling the dozen blocks up the hill to her place.

The next morning, feeling no effects from the ordinarily toxic combination of shots we'd done, I stepped up to the plate with my bat in hand and drove the first pitch out of the park. We went into extra innings that day and returned to the king-size sideways diamond to sleep off our nights on the town before engaging in daily double-headers over the weekend and into the next week, with plenty of heartfelt pillow talk between sessions—no need for drugs to heighten our emotional and physical communion.

That Sunday, which happened to be Mother's Day, she returned from what I assumed was a trip to the bathroom. She opened the lid of a box she carried and shared with me its contents: a birth certificate and photos of her as an early teen with a newborn. As we gazed at the items in mutual tearful silence, whatever had dampened our connection seemed to have evaporated.

Everything changed on Tuesday, starting with the weather, which took a cold and wet turn that would last through Memorial Day. As I left her apartment that afternoon to go get mine ready for my semifinal viewing party, the gloomy sky overhead appeared to portend a coming storm. And did it ever.

"Why don't you call her?" asked Scott, when Angie hadn't arrived by the end of the Jeopardy round.

"If she hasn't left by now," I replied, "she wouldn't make it in time for Final Jeopardy." That actually might not be so bad, I thought. "I bet she was running late and decided to watch at home. She'll meet us after."

"Why don't you call her and suggest that?" asked Becca. "So she doesn't try to rush over and miss your tragic demise."

Thanks, roomie. I knew how she meant it, though. If I could count on anything, it was Becca's understanding—and calling me out on—my insecurities. And she had a point about Angie.

I stepped into the kitchen, picked up the handset from the wall-mounted base, and pushed the familiar sequence of buttons. After eight or ten rings a connection was made and quickly broken. I dialed again. This time it was answered after the first ring, and just as quickly disconnected. I tried once more. Busy signal.

142

"Struck out," I said after hanging up the receiver.

"She probably doesn't want to be disturbed," Johnny replied, indicating with a tilt of his head that Double Jeopardy was about to get underway.

Yeah, I thought, the storm inside me intensifying. I opened the cabinet, took down the whiskey bottle, and poured myself a fistful. By the time the show—and my short-lived victor status—ended with my big choke, I'd swallowed the entire fist.

"Don't go," said Melissa when I took my keys off the hook, as I was certain Angie had done to her phone, after my repeated attempts to reach her between Double and Final Jeopardy had met with steady busy signals.

"I'm fine."

"It's not your driving I'm worried about."

"What's that supposed to mean? You know something?"

"No."

"Why don't we all go?" asked Scott. He meant the four of us, since Becca would no doubt opt to mind her own business, and Dina and Sabine were also no-shows.

I shook my head. "I gotta do this on my own."

As I approached Angie's apartment, I heard Guns N' Roses welcoming me to the jungle. I knocked, then banged on the door until it opened.

In the time it took Angie to step out and close the door behind her—wearing her new lucky sweatshirt and seemingly nothing else—Axl sang, "And you're a very sexy girl / That's very hard to please."

That fits, I thought.

She directed her gaze toward the hallway carpet. We each waited for the other to say something. She won.

"We missed you at my place. *I* missed you."

"Sorry."

"Will you look at me for a minute?" I asked.

She shook her head. "Sorry."

"It's okay. No big deal. Whatever happened, I forgive you."

Her head snapped up. "I don't want—or need—your forgiveness."

I didn't recognize the glassy look in her eyes. She wasn't rolling, or tripping, or stoned.

"You should go now," she said.

"Come with me. Everyone's waiting for us."

"Everyone?"

"Well, not Kirk," I said, hoping a little levity would lighten the moment. It didn't. "And not Sabine or Dina. Are they in there?"

The door swung open about a foot. I heard the frontman's melodic voice sing, "And when you're high you never / Ever want to come down."

Too perfect. You could not make this shit up.

"Leave," said Angie. Then she slipped through the crack.

As the door closed after her, I wedged my foot against it. It opened wider, and Christian filled the gap. Perhaps I should say he *blocked* it. He'd traded his boy-next-door costume for an ensemble that expressed his sole (soul) true color: black.

On the stereo inside, Slash and crew launched into an extended instrumental.

"I'm gonna tell you this once," said the dealer.

Don't say it, I thought, somehow anticipating the words about to escape his mouth.

He said them anyway: "Don't come 'round here no more."

I shook my head. "You really shouldn't say that unless you're wearing your Mad Hatter outfit. Makes you seem ... *petty.*"

He looked at me with a frown, which, after a moment, transformed to a grin. "Oh. 'Cuz of that video. You're a real smartass."

That I am. Smart and an ass.

He pulled up his shirt to show me a handgun tucked

144

into his waistband. "I don't like smartasses."

"You know where you are? / You're in the jungle, baby / You're gonna dieee," cried Axl, elongating the last word until it transformed into an anguished scream.

This couldn't get more surreal, I thought. Even if I were on acid.

"Raaaarrrr," my Inner Lion said straight into Christian's face. I waved a paw at him as I turned away. "See you around." I strode majestically down the hall.

"You better hope not," he called after me.

"Welcome to the jungle / Watch it bring you to your / Nuh-nuh-nuh-nuh-nuh-nuh-nuh-nuh-knees knees!"

The door slammed shut.

"Kneel down," said Angie, then waited for me to comply. "Now ... what is it they say? During mass?"

"Uh ... something about the wine and the wafer being the blood and body of Christ?"

"Right! Okay. Here we go. *This Is The Body Of Christ*." She gave me two pieces of bread stuck together with peanut butter.

"You sure that's the right amount?" I asked. It was my first time.

"I put like a gram and a half in there. I'm taking twice that."

Of course you are, I thought.

I peeled open the bread and counted the stems and caps. I had no idea how many was too many. With a shrug, I flattened out the bread, bit into it, and started to chew.

"This is disgusting," I said, my mouth full of peanut butter and mushroom sandwich.

"Wash it down with this," she replied, handing me a big glass of liquid. "I mean, *This Is The Blood Of Christ*."

I sipped and swished, trying to soften the glob enough to swallow it. Once I cleared my mouth, I finished the rest in smaller bites, with plenty of sugary water.

"Congratulations, Drew-Drew. You're about to have

145

a religious experience."

As Angie nibbled on her consecrated concoction and gulped her sacred solution, her face contorting with every blessed bite, I reflected on the Sunday sermon immediately preceding our proceedings. It had been our first exchange in the twelve days since my rumble in the jungle with Christian, whose "advice" I'd decided—once the liquid courage had drained from my fortunately still flowing blood—would be best to heed, an epiphany brought on, at least in part, by my realization I wasn't meant—much less cut out—to save her, from him or from herself.

"Holy hell," I'd said maybe ten minutes before this, after opening my apartment door to her pale and gaunt countenance.

"It's been a rough couple of weeks," she replied. She didn't offer details, and I didn't ask.

"I'm worried about you," I said, once I'd closed—and bolted—the door with her inside.

"What do you care? You're leaving soon enough anyway."

Ah, I thought. So that's it.

"Come with me," I said, taking her hands, and surprising myself as much as her.

"For God's sake!" she cried, breaking free. "Why does everyone want me to be theirs?"

If I'd thought she wanted an answer, I would've rattled off all the reasons I could come up with—and might've *still* been listing them.

"Why can't people let me be me? Just give me some fucking space." Once I'd literally done just that, stepping back from her, she started to pace. "I'm failing all my classes."

No surprise there. With only a week before final exams, it was too late to change that, or I would've offered to help her with her coursework. So much for not trying, or at least wanting, to save her.

"They'll probably kick me out." She stopped pacing

146

and faced me. "But Florida?"

"I think a change would do you good." Being with me would do you good. Do *me* good.

"Maybe you're right. That's so far from here, though." She'd lived in Seattle all her life, and her entire family—including, as far as anyone knew, her son—was still in the area. "Can we talk about it more later? Like in the summer?"

"Of course. It's a big decision."

"Thank you. For the offer, and for giving me room." She sighed out a breath. "For now," she said, removing a baggie from the little purse she carried, "all I wanna do is have some fun!"

It's pure coincidence the above dialogue makes allusions to two Sheryl Crow songs not released until several years later. Or is it? Seattle is home to an unusually large population of the bird by that name. Members of the flock often congregated on the power lines outside my apartment building, and the windows of my second-floor living room were likely open at the time. You know, if you believe in that sort of thing.

"I like fun," I said.

"I knew I could count on you! 'Shrooming alone sucks."

I wouldn't know, I thought.

"Don't worry, these didn't come from Christian. He means nothing to me, by the way."

You seem to mean a lot to him, I started to say. But she knew that, and I held my tongue.

We were still waiting for the psilocybin to take effect, biding time by watching MTV, when a second seeker came knocking at the gate to my sanctuary. Our initial sense of alarm faded a bit once we considered how little force was applied to generate the sound. Even so, Angie slipped down the hallway while I went to the door, wishing for the magical appearance of a peephole.

I fastened the security chain before unlocking and cracking open the door.

147

"Where is she?" asked Sabine.

"Becca? She went out of town for the long weekend."

"Don't be stupid." She raised her voice. "I know Angie's here. And so does Christian."

"I wish he'd let me off my leash!" shouted the wayward follower, returning from exile.

"He wants to see you. Right away."

"Sorry," said Angie. She pushed the door shut, then bowed her head.

I lifted her chin. We held each other's eyes for a long moment.

"This is how it has to be," she said. "You know that, right?"

I nodded.

She unhooked the chain and opened the door.

Once they'd gone, I crashed onto the sofa and stared at the TV screen. The video for a recent hit by Fine Young Cannibals came on.

"I can't stop the way I feel / Things you do don't seem real," sang the lead vocalist, Roland Gift ("roll and gift"?).

I got up, approached the console, and raised the volume, which I'd lowered in an instinctive response to Sabine's arrival.

"She drives me crazy / And I can't help myself."

Oh, come on.

Angie was right: 'Shrooming alone sucks, especially when you start already freaked out. It didn't take long for me to realize I needed to act to control the direction of my trip. I knew exactly what to do. Alcohol would temper the intensity of my high, and a friendly environment would soften its edge. That's how I found myself, maybe two hours after her departure, sitting at the bar in a favorite tavern right down the street from my apartment. The location wasn't its only serendipitous feature. This place was known as a haven for artists and radicals. Back in the day, Dylan Thomas and Allen Ginsberg—and, according

148

to legend, Jack Kerouac—hung out there.

I took my time with the first beer, knowing nausea was a common reaction to the drug. A second sat in front of me now. I sipped and listened to the music from the jukebox. While the lyrics didn't match up directly with either my internal or external experience—thank the gods!—the vibe of most songs, particularly those by the Grateful Dead and the Allman Brothers Band, suited my state of being. A few tunes, ones I would've enjoyed under other circumstances—by Led Zeppelin, the Rolling Stones, and other classic rock groups—rekindled my agitation when they played. I was calm at the moment.

I noticed a middle-aged man down the bar gaze across the two vacant stools between us in my direction. When he nodded at me, I slid one seat toward him. "Can I buy you a beer?"

"Sure thing," he replied.

I slid onto the stool beside him as I motioned for the bartender. I waited for his draft to arrive. We raised our mugs in communion.

Here goes, I thought. "Can I ask you something?"

"I knew there'd be a catch."

"No no no. It's not like that."

"Like what?"

"Uh ... like whatever. Whatever you're thinking."

"How do you know what I'm thinking?"

"I don't. Of course not." I shook my head. "Sorry to bother you."

I slid one seat away. But I couldn't help glancing at him what seemed like every now and then but might have been more often. He was perfect. Penetrating eyes set into a wizened visage. Long gray ponytail. Well-worn leather jacket.

"What is you want from me?" he asked. "Really, kiddo, I mean it." He patted the stool next to him.

I slid back over. "I'm fucked up."

"I can see that."

"I mean my whole existence. It's a mess. I need ...

advice."

"Advice?"

"From a mentor. No, that's not right. From a life coach. No, that's wrong, too."

"From a guru?"

"Yes! That's the word. A guru. I need advice from a guru."

He smirked. "I'm no guru. But I'll tell you where to find all the advice you need."

I took in a breath and held it while I waited for him to guide me to the source of truth.

"*Poor Richard's Almanac.*"

I exhaled in disbelief. "Don't you mean, '*What is* Poor Richard's Almanac?'" I asked. In response to his blank stare, I added, "You know, like on *Jeopardy!.*"

"I look like I watch *Jeopardy!?*" he replied.

He didn't, come to think of it. Not a bit.

"You heard, though, right?" I asked. "About the UW student who was on it. That's the question he missed. That's what he choked on."

He nodded in thought, then shrugged. He chugged the contents of his mug. "You really do need a guru," he said, climbing off his barstool. He patted me on the back. "Meantime, check out what ol' Dick has to say about life—and other things."

I shook my head as he walked out of the tavern, glad to be rid of that false prophet.

"*Early to Bed, and early to rise, makes a Man healthy, wealthy and wise,*" I read aloud from an anthology I found on my bookshelf. I'd heard that passage quoted more than once. Its origin, I'd just learned, was the preface to the final edition of the almanac, published in 1758 with a title, *The Way to Wealth*, that told me everything I needed to know. Another of its pearls of wisdom: "*There are no Gains, without Pains.*"

So that's where Jane Fonda came up with the

exercise motto!

I scanned the pages, searching for something—anything—to transcend Poor Dick's general triteness and his focus on material success. Near the end I hit upon a pair of phrases with surprising resonance. The first—"*we may give Advice, but we cannot give Conduct*"—seemed applicable to my quest, even if I couldn't grasp exactly how. The second—"*They that won't be counselled [sic], can't be helped*"—nailed my current feeling toward Angie.

I flipped to the anthology's other excerpt, the preface to the first edition, published in 1733. I'd started reading it earlier but hadn't made it past the opening paragraph, which was bogged down with an account of the relationship between the eponymous—and fictitious—author and his wife. The only part of genuine interest to me was Richard Saunders' love for stargazing, which was not only something I still shared but also information that might've helped me achieve a different outcome on *Jeopardy!*. (The clue mentioned astronomy.)

This time my eyes landed in the middle of a sentence in the next paragraph, which from that point read, "inexorable Death, who was never known to respect Merit, has already prepared the mortal Dart, the fatal Sister has already extended her destroying Shears, and that ingenuous Man must soon be taken from us."

Now *that* is some weighty prose. I could spend hours pondering the implications of that. And perhaps I did.

The next thing I remember, someone was banging on my door. I wandered over to it, in a trance of sorts, and, after struggling a few moments to unlock it—wondering what in the heavens possessed me to turn the deadbolt—threw it wide open.

"Fuck the world!" I yelled from the rooftop of Angie's apartment building.

"Fuck the world!" Scott echoed me.

"Fuck life!" I shouted.

151

"Fuck life!" he repeated.

"Fuck death!"

"Fuck death!"

"Fuck everything!"

"Fuck everything!"

I know I promised to explain how this scenario came about. Many details of what transpired between Scott's arrival at my apartment and this moment don't matter. What does matter is that he spotted the half-full baggie Angie left on my counter and offered to "catch up" with me so I wouldn't have to trip alone any longer.

Once he wolfed down a hefty serving of mushrooms, I realized it had been almost six hours since my initial dose, meaning he would be the one tripping alone soon. So I finished off the remaining caps and stems, literally choking them down with chocolate milk, since my supply of peanut butter had been exhausted in making Scott's sandwich.

Sometime later, the phone rang. I'd filled Scott in on the situation with Angie by then, and he insisted on answering the call, certain it would be her. It wasn't. It was her sister. In a frantic voice, Dina told him Angie needed our help, and to get over to her place right away, or it would be too late.

Despite the urgency, neither of us dared drive—a wise choice—which left two obvious options: a seventy-five-minute walk or a forty-five-minute bus ride with a transfer downtown. Averse to being confined with strangers in a packed tube on wheels, we put on our thinking caps and came up with option three: run as fast as our rubbery stems would carry us.

We ended up walking briskly more than running, and we paused to puke twice each. By the time we did get there, however long it took, it *was* too late. We found Angie's door busted open. Her apartment showed signs of a struggle, including what looked like bloodstains on the carpet. We waited inside for a while, then headed to the roof for air.

152

I hoped to find solace—or at least lose myself—in the constellations above, but I had to settle for the sense of cleansing I felt standing in a gentle mist as I came to accept I had no control over Angie's fate. What would we have done to rescue her from Christian in our condition anyway? Maybe we'd all be dead.

"Fuck the world!" I shrieked in silence.

"Fuck the world!" echoed a voice that wasn't Scott's.

I turned and saw the embodiment of beauty—now more beautiful than ever—emerge from the roof access enclosure. I rushed toward her.

"Fuck life!" she shouted, dodging my embrace and racing across the rain-slicked surface of the building top. "Fuck death!" Angie hopped onto the roughly two-foot-high, ten-inch-wide barrier lining the perimeter of the roof, her momentum nearly carrying her over the edge. "Fuck everything!"

She must've heard us on the ground below or coming up the stairwell as we screamed that sequence over and over.

"Christian's dead," she said without any sign of feeling. "They killed him." She gazed out toward the Space Needle. "Maybe I'll fly away next."

"Please don't," I said, inching forward as Scott did the same from the other side.

"Why not? Give me one good reason. And don't say your love. Don't you dare presume to be reason for me to live! Don't you dare." She jumped into the air and rotated one hundred and eighty degrees while elevated, landing so she faced us. She raised her palms, warning us to stay back, but also to regain her precarious balance on the wet concrete.

"I wouldn't dare," I said, a tidal wave of clarity, and composure, engulfing me. "I do love you, but that's only reason for *me* to live. Who do *you* love? That's your reason."

"Nobody. I'm dead inside. So what's the point of breathing?"

153

"What about Danny?" I asked. That caught her attention. "You promised your newborn son you'd find him and be together again one day. You're gonna break that promise?"

"That might not even be his name anymore."

As she drifted into thought, Scott and I each took a step toward her.

"Besides, what kind of mother would I be?"

"You can't contact him until he's eighteen, right? That's almost twelve years from now. You have plenty of time to turn your life around. We're practically kids ourselves. We're not the people we'll become. You could be anything you want by then. With what I've seen in you, with what's in your heart, you'll be the best damn mother who ever lived."

"You really think so?" she asked.

I nodded, and meant it.

Angie wiped away tears and tilted her head back, letting the tears of heaven drizzle onto her face as Scott and I shuffled forward. As we reached for her, she lifted a foot to step down onto the roof and then—in what seemed like slow motion—slipped and fell.

I gasped, then felt the flow of my own tears as I gazed at the newest, and truest, redefinition of beauty looking up at me from Scott's arms.

CHAPTER TWELVE

INTERNATIONAL INDEPENDENCE

As far as I know, the body of Christian was never found, nor were his killers ever held accountable, at least not by public authorities. Angie's landlord was less than pleased about the broken door and carpet stains, which it turns out were not from the blood of Christian—or anyone else—but from red wine. Whatever her involvement in the crime, which she refused to discuss, Angie got off—aside from having to pay for the damages—scot-free.

But she did not get off Scott-free, as I'm about to tell you.

We stepped out of the train station into a bustling plaza at noon on July Fourth, greeted not by exploding fireworks but by the melodic rhythms of steel drums. Welcome to Amsterdam!

Minutes later we were greeted by Sabine, who, as promised, awaited us in one corner of the square. We dropped our bags at the hostel where she'd booked us a private room with four twin beds. Then we headed to a museum. *Yeah, right.* For we three young Americans, the liberal Dutch drug laws—or, more accurately, their tolerant enforcement policies—were the main attraction and most obvious reason for making the Netherlands our first stop in Europe.

We *did* visit a pair of museums that afternoon, but not together. Whereas the other three musketeers were roused by the appeal of the Sex Museum, I was drawn by Van Gogh. Also, I was eager to part ways with my companions, as I'd been waiting for an opportunity to reflect on an incident from our overseas travel that left hanging over my head a cloud thicker than the smoke circulating through the "cannabis café" where we landed and sampled the merchandise.

One of the first paintings to catch my eye—descriptively titled "Skull of a Skeleton with Burning Cigarette"—seemed apropos to the event in my mind. About midway into our ten-hour nonstop flight from Seattle, somewhere over the Arctic Circle and near Earth's crown, Angie excused herself from the middle seat she occupied between me and Scott.

"I need a pee and a butt," she said.

"While I'm up ..." Scott replied before following her down the aisle toward the lavatories and smoking section in the back of the 747. (In those days, you could still light up on international flights.)

I didn't share their addiction to nicotine, and I'd restricted my fluid intake. Once they disappeared, I leaned my head against the pillow I'd folded against the lowered window shade and closed my eyes.

When I opened them, the seats beside me remained vacant. I checked my wristwatch and saw they'd been gone half an hour. Must be trying to get a sufficient fix to last the rest of the trip, I thought, then rejoined the majority of our fellow passengers in fitful slumber.

I was awakened after another thirty minutes by exhilarated giggling as Angie and Scott slid into the row. They seemed oblivious to the fact they were causing a disturbance to others, and particularly to me. As they continued to demonstrate signs of euphoria, I wondered if one of them had dared bring ecstasy through security.

Granted, exiting the United States didn't entail the level of scrutiny we'd be subject to on re-entry. But what was the point of taking even that risk when we were en route to Amsterdam?

Angie flagged down the next flight attendant to pass through our cabin and ordered champagne, specifying she wanted two cups. I peeked below a single fluttering eyelid as Scott divided the contents of the miniature bottle.

"To joining the club," she toasted. They pressed their supple plastic shells together and sipped with satisfaction.

It took every bit of my resolve to suppress my sudden nausea, which had nothing to do with airsickness. I knew full well what club she meant. Its title shares words with a nickname for Denver and its initiation involves what Debbie did in Dallas.

I spent the remainder of the flight second-guessing my decision to go through with the trip despite everything that transpired between us since Memorial Day. What had driven me to make that choice? The simple answer was we'd booked our nonrefundable plane tickets during the peak of our ecstatic Easter celebration, after Sabine expressed separation anxiety in regard to her scheduled June return to the south of France. We were the four musketeers, after all! The more complicated—and truthful—answer was I hoped I could win what had become an obvious competition between Scott and me for Angie's affection, if not her love, which she still claimed she was incapable of feeling. I boarded the plane believing I had a fighting chance.

I've lost a key battle, I now thought, as I stepped up to the velvet rope keeping museum-goers from getting too close to one of the precious works of art. What next? Accept defeat and try to salvage our friendships? Or adopt a Machiavellian strategy and try to sabotage their union before it comes all the way into being?

The canvas before me depicted a path leading into a field of wheat without a destination. Depending on your perspective, it either curved out of sight in the distance or got swallowed up by the wind-swept stalks. Against the dark and foreboding sky above, dozens of birds flew in different directions, as though the flock had no collective sense of where they were going.

I looked at the nearby placard, which listed the painting's title—"Wheatfield with Crows"—and quoted a passage by Jules Michelet, one of Van Gogh's favorite authors: "The ancients, who lived far more completely than ourselves in and with nature, found it no small profit to follow, in a hundred obscure things where human experience as yet affords no light, the directions of so prudent and sage a bird."

I contemplated the implications of this juxtaposition of text and image, which the placard noted was finished during the last weeks of the artist's life and might have been his final work.

I'd never felt so lost and alone.

I opened the door to our hostel room and flipped on the light switch, resolved to wait there until the others returned. These people—Scott and Angie at least—meant far too much to me to let a little confusion and hurt dissolve our bond. Okay, *a lot* of those things. Even so.

I froze in the doorway as I took in the scene. At first, all I saw was Angie and Sabine kissing as their naked bodies leaned toward each other on one of the beds. Then I noticed Angie rocking up and down in a familiar manner. Sure enough, she sat astride the pelvis of a man whose head was obscured by Sabine's angled crotch. Not that his identity was a mystery.

The women turned toward me, alerted to my presence by the sudden illumination. Angie extended a hand in my direction as Sabine bent to suckle one of her breasts. The room began to spin. Angie closed her eyes and tilted her head back with a moan.

"Yeah, baby," I heard a distorted version of Scott's voice say. "Let me hear you scream. Come on, girl! Come on!"

And that's exactly what she did, crying out in a way I'd never heard from her.

I collapsed to my knees and gripped my head until I felt a hand touch my shoulder.

"Join us," said Angie. "I always cum more easily the second time."

I looked into her face. It blurred.

Behind her, Scott sat up and swung his feet onto the floor. "Hey, man. Ange told me everything. No need to be ashamed. My first blow job was from a guy. You wanna suck my dick, that's totally cool." He spread his knees apart, as if he expected me to crawl right over. "Assuming you can handle all this."

His face blurred.

I staggered to my feet and backed into the hallway, pulling the door shut after me. I held it closed by the knob while Angie tugged on the other side. I took a series of rapid breaths. As soon as I felt the opposing pressure ease, I let go and fled down the corridor.

If the bridges crossing the numerous canals in Amsterdam were much higher, I might've jumped from one as I wandered the city streets. Instead, as late night turned to early morning and after several stops in taverns for whiskey shots, I found myself in *De Wallen*, the name of which translates as "the quays" but which is known more commonly as the Red Light District.

My travel budget didn't include spending on a prostitute. Besides, I thought, real men don't pay for sex. I hadn't since my first time. Come to think of it, *I* hadn't paid for it then either.

On the other hand, I had to do something to release my pent-up tension. And when in Rome ...

I roamed the maze of narrow pathways, eyeballing half-naked bodies on display through windows lined with glowing bulbs, wondering what perverted acts were

159

transpiring behind the closed curtains of the darkened ones. The lingerie-clad transvestites (a term still in common usage then and one that conveys my limited awareness at the time) held particular fascination. They seemed so ... natural. One smiled at me every time I walked by her—*his*—window.

Okay, I thought, that's enough. Not my type. Just looking. No urge to explore *those* nether lands.

On my next pass, she—*he*—waved, beckoning me.

I considered the similar spelling of the words "deviant" and "defiant" and wondered if they had common origin. (They do not.) Maybe their meanings were more similar, at least in certain contexts, than I'd understood them to be.

A moment later, I made my decision. I approached the chosen door and rang the bell. I soon entered the cozy chamber of a real woman, turning my back on the *freak* across the street—and on the one inside my own skin.

I waited outside the hostel until I saw them leave, then darted in to collect my things. I knew we'd be on the same train to Paris, as we bought our tickets together before leaving the station the day before. After the unbudgeted expense I incurred in *De Wallen*, I couldn't afford to squander more money on a new fare. (Given my state of inebriation and my propensity for "whiskey dick," the hefty sum she charged—in advance—truly had been squandered.) Upon boarding, I found a window seat near the back of the rearmost car, hoping to avoid contact until I could secure conveyance to my next destination, which most definitely was no longer Sabine's hometown in the south of France.

Between the time of my meditative visit to the Van Gogh Museum and my walking in on the threesome *in flagrante delicto*, I'd thought about the movie *The Return of the Musketeers*. It had been filmed the year before by the director of the earlier pictures, with a script by the

160

same screenwriter and featuring largely the same cast, and I was anticipating seeing it as soon as it was released. I'd never read the Dumas sequel on which the new movie was based, but I'd heard the plot involved the musketeers turning against each other before reuniting to defeat a common foe. I'd hoped by returning to the hostel I might effect a similar reconciliation.

Now my thoughts were on how I might revise the narrative as "The Solo Adventures of D'Artagnan." The way I figured it, he was the main character of the novels anyway. Dumas even called the series the *D'Artagnan Romances*.

I'd read that one of the actors had a fatal accident during the film shoot in Spain. Roy Kinnear, who played D'Artagnan's loyal servant Planchet, fell from a horse and broke his pelvis, then suffered a heart attack. I could relate to both.

I'd long wanted to visit Spain, an interest dating back to my secondary school studies of the language and culture, through which I'd been exposed to the work of the poet and dramatist Federico García Lorca. I'd since learned of Lorca's close, and often troubled, relationships with Salvador Dalí, one of my favorite painters, and filmmaker Luis Buñuel. The writer's hometown—and site of the famous Alhambra palace—was near the southern tip of the Iberian Peninsula. Perhaps I could turn my misfortune into an opportunity to make a pilgrimage of sorts. I could travel down the Mediterranean coast before going west to Lorca's Granada, then head north to Toledo, where the man who performed as faithful companion to my alter ego had slipped into the arms of death.

As I watched the countryside roll by and formulated these plans, I listened to music on my Sony Walkman. The cassette playing at the moment, a regular in my rotation, was the latest album by the band INXS, whose name—which is not a strange spelling of "inks," as I assumed until the first time I heard it pronounced—summed up the nature of what I now sought to escape.

161

A hit single from the year before came on. "Here come the woman / With the look in her eye / Raised on leather / With flesh on her mind." So much for escaping *her*, I thought. "Words as weapons / sharper than knives / Makes you wonder how the other half die."

"Makes you wonder," I repeated along with the song.

The vocals continued. "Here come the man / With the look in his eye / Fed on nothing / But full of pride." Nailed him. "Look at them go / Look at them kick / Makes you wonder how the other half live." Hmmm.

"The devil inside, the devil inside," sang Michael Hutchence, whose accidental death by autoerotic asphyxiation years later made me wonder what devil he had inside.

I recalled Angie's quip about not being costumed as Wonder Woman when we met. That made me wonder how I allowed myself to ignore the warning signs.

Blinded by love, I thought, as I remained deaf to the song's most relevant words: "Every single one of us / The devil inside."

I shouldered my backpack and turned from the window with passport and ticket in hand.

"Where you off to?" asked Angie. No escaping her indeed.

"Barcelona and points beyond."

"Would you like to talk first?

"Not really. But I'll listen to anything you want to say."

"Would it help to know we were way high? One piece of space cake between the three of us! That shit is *potent*," she said.

Words as weapons, sharper than knives, I thought, chuckling as I shook my head.

"I wish you'd come with us," she continued, "but I understand why you won't. Will you meet us back here next week? Sabine says the Bastille Day celebration is not to be missed."

We'd scheduled our return flight so we could spend the French national holiday in Paris. But now D'Artagnan had fortresses of his own to storm.

"I'll see you at the Amsterdam airport," I said. And it felt good.

I never made it to Toledo, or even to Granada—although I did take in the Dalí Museum in Figueres—abandoning my quest for whatever I sought in those places in favor of quenching my thirst from another Holy Grail. Before I get to that, I'll share a few words about Barcelona.

If I could choose any city in the world as my home, it might well be the capital of Catalonia. I've never seen anything like its combination of medieval and modern architecture or felt such a simultaneously cosmopolitan and quirky vibe. The two other major European cities I'd visited by then—Amsterdam, even with its quaint charm, and Athens, even with its splendor of antiquity—didn't compare in my estimation. Nor does anywhere I've traveled—in physical form—since.

I spent days ambling along stone alleys beneath archways and ornamental facades in the Gothic Quarter, rambling along La Rambla past the array of street performers and sidewalk cafés to the Columbus Monument, basking on beaches and parking myself in parks, and tramping to the top of Montjuic, with its cliffside view of the harbor and where preparations were underway to host the Summer Olympics three years later. With the substantial investment being made in its infrastructure in advance of those games—a festival of international goodwill through spirited but gracious competition—the city seemed like a butterfly about to emerge from its cocoon. I crawled my way through it as though it were my entire world.

I'll never forget the feeling I got at one particular construction site. *La Sagrada Família*—"the sacred

163

family"—is the abbreviated name for the crowning achievement of Catalan architect and engineer Antoni Gaudí, whose distinctive works, borrowing techniques from the Gothic Revival movement and from various Asian countries—including India, Persia, and Japan—and integrating them with natural elements to form an organic whole, pop up all over the city. This specific project is a massive Roman Catholic church, designated in its full name—and by a recent pope—as a basilica, the erection of which started in 1882 and remains underway. It's now expected to be completed in 2026, which will mark a century since the death of its creator. I was inspired and awed by the sheer ambition of its immensity and complexity, as well as by the concept of something being, in essence, a perpetual work-in-progress.

From Barcelona, I trained to the tourist mecca of Alicante, where my pilgrim's progress came to a halt. My soundtrack on that ride featured Def Leppard's *Hysteria* album. By the time we docked in the port town, my pump was primed by songs like "Love Bites," "Pour Some Sugar on Me," "Animal," and "Women"—no need to quote lyrics with those titles.

A bit after midnight, a crowd finally began filing into what my *Lonely Planet* guidebook proclaimed the hottest nightclub in town. I'd spent the last hour chatting with a fortyish man who could've been the official spokesmodel for *machismo*, his shirt unbuttoned almost to his belt, showing off a furry chest and ample gut, as well as a thick gold chain with crucifix pendant. Our conversation had been as clichéd as he was, but at least I was practicing my oral skills.

I was about ready to blow when two *señoritas bonitas* entered. The gypsy eyes of one gazed at my longish hair, streaked blond by the Mediterranean sun. Unlike the *hombre* beside me, despite my decent command of the native tongue, for a local I could not pass.

Gypsy and I rolled our eyes as *mi amigo* performed a versatile display of cheap bar tricks. In the presence of women, he became tolerable, even if mostly as a diversionary tactic. He kept the *otra señorita* occupied while I showed Gypsy my best moves. There weren't many. But judging by what came next, my awkward disco-technique seems to have added to my *americano* charm.

"I want your sex," sang George Michael on the dance remix of that song, as I nodded at her. "I want you," the former Wham!—"bam, thank you"?—man vocalized, as I pointed at her. "I want your sex," he sang again, as I put my hands on her hips and grinded my pelvis against her.

"*Te quiero*," I said a few minutes later, as we sauntered in the direction of the *pension*, or small rooming house, where I was staying.

Gypsy looked at me aghast, and I thought I'd blown it. She conveyed to me, in a roundabout Spanish explanation I could grasp, that the phrase I used—which translates literally as "I want you"—was an idiomatic expression for "I love you."

"No no no," I replied. "Fuck love."

She smiled. She clearly understood a few words of English, even though she never spoke any to me.

Actually, she did speak one word: a well-timed "*Wow!*" as I first penetrated her. I knew it wasn't in reaction to the *size* of my manhood, but it was gratifying all the same.

The next day she guided me to local sights: *El Castillo de Santa Bárbara* atop a mountain rising from the city center; the colorful *Barrio de la Santa Cruz* on its slopes; and *El Parque de Canalejas*, where lions sculpted from stone stand guard over hundred-year-old fig trees. That evening, as we strolled the palm tree-lined, marble-tiled promenade of *La Explanada de España*, she asked if I wanted to hop a train with her to Valencia, where she lived, in the morning.

"*Claro*," I said. Sure.

We spent nearly every minute of that week, her

165

summer holiday, together. I'd never felt so at ease with someone. Despite the language barrier, which often required us to speak extra words, communicating felt effortless.

Gypsy took me places no typical tourist gets to go, including the private office of the President of Valencia, a friend of her family. A member of the Spanish Socialist Workers Party, he was the province's first elected leader since the restoration of democracy after the death of Francisco Franco. The entire government palace was a sight to behold, especially the ornate gold ceiling in the hall where *el presidente* welcomed visiting dignitaries. In the presence of its luminosity, and her radiance, I felt like one of those special guests.

At the time appointed for us to part, Gypsy and I did so without any hint of pain or regret. We'd shared genuine connection, and that was enough. It didn't have to last forever.

"*Adiós,*" we said, wishing each other endless wellbeing. You're going to God.

I considered changing my seat assignment before deciding I was up to the test. In fact, after Angie and I made eye contact across our departure gate, *I* approached *them.* We exchanged convivial greetings and summaries of our travels.

I wasn't all that surprised to learn their European vacation had been filled with misadventures and chaos befitting the National Lampoon film by that name. Starring Scotty Chase and Angela D'Angelo, I thought. I recalled how, during the Griswold family's return flight to the United States, Clark causes their plane to knock the torch from the hand of the Statue of Liberty. I remembered, with a wry smile and a glance at Scott, Becca's comment the morning after the Halloween party. My grin widened as, gazing at Angie, I imagined our plane knocking the halo off the Space Needle.

Like the movie before its comic ending, their narrative had taken a serious twist when they were robbed while in the French Riviera.

"Sorry to hear that. Glad everyone's okay," I said, and meant it. When turn came for me to describe how my solitary flight had gone, I kept it short and sweet. "Perfect."

Soon after, I handed my boarding pass to the gate agent, relieved to be on my way home. Even though I wasn't yet sure where that was, I was convinced I had nowhere to go but up.

When I waved goodbye—*adiós*—to Scott and Angie as I drove away from my apartment building, I figured it would be the last time I saw them. It wasn't. We met again, a decade later, when I made my first return to Los Angeles since my episodes of *Jeopardy!*, to give a paper at an academic conference. They'd relocated there, as a married couple, some years before.

We had dinner. We knocked back a few drinks. Then we went to my hotel room, where—for old times' sake—we smoked a joint they'd brought along. While we didn't quite party like it was 1999 (which it was), we enjoyed a pleasant enough evening. We reminisced about our joyful escapades. We avoided raising the specter of our more painful ones. With two more years to wait before she could contact Danny, Angie already had leads on his new identity from information she found on the emergent World Wide Web. Our one-and-done reunion reached its climax with the three of us passing out on the king-size bed in a fitting tableaux: Angie and Scott lying in each other's arms a few feet away from me.

After leaving them behind in Seattle back in 1989, I navigated my way south on I-5, then turned east onto I-90, an open atlas riding shotgun on my solo trek to Florida. I'd circled my first stop, on the other side of the state: Spokane, where a stepbrother was eager to host me.

167

My temporary family disbanded, I was resolved to strengthen ties with my permanent one. After my departure from Fairchild Air Force Base, I'd spend several days in Janesville, where my only actual (half-)blood brother would be home from boarding school for the summer, no doubt eager for a Trivial Pursuit rematch. I hope he wins, I thought.

In between those encounters, I'd scale the Rockies, traverse the Continental Divide, and cruise across the Great Plains, making frequent stops to gaze around me at the infinite sky.

THIRD MOVEMENT
RE-VISIONS

CHAPTER THIRTEEN

ANDRE(W) THE TITAN

"Ad in," I said, following convention and announcing the scoring advantage I held over my opponent after winning the deuce point. I bounced the ball four times, then rocked back and forth twice with the outside of my left foot toeing the baseline. As I shifted my weight back for a third time, I circled my racquet down and around and tossed the ball up to where my sweet spot would connect with it over and slightly in front of my head. Textbook.

My perfect form showed in the result: My serve landed right in the spot I'd aimed for in the corner of the box along the center line, where it skidded hard and low off the acrylic surface of the concrete court.

My adversary, a leftie, had to stretch to attempt a backhand stab of a return. The ball popped off his frame high into the air.

Having followed my initial strike midway to the net, all I had to do was step up and put away the volley. I adjusted my sweaty grip and smashed the ball down the sideline away from where his momentum had carried him.

"Game. And. Set," I said.

"One apiece," he replied, joining me at the net. "I'd suggest we play a third, but I'm fried. Heat index must be one twenty."

"Ties are like kissing your sister," I said.

Truth be told, I wasn't about to play another set, lest it end with my melting or collapsing onto the court. His estimate of the combined effect of the heat and humidity—on this late August afternoon in Tallahassee—actually felt low to me.

But I also wasn't about to give him that satisfaction. "I suppose if you wanna forfeit ..."

"You know what? Sure. You win." He held out a hand, which I clasped with my own. He pulled me over the net so our bare chests and shoulders bumped together. "Happy birthday."

"Aww. You remembered. Thanks, Jack. I'm touched."

"Don't get too weepy, Goldilocks. Not like I baked you a cake. Or bought you anything."

"Goldilocks? More like Andre Agassi," I said.

In addition to a similar first name, I did have the rising superstar's hair, which I hadn't cut since leaving Seattle three years prior and now wore in a sun-bleached ponytail. I'd been a big Agassi fan since long before he won his first major tournament earlier that summer—in, no less, the most unlikely of places for his style of game and his aversion to the bounds of tradition: the hallowed grounds of Wimbledon. I was disappointed he'd decided to skip the upcoming Barcelona Olympics. I'd read his withdrawal from consideration was a gesture of sportsmanship to open a spot on the team for an elder statesman playing his last full season on the tour.

"And you're an aging McEnroe," I added, naming that elder statesman, who, regardless of Andre's intentions, was passed over by the selection committee for the young Michael Chang, himself quite an admirable underdog. I'll never forget Chang's 1989 French Open match against Ivan Lendl, played a week after the most eventful Memorial Day weekend I've ever had, in which, suffering from severe cramps, he hit an underhand

172

serve—and won the point, surviving that day and going on to claim the title.

"Whatever," replied Jack, who did have three years on me. "I'll run home and clean up, then meet you at the pub. First few rounds are on me, but I'm not letting you win at darts."

"Take all the time you want in the shower," I said as we collected our gear. "Seriously. I promised Kessler I'd make an appearance at the welcome party for new grad students. She likes to show me off."

Within the program, *I* was something of an elder statesman, and definitely the golden boy, having won a highly competitive university-wide fellowship each of the past three years. I had no objection to hearing my praises sung in public. Besides, it gave me an opportunity to scope out—and impress—the pool of potential bedmates.

Who would be the lucky lady tonight?

I made my move. I'd observed the school of minnows and was ready to feed. For my prey, I'd chosen a wholesome-looking brunette, a real sweetie petitie. I timed my approach to arrive at the buffet table right when she did. Our hands touched as we reached for plates.

"Sorry," I said, after we pulled our hands back and exchanged a look of surprise—in my case, of course, feigned. I separated a plate from the stack and offered it to her with a smile, both of which she accepted. "Welcome to the program. I'm Drew."

"So I heard," she said, reciprocating the smile wryly. Kessler had delivered quite the aria. "Short for Andrew? As in that awful storm?"

A Category Five hurricane sharing my name had devastated the Miami area the previous day and was at that moment churning back up to speed in the Gulf of Mexico. For all we knew, it might turn toward the Florida panhandle and head in our direction. (It ended up making its final landfall in Louisiana and had little impact on us.)

"I'm no force of nature. Just an ordinary guy." At least that's how I liked to play it.

"I don't quite believe that. Let's hope you're not so destructive." She spooned several meatballs onto her plate and gestured her willingness to do the same for me.

"No thanks. Seafood only. Except for turkey on Thanksgiving. I stopped eating mammals and other birds a couple years ago. Ever kill an animal yourself?"

"Uh ... no."

"If you ever do, you might go vegetarian."

"I think you're what's called a pescetarian," she said.

I smiled. "Yes. *I* am a pescatarian. But I was talking about *you*."

Her turn to smile. "Ah. Well, I have *thought* about it. But in Wisconsin, even fruit salad has bacon."

Wisconsin. Interesting. "I'm from there, too," I said. "Born there anyway. 'On this date in history ...'"

"Today? Happy birthday!"

"A quarter century in the books." Pun not intended, I thought, but I'll take it.

"You turned twenty-five? On the twenty-fifth? Then it's your *golden* birthday."

That's the spot on the podium I'm targeting, I thought, even if my complexion is closer to bronze. I took a good look in the mirror before leaving home, and I liked what I saw, especially after swapping out my usual diamond stud earring for the dangly Ankh symbol I reserved for special occasions. I'd been fascinated by Egypt since taking in the King Tut exhibit in Chicago when I was ten years old and even more so since being taken to that country by my mom, along with my siblings, when I was thirteen.

"I turned eleven on mine," she said. "November eleventh. Easy enough to remember. Eleven eleven."

Her eyes, which had held mine since they met—when we did—at the start of the buffet line, sparkled with a sheer genuineness I found compelling.

"What's your name?" I asked.

174

"This place must have low standards for admission. Not to mention that fellowship." In response to my raised eyebrow, she added, "A doctoral student who can't read?"

I chuckled, then forced my gaze down to the tag she'd stuck to her blouse above a perky breast. Handwritten letters spelled *Joy*.

"I saw Drew bantering with a little cutie," said Elijah, my best friend in the department, once our late-night conversation made its inevitable turn to assessing the new grad class—or at least its female members.

"King of the jungle smells fresh meat, eh?" asked Jack, who was an outsider of sorts in our circle by virtue of not being a student in the program.

"Here I am, rock you like a hurricane!" sang Dave à la the Scorpions tune. He'd been our other regular drinking buddy for some time.

I shook my head as the three of them enjoyed a hearty laugh. I turned the assortment of beer bottles in front of me so their labels all faced the same way. "Actually, I wouldn't want to hook up with her," I said.

My companions grew silent.

I stacked the empty shot glasses into a precarious tower and considered making a pun about their proximity on the table to a box that had recently held—until we devoured it—a pizza. Instead, I stayed the course. I took in a deep breath. "I'd want to date her."

The silence endured the length of my exhale, then my mates burst out in hysterics.

"I mean it," I said. "Something about her."

"Well," said Dave, "that song *is* off the *Love at First Sting* album."

I smiled at his wit. Three English doctoral students— soon-to-be doctoral candidates!—walk into a bar ...

"And she *is* a Scorpio," I said, allowing his playfulness to permeate me for a moment, albeit a short one. I regained my solemnity. "But y'all know exactly how

I feel about love."

"Fuck that shit!" they shouted in unison.

Each of us grabbed a bottle, and we knocked them together, brought their mouths to ours, and tilted their bottoms up, empty or not.

"Fuck love," I said, repeating the motto I'd articulated when I embarked upon my solo adventures and which had remained my guiding principle to that day. The life I envisioned for myself as a bachelor writer and professor, encountering fresh young faces—and other body parts—every year, did not include a long-term commitment or any kind of serious relationship.

My three pals were amused by my stance and perhaps admired it, even if none of them shared it. Dave, similarly unattached, wanted—and strove—to change his status. Elijah lived with a girlfriend he met through the program and who'd finished her MA degree that spring. And Jack, a high school science teacher, had married a former student the previous summer.

Seattle's rise to cultural prominence since my departure hadn't made it easier to forget what I experienced there. The emergence of grunge—with Nirvana leading the way—had given voice to my generation, the one marked with an X, bringing what smelled like authentic spirit and sounded like social relevance to the music world. But for this member of that cohort it also became a source of ever-present emotional triggers. I'd heard from Melissa, with whom I'd stayed in sporadic contact, that Dina had a fairly lengthy fling with a well-known guitar player from one of the city's hottest bands. "Rock" (not quite his real name) had flown what remained of our once happy family—Dina, Angie, Scott, Johnny, and Melissa—from Seattle to Key West to ring in the most recent new year. Not even Florida was safe from them!

Besides grunge itself, which precipitated more of a general ache, a number of specific popular tunes from the early '90s reopened deep wounds, although sometimes

176

with a cathartic effect. Pick a track from Red Hot Chili Peppers' *Blood Sugar Sex Magik*—especially "Give It Away" and "Under the Bridge"—or from U2's *Achtung Baby*—just about any of them—and give it a careful hearing, and you'll get a sense of what I mean.

The hit single "Silent Lucidity" by Queensrÿche, combining a Jet City connection with lyrics at least obliquely resonant to my time there, had a particularly powerful impact on me—and even more of a healing one, with its emphasis on freedom from fear and pain through escape into a mystical dream realm. It's a remarkable song, a heavy metal power ballad blending the simplicity of a melodic lullaby with the grandeur of classical orchestration, even borrowing from Brahms' famous "Lullaby." I listened to it *a lot*.

And then there was *Singles*, the Cameron Crowe film coming out the next month. From what I'd read, it chronicled the messy love lives of a group of Seattle twentysomethings. I was willing to bet it ended happily, especially for the character played by Campbell Scott, who bore more than a passing resemblance to my former friend with the actor's last name for a first one.

"Fuck love," I repeated, then picked up a beer bottle in the hope it wasn't empty.

"Fuck that," I said.

I pulled away from the peephole and turned my back to the door, then leaned against it as a wave of nausea shot up into my throat. My head throbbed with each clang of the brass knocker. If this continues much longer, I thought, my brain might literally explode.

I turned the bolt, then twisted the knob and pulled open the door. The sudden infiltration of light through my blurry—and I would imagine bloodshot—corneas and dilated pupils and into my sensitive retinas caused me to shield my eyes with one arm.

"Am I that repulsive?" asked Joy.

177

"What are you doing here?"

"Tracked you down. Hope you don't mind," she said. "Happy belated birthday!"

I placed an open hand across my brow and peered under it. I saw she held a decorated cake in front of her like an offering. "I can't accept that."

"No animals were harmed in the baking of this cake. It's vegan!"

"That's really sweet ..."

"I hope so. I did use a lot of sugar."

"... But I just can't."

I shut the door, then turned with a sigh and leaned against it again. I counted to fifty and checked the peephole: all clear. *Phew.*

What I couldn't see, and wouldn't realize until later, was she'd left her confection right outside my door.

CHAPTER FOURTEEN

COMPREHENSIVE OVERHAUL

I turned the corner and saw Joy.

Fuck. I considered reversing direction and circling the floor to my destination, but she was surveying the bulletin board outside the door next to Kessler's office and might still be there when I arrived. Besides, I was practically late already—which, for this Virgo, meant only five minutes early. And I couldn't avoid her forever.

As I took in a breath and stepped forward, she looked down the hallway and saw me. "Hey there!" she called. "How's the celebration going? I think birthdays should be birth weeks."

"Kinda sucks to know a third of my days—maybe my best ones—are behind me." I based that figure on the national average life expectancy, not Madame Cherie's reading of my rascette lines, which suggested I might still have three quarters of the game ahead of me. "But I am enjoying the delicious cake. Thank you." I'd nearly reached her. "What are you doing?"

"Oh. I'm trying to decide how to rearrange the layout of this board."

"That's how you spend your days? You wander through campus buildings and adjust how people have hung fliers?"

"Nooo. But that might be fun some time. My assistantship is with the student lit journal." Sure enough, we stood outside the journal's editorial office.

I gestured to the adjacent door. "Got a meeting. See you around."

"Kessler's your advisor?"

I nodded.

"And you're taking your qualifying exams this semester?"

I nodded.

"Maybe we'll run into each other here on a regular basis."

Or maybe not, I thought. I wondered how tricky it would be to schedule all my meetings outside Joy's work hours.

"Well, I won't keep you." She smiled and stepped inside.

I stared after her, contemplating whether her kindness could really be as uncomplicated as it seemed.

"Sounds complicated," said Kessler, in response to the second area of study I'd proposed.

"They're supposed to be comprehensive," I replied.

"All together, yes. Not individually."

The program's approach to evaluating a doctoral student's proficiency and preparedness to advance to the dissertation stage involved the student choosing—with an advisor's approval—four areas to master through extensive reading and then demonstrating that mastery through in-depth written examinations over four consecutive weekends in the latter half of the semester. One area was practical: techniques of a creative writing genre. I'd spent the last three years living and breathing fiction, but on a whim I'd decided to branch out into memoir.

Kessler hadn't objected to that. Her apprehensions were over the literary period. I'd selected American

Romanticism, and I wanted to explore the transcendentalism of Emerson and friends in contrast to the German and French versions, as well as the ancient Sanskrit texts many of those writers cited as influences.

"Let's drop the Continental Europeans," she said. "After all, this is a department of English, not Comparative Lit."

Fair enough, I thought. It was time to bid *adieu* to Dumas and all four of his musketeers, and I'd have to overcome my sorrows in a way Goethe's titular—and suicidal—Young Werther never did.

"What about the Brits?" she asked.

"I like some of the poets. Shelley and Keats. As for novelists, Austen's too conservative, and the Brontë sisters too gloomy. I mean their *lives*, not just their works. But you're right. Let's keep it a more focused analysis of how Eastern philosophy took hold right here at home."

"And for your author?"

"I was thinking John Irving."

Kessler's matronly face crinkled into an expression I knew all too well.

But I was ready to make my case. "I realize by some standards he's not a *major* writer. How many living ones are? He should've won the Pulitzer for *Garp*." (He truly should have.) "His work really speaks to me. We both grew up in New England. We both captained our high school wrestling teams."

Kessler ruminated.

"And he writes about writers. And outsiders."

She nodded. "And your critical methodology?"

Here we go. "I'm intrigued by this emerging field of 'queer' theory. How sexual desire and behavior relate to gender and biological sex. And mismatches between them. In discourse and in practice. Normative versus deviant."

"Most of that work is being done by women and gay men," she noted. "So you'd like to interrogate it from the perspective of a straight male?"

181

Well, I thought. *More or less.* I nodded.

She pondered a moment. "I'm not sufficiently familiar with the seminal texts."

I nodded and sighed. I'd been fairly certain she'd reject the topic, which I knew would be a stretch for her.

"But if another faculty member will agree to mentor you in that area," she added, "I'll allow it."

Any legitimate natural or social scientist conducts empirical research to verify or refute accepted knowledge. That's how I found myself sitting behind the wheel of my VW Cabriolet, convertible top raised, in the parking lot outside the only gay bar—as far as I knew—in town.

Over the past month, I'd read and re-read the texts on the list I put together with the help of my queer theory mentor. It hadn't been hard to find one in a department with several youngish faculty members who'd completed their own doctoral studies and joined the ranks of tenure-credit-starving assistant professors in recent years.

If the field had a founding mother, it was Eve Kosofsky Sedgwick. Her work introduced me to the concept of male "homosocial" bonding, which she argues blurs boundaries between gay and straight identities through fluctuating definitions of what constitutes "erotic" behavior. In certain contexts, some of what seems like wholly heterosexual relations, including—especially?—ones exhibiting overt homophobia (team sports, fraternities, etc.), could be read as expressing latent homoerotic desire. She further dismantles the notion of a natural—versus socially constructed—binary opposition when it comes to sexuality, suggesting everyone has some "bisexual" traits of mind and personality, if not sexual desire.

If these ideas seem obvious to you, remember they've had three full decades to spread throughout our culture. For me, they were radical and liberating.

I had another month until my four straight weekends

of examination got underway. It was time to apply and test the theory I'd studied—which also encompassed more fundamental LGBTQ, feminist, and post-structuralist thought—through praxis.

Past time, really. I'd parked in the same lot on two prior occasions but succumbed to nerves and remained in the car, limiting observation of my subjects of study to interaction occurring outside the entrance to their protected environment. I was resolved to go all the way this time. I closed my eyes and took in a deep breath.

A minute or so later I sat down at the bar and let out the breath I'd held since before stepping through the door. I'd chosen a Tuesday, which I correctly hypothesized would be a slow night, for my initial foray into the wild, hoping to avoid an encounter with anyone I knew.

Even so, I'd barely slid onto the stool when a cute guy approached, asked what I was drinking (bourbon, neat), and bought me one.

I like this already, I thought.

Over the next couple hours, I engaged in small talk with half a dozen men who stepped in right beside me to place their orders, even though there was plenty of empty space along the bar. A few paid for my refills or lit my cigarettes, facilitating the more regular smoking habit— especially when drinking—I'd acquired in grad school.

Conscious of my power as the "object of desire"— having so often in my pick-up bar experience been the one on the hunt—I was careful not to abuse it. I accepted drinks from only those suitors I found in some way appealing. I didn't allow flirtatious banter to go too far unless I meant it. If I wasn't interested in someone, I let him know in a polite but straightforward manner.

Eventually I made my decision. I led the Chosen One out to the parking lot and instructed him to follow me home, where I had condoms and lube waiting on the nightstand beside my bed. AIDS awareness had increased dramatically since my HIV scare: Red ribbons were everywhere; Magic Johnson had helped the mainstream public realize it was an equal opportunity disease.

Afterward, we exchanged a "nice meeting you" and a handshake.

And with that, he was gone.

Over the next eight weeks, whenever I needed to relieve stress from my intensive, high-stakes studying—which was almost nightly until the exams started, when I slowed my pace due to the need to get some rest—I snuck over to the secret gay lair. I sauntered in the door, cruised around the floor, and headed to the bar. By the time I finished my first drink, I'd be ready to leave with that evening's Man of the Night. I got fucked—always safely—by a faceless blur of white dudes, Black dudes, Latino dudes, Asian dudes, and at least one Native American dude. I got fucked by men of various ages—as old as fifty—and assorted shapes and sizes. (I preferred *substantial* ones; I liked how it felt to be held by a man bigger than me.) Simply put, I did not discriminate. I never got fucked by a dude in a wheelchair, but if the opportunity had arisen ...

By the start of my written examinations in late October, I'd conducted a thorough investigation into the sexual characteristics and routines of the gay or bisexual North Floridian (and occasional South Georgian) human male, disproving some personal and cultural biases and seeming to confirm others. I won't be more specific, as my sample size was too small—unlike some of its members—to support definitive comparisons.

I'd read a lot of literature and criticism, too, for my queries into queerness and my three other exam areas. But I hadn't come up with ways to put any of that other learning into practice. Still, immersing myself in the *Bhagavad Gita* for the first, and second, time had been quite an experience. It was almost overwhelming, in fact, as I got swept up in the poetic and spiritual depiction of existence that so enthralled Emerson and Thoreau a hundred and fifty years earlier.

As a side note, I'm aware of the irony in my becoming

184

an expert in a critical approach for uncovering and advancing marginalized voices while simultaneously restricting my study of American Romanticism to the works of (rich) white men. Emily Dickinson lived—and died—in the town where I grew up, for goodness' sake. My classmates and I got high beside her grave! But she wasn't a transcendentalist, and that's what most interested me about the movement. I did notice some overlap in the poetry of Walt Whitman, who promulgated among his multitudes an unabashedly masculine vision of homosexuality.

Likewise with John Irving, whose work delves into sexual and other deviance without passing judgment. His more recent novel *In One Person* even features a bisexual narrator. If only he'd written it twenty years earlier!

Returning to the *Gita*, I couldn't quite get my mind around everything Krishna says, but I found Arjuna's dilemma gripping and provocative. Should he fight a "just" war even though it will result in so much death? One analysis I'd come across interpreted the battlefield setting as a metaphor for the universal inner struggle between clinging to ego and letting go.

Huh, I thought.

One thing I hadn't done since late August was interact with Joy. That would change soon enough.

"WOOOO!" I shouted, shaking my fists in the air.

"WOOOOOO!" Elijah answered, doing the same, then opening his palms for a high-ten, which I delivered.

"WOOOOOOOO!" we shouted in unison before wrapping our arms around each other in a fierce embrace.

Technically, our celebration was premature. We still had to pass an oral defense of our written answers. But that was generally understood to be a formality. Quite frankly, merely surviving the four straight weekends of sleep-deprived scholarly production—a form of academic hazing if there ever was one—was a victory in its own

185

right. Over each of those weekends we'd had to generate two essays, suitable for publication in terms of both length and quality, in response to questions we were given on Friday afternoon.

It meant a lot to share the moment with Elijah. We started the PhD program at the same time and had taken many classes together. We often showed up to campus wearing matching outfits—totally by coincidence—and many of our professors consistently mixed up our names, even though we looked nothing alike. He was shorter and stockier and had dark, curly, receding hair. Some of our more hip profs had taken to interchangeably calling us Drewlijah, an appellation we'd come up with for ourselves after reading Donna Haraway's feminist "Cyborg Manifesto"—which employs a technological human-machine-hybrid metaphor to envision a world in which people construct alliances based on "affinities" rather than subscribing to culturally imposed categories of identity and boundaries of identification.

Jack approached, bearing shots. We wasted no time downing them, or the round brought to us by Elijah's girlfriend Heather, whose personality bore no resemblance to any of the trio of so-named characters in the movie *Heathers*. Or the one provided by Jack's wife Anna. Or the one carried over by Dave.

A couple hours later, Elijah, who also consumed most of a bottle of Jägermeister, passed out on a deck chair, apparently not a true "hunting master" after all, while the rest of us, which included a pair of young, undergraduate women Dave brought with him, soaked in the hot tub in drunken—and naked—glory. We played an innocent enough version of "spin the bottle" with an empty beer bottle floating in the center of the tub without the jets on. Jack had to be persuaded to participate, due to his anxiety over the possibility of kissing a man.

"It's just your lips," Anna said, her native Russian accent—as usual—accentuated by her consumption of alcohol. In case you're wondering, she was *not* named

186

after Tolstoy's Karenina. "And maybe a little tongue."

"What's *she* doing here?" asked Dave, when Joy appeared in Jack and Anna's back yard.

"I invited her," I replied. I slid out of the water and over the edge of the tub and wrapped myself in one of the towels someone—most likely Anna—had the foresight to place nearby.

"Hey," I said as Joy reached the patio. "Everybody, this is Joy. Joy, this is ... everybody."

"I seem to be interrupting," she said, looking past me at the crowded hot tub.

"Not at all," said Dave. "Hop in. We'll find a spot for you."

"I didn't think you were coming," I said.

"I probably shouldn't have. And I can't stay long. My flight leaves pretty early."

"I'm glad you're here." I led her out into the yard away from the lights of the house—and the sounds of the hot tub fun and games, which had already resumed.

As you've no doubt surmised, there'd been a major shift in my attitude toward Joy since I started taking the exams. Don't feel bad if you didn't see it coming. Neither did I.

On the Monday morning after my first marathon writing weekend, I'd staggered down the hallway to Kessler's office and dropped my exam answers—thirty-six pages (not including the "works cited" list) of typed, double-spaced brilliance—into the box on her door, which I was grateful to find closed. I noticed the one next to it was open, though, as I started back the way I'd come.

Inside the journal office, at a desk with an empty chair on its near end, sat Joy. "Hey," she said. "Long time, no see. Wanna sit?" she asked, as if reading my mind.

I nodded, then stepped through the door and collapsed into the chair, which—despite being made from hardwood—felt like the most comfortable seat I'd ever set my ass down on.

"You look exhausted."

187

I sighed and stroked my face, which was rough with beard growth. *Uh huh*.

I don't recall everything we said during the next hour or so, or all of what we discussed on the three following Mondays. I know I rambled quite a bit, mostly about the ideas I'd been contemplating and expressing in more articulate prose for the past sixty-six hours, including the ten or so total hours I'd slept, dreaming about those same ideas, over the three nights of each weekend.

But I also listened a lot, *really* listened—perhaps because, in the wake of an extended adrenaline rush, I was too fatigued to think about what I might say next. And I truly heard her.

I learned right away she had a boyfriend in Wisconsin. That didn't bother me in the slightest. Quite the opposite. It meant she was safe. I could drop my guard and be my real self—as her openness encouraged me to do—without fear of alienating her or, worse, attracting her.

The next week we celebrated the election the previous Tuesday of "a man from a town called Hope" as President of the United States, no thanks to Florida, which had gone for Bush the Elder, as it would do—according to the Supreme Court anyway—for his son eight years later, and far more pivotally.

I surprised Joy—and, to be honest, myself—that same Monday by wishing her an early happy birthday. Her twenty-third was two days later.

"Easy enough to remember," I said. "Eleven eleven."

It didn't hurt that it happened to fall on Veterans Day, the American evolution of the more international Armistice Day commemorating the November 1918 end to hostilities in World War I, "the war to end all wars."

"I guess that makes you Number One," I added, "to the fourth degree."

"I've never looked at it that way," she replied.

Of course not, I thought, wishing I could retract the words—or at least their narcissistic implications, which didn't at all apply to her.

When I made my punctual appearance the morning after the final weekend of my exams, on the Monday before Thanksgiving, she wasn't seated at her desk. She stood in the hallway outside Kessler's door. She held a dozen white and red carnations, the flower of coronation (and incarnation), pressed to her chest.

"Congratulations, friend," she said, handing me the bouquet, which I accepted.

And that's how I came to invite Joy to the party.

Moving from the steamy hot tub out into the crisp, cool night air had sobered me right up. As we sat on the stone wall circling the pond Jack had built and stocked with varieties of koi, Joy gazed overhead.

"There's Andromeda," she said. "The constellation, not the galaxy."

"And there's Perseus," I replied. "Let's hope Pegasus gets him there in time to save her from Poseidon's sea monster. Where is that winged horse anyway?"

"There!" we said in unison, pointing, then laughing together.

"When I was a kid," she said, "my aunt and uncle would take me stargazing in the field behind their house. I begged my mom and dad to let me sleep over every summer weekend." She paused. "He's dead now. Uncle Pat. Cancer. He had exposure to Agent Orange. In Vietnam."

"I'm sorry," I said.

She nodded. A single tear glistened in the corner of her blue-gray eye.

"So pretty," I said, unintentionally speaking the thought.

"Thanks." She wiped away the tear as it started to run down her cheek.

I gestured to the pond, where colorful carp swam below the lily pads on its surface. "I meant the koi." After

189

she chuckled in response, I added, "But since you're *fishing* for a sympathy compliment, so are you." When she remained silent in response this time, I thought it best to clarify myself. "I was kidding. About fishing for sympathy."

"I should go soon," she said. So much for my smooth-talking charm. "Before I do, I came here to tell you something." She paused. "I'm breaking up with Tim."

Well now. That was a game changer. And not in a good way. Why had I told her she was pretty?

In truth, the news didn't come as a total shock. At one of our recent weekly chat sessions, she'd expressed concern about the state of her relationship and its ability to survive long distance for two years after only two years together. Apparently Tim had no interest in leaving Madison, where he'd gotten a job teaching music at a middle school.

"I'm sorry," I said.

"Don't be. It was inevitable. Better to get it out of the way and move on with our lives. That's what I want to talk to you about."

Uh-oh, I thought. Here it comes.

"I know you don't want a serious relationship."

I waited for the other shoe to drop.

"Neither do I."

"No?" I asked. The shoe had turned out to be more of a soft sandal than a spiked heel.

"You've got a dissertation to write."

"Ugh. Did you have to bring that up *tonight*?"

"Sorry. My point is we both need to focus on why we're here."

"Indeed. And where we're headed."

"Exactly. In eighteen months, you'll have your doctorate, and I'll have my master's."

"Knock on wood," I said, rapping my knuckles against the side of my skull.

"And we'll be going our separate ways for our careers." She looked me in the eyes. "But that's a year and a half from now. Why not make the most of our time together until then? I feel a connection with you. I think you feel it, too. And I like it. I think you like it, too."

"What exactly are you proposing?"

"I'm *proposing* we hang out together. As much or as little as we feel like. No strings."

"No strings," I repeated.

I wondered if it were possible—especially for a woman, even one as grounded as Joy—to "hang out" with someone for long without forming a deeper bond. Several of my female fuck buddies had claimed that was what they wanted even as they grew more and more attached. Now if she were a guy, maybe. Then a realization hit me. *Dude,* I thought, you're totally reaffirming your culturally inscribed gender bias.

"Okay," I said.

She was going home for Thanksgiving, then she'd have finals, then she'd go home again for Christmas. We'd see what came of hanging out together in the new year.

In the meantime, the hot tub—and all those lips and tongues—awaited.

CHAPTER FIFTEEN

CARPE CEREBRUM

"*Laissez les bon temps rouler!*" I shouted from the hot tub in our hotel courtyard as I raised my plastic cup toward where Jack sat on the steps in the swimming pool.

Once he reciprocated, we chugged the contents. We were letting the good times roll, all right. Welcome to N'awlins!

I looked over at the row of chaise lounges between the pool and the courtyard wall, where Anna and Joy basked in the late December sun. By which I mean they caught its rays on their faces while their bodies remained covered by jeans and sweatshirts. The temperature hit the mid-sixties earlier that afternoon but was already falling as the short winter's day wound down. It was perfect weather for relaxing with an adult beverage in either of the establishment's heated outdoor baths—or for poolside reading and girl talk, if that was your preference.

I know I said I didn't intend to "hang out" with Joy until January. But, indicative of her typical work habits, she finished all her term papers well in advance of their due dates, and her only final exam was a take-home essay she knocked out in a day, leaving a two-week stretch before her Christmas trip during which the two of us had few school-related obligations.

We'd seen a couple movies, we'd had drinks and played euchre at a favorite bar with Jack and Anna one night and with Elijah and Heather another, and she'd cooked me dinner—on the day of my successful oral comprehensive defense—at her place. We ended that evening by making out for fifteen or so minutes. That was as far as our physical intimacy had progressed.

When I found out she'd be back for New Year's, I figured it made sense to invite her to join us for the two nights of mild debauchery we had planned in the Big Easy. Even though we'd share a room—and a bed—I didn't expect the city's nickname to rub off on her. In fact, I hoped it wouldn't. The thought of having sex with her engendered in me a kind of "double-bind" anxiety: It might go poorly, but it also might go well; neither outcome seemed conducive to maintaining the "no-strings" arrangement that, so far, we both seemed to find satisfying.

Maybe that's at least partly why I was well on my way to getting too fucked up to fuck. Our first stop after checking into our French Quarter lodgings had been the legendary Pat O'Brien's. A couple Hurricanes later—a couple each for me and Jack and one each for Anna and Joy—we returned to the hotel and smoked a little weed.

As we walked down the stairs to the lobby, where we would stop at the bar for a round of beers to take to the pool, Anna gestured toward Joy while whispering to Jack—in her usual easy-to-overhear fashion—"Better, not worse."

I knew exactly what she meant, and I was in wholehearted agreement.

My last road trip with the two of them had taken place seven months before this, when we traveled to Atlanta for a Cure show at the Omni. My companion then was the only woman, prior to Joy, I actually "dated" in the time I'd known them. Bridget taught English at the high school in Thomasville, Georgia, about thirty minutes north of Tallahassee. She'd graduated from FSU, and we

194

met at a reception for a guest writer the program brought to campus to lead master classes and read from their own work.

After we'd settled in at our hotel—walking distance from the downtown venue—Jack revealed his intention to take another "trip" to enhance his enjoyment of the concert. And he'd brought enough LSD to share. He proceeded to do a whole hit, while Anna, Bridget, and I each did half of one.

That had been a perfect dose to intensify the colors of the stage lighting and add texture to the music without sending me into deep reflection—even when the group played songs I associated with the ecstatic dance sessions we'd held in Angie's apartment. The band's main set and first encore were a wonderful experience. But the show didn't end there.

I suspect it was a fusion of the lyrics with the acid in her brain that led Bridget astray as Robert Smith launched into "Lovesong" to open the second encore. "Whenever I'm alone with you / You make me feel like I am home again," he sang, "Whenever I'm alone with you / You make me feel like I am whole again."

She grabbed both my hands and turned me to face her. "I just heard your heart open."

I have no idea what my expression replied. I know what I thought: *You* are not the *cure* for my woes.

Later that week, I broke up with her.

Better, not worse, I now thought, gazing at Joy from the hot tub.

"Hey," called out Jack. "How many times you think you can swim back and forth across the pool on one breath? Side to side, not the long way."

I considered the distance. Until my mid-teens, I'd been deathly afraid of the water, an anxiety my stepbrothers attempted to help me overcome by pushing or throwing me into swimming pools whenever they could. My obsession with the Frogger video game didn't help, as it inevitably ends with death as road kill or 'gator

195

bait, or by drowning. Even if you filled the entire row of lily pads with frogs, you didn't "win"; you simply advanced to the next, faster level. On the other hand, you did get multiple lives for every quarter you fed into the slot. In any case, since moving to Florida, I'd become a strong swimmer, on many mornings doing fifty or more laps in my apartment complex pool.

"I don't know. Five?"

"Wow," he responded, with more than a trace of doubt in his voice. "I tried and only did two."

I shook my head with a sigh, then rose from the soothing waters to meet his challenge.

Once I'd acclimated to the conditions of the larger arena, I took in a deep breath, dropped below the surface, and glided away from the wall. By my fifth crossing, I could feel a decent amount of internal pressure. I'd survive another pass or two, but why bother? I'd proven myself.

"Wow," he repeated, the earlier inflection of doubt replaced by a sharper tone.

Whatever, I thought, and went back to chilling out, smiling at Joy with my arms folded on the edge of the pool and my torso and legs floating behind me.

A few minutes later, heavy breathing prompted me to glance over my shoulder. Jack bobbed up and down along the far wall in time with deep inhalations and exhalations. Once he saw he'd attracted my attention, he slid underwater and launched his bid to top me.

Whatever. I watched his stocky form barrel across the pool on his initial lap, and then a second and third time. *Way to go, man*, I thought, as he touched the wall near me. *You've achieved a personal best.*

He soon completed cross number four and started a fifth, drying up my sarcasm. He appeared to struggle mightily as he approached my wall. Even so, he made it across—and back to the far side for a total of six. Once he'd caught his breath, he shrugged across the pool at me.

Six! The bastard had low-balled me!

196

So I took another shot. But I knew from my initial thrust I didn't have it in me.

"You win," I conceded, then went back to chilling out. But I was *far* from chill.

I looked up at Joy, who smiled and shrugged as if to say "silly boys." It turns out she was dead right—or nearly so. Our boyish behavior was absurd. And self-jeopardizing.

I waited a few minutes, then looked up at Joy again. *We'll see who's silly.* When I caught her eye, I nodded and flashed my trademark grin. *Watch this.*

Then I stole a page from my opponent's playbook and induced hyperventilation. After working my bronchial openings good and loose, I took all the air I could into the deepest reaches of my being. I dipped my head below the water, and off I went.

Three crosses in my chest cavity tightened. At five my lungs throbbed and my eyes bulged. I powered forward, letting the breath trickle out. As long as I timed it right ...

I tapped the wall to tally six—my body and brain starved for oxygen—and made the turn. There would be no sister-kissing on this day. I was resolved to win.

Once I touched the opposite side, I exploded upward, pumped my fist in the air, and gulped in a mouthful of victory.

At least that's how it felt.

How did I get here? I wondered. I dragged my gaze from the needle taped to the back of my hand near the wrist, its point penetrating my skin, along the plastic tubing to the bag of clear fluid hanging overhead from a branch of the metal tree beside my bed.

Joy stood nearby. "Hey," she said.

"Where are we?"

"Emergency room. Do you know what city?"

"N'awlins?"

"Good. Doctor said to ask. It's good you can

197

remember."

"Did I win?" I asked.

She responded with a circular nod as she broke into sobs.

I looked down at my chest through the open front of the gown I wore and saw discs taped there. More were attached to other parts of my corporeal form, all leading to a monitor on the side of the bed opposite Joy.

My vital signs registered on the screen. My cardiac rhythm spiked and dipped.

Once the wave of feeling subsided and Joy restored her equilibrium, she told me what happened from a spectator's perspective. From *her* vantage point, I raised my celebratory fist only about a forearm's length above the water before collapsing backwards. Jack ignored me, assuming I was exaggerating the toll taken on me as a result of my Herculean efforts—a reasonable inference based on my track record—even as Anna yelled at him to save me.

As I sank to the bottom of the pool, unconscious, Joy freed the life preserver from its housing and flung it in my direction. When Jack saw she intended to dive into the water fully dressed, he realized the seriousness of the situation. According to the testimony of this eye witness, who stood poised for further action while Jack splashed to my rescue, foam spewed from the lips of my purple head as Jack lugged me to the shallow end in a rear-mount bear hug.

Joy and Anna helped lift me out of the pool. Jack ejected fluid from my lungs by pulsing his fist into my diaphragm and pounding me on my back. They laid me out on the concrete slab of the deck, where Joy administered mouth-to-mouth resuscitation while Anna ran to the lobby to summon an ambulance. I regained consciousness long enough to crawl into a nearby patch of decorative vegetation, where I puked before passing out in the bush.

Sounds like quite a scene, I thought. Sorry to have

missed it. But it'll make one hell of a story someday.

Joy was soon exiled from my curtained quarters in the ER, when technicians arrived with equipment to measure the activity in my brain—apparently believing they'd actually find some.

"Your cortex isn't as *fluffy* as it should be," said the neurologist I'd been referred to back in Tallahassee, as he studied my cerebral MRI. "Are you a heavy drinker?"

"Kinda. Not as much as I when I was younger."

"Had you ingested any drugs on the day of your seizure?"

"Just a little pot."

"No alcohol?"

"Well, yeah, sure. I thought you meant real drugs." Another thought occurred to me. "Hey," I said. "Could previous drug use have caused this?"

"What drugs?" he asked.

I listed all the ones I'd ever done, most of which I've told you about and which did *not* include crack, meth, or heroin. You have to draw the line somewhere.

"My best professional opinion," he replied, "is a distinct maybe." He proceeded to caution me against taking any more psychedelic mushrooms—a warning I've since disregarded without any adverse effects—which he said were hard to dose and, if the wrong ones were picked, deadly poisonous. "They're not known as the 'devil's toadstool' for nothing."

Devil's toadstool, I thought. Then I thought about *The World According to Garp* and the Under Toad, which from its origins in an innocent mispronunciation of "undertow" evolves into a symbol for anxiety and death. *Easy enough to drown in that*, I'd realized long before. I wondered how I missed the connection to mushrooms during that late May day in Seattle when I'd been so out of my depth. Or maybe I *had* made the connection then and didn't remember.

199

"About the seizure," I said. "You think I'll have more?"

"Hard to say. Nothing structural to worry about on your MRI. The EEG from the New Orleans ER does show abnormal brainwave patterns in one hemisphere."

Abnormal brainwaves.

"On the other hand, you're in an age range less likely than some to develop a seizure disorder, and—in the combination of caffeine and alcohol intake, low nutrition, and oxygen deprivation—you more or less created a perfect storm of behavioral triggers."

"I'll try to avoid that in the future."

"That would be my recommendation. We'll do another EEG in six months to see if the abnormal patterns are typical. In the meantime, I'm prescribing a mild anti-seizure medication."

"No no no. No meds. Not if it's what they gave me in N'awlins, or anything like it. I was foggy for days, even after I stopped taking it."

"You'd rather risk another episode?"

"I'm a doctoral candidate. I need absolute clarity to finish my dissertation. To come up with an idea for it." I'd been feeling pressure from Kessler about that.

"Do I have your promise to take better care of what's inside that thick skull of yours?"

My hair, its elastic removed, fluttered around my head as the Cabriolet, its top lowered, zoomed south on Highway 319 where it skirts the boundary of the Apalachicola National Forest. I raised both arms overhead and felt resistance from the wind on my palms. I imagined myself becoming permeable enough for currents of air to pass through me. It was a great day to be alive.

I looked behind the wheel at Joy, who seemed to be enjoying driving as much as I was enjoying not. I didn't have much choice about it. Florida law barred me from operating a motor vehicle until I remained seizure-free for six months, with or without medication. Legality aside, I had no desire to assume liability for the death of anyone else due to my fragile condition.

We cruised right through Panacea and out Alligator Drive toward the point by the same name. Along the way, I thought back to New Year's Eve.

Joy had stayed with me at the hospital until my release in the early morning hours. We realized midnight had struck only when we heard cheers from across the floor of the emergency room. Much to my surprise—and delight—she leaned over the bed and planted her two lips against mine.

"You sure you wanna hang out with me?" I'd asked.

"You don't have to prove anything," she'd said. "Not to me."

We now parked near the lighthouse, walked out to the beach, set down our picnic basket and cooler, and spread our blanket on the sand close to a patch of sea oats concealing us from the lot. It was warmer than average for late January in North Florida, but it was still a weekday, and we had the stretch of beach to ourselves.

"Are you afraid?" she asked once we got settled. "I would be. If I thought I might have something wrong with my brain."

"I've had worse health scares," I replied without thinking. *Fuck.* Not ready to go there.

"Like what?" she asked, then took in my expression. "Forget it. I shouldn't have asked."

Before long, we'd eaten all the cheese—we're native Wisconsinners, after all—and most of the smoked fish spread and fresh fruit we'd brought and sipped half the bottle of white wine we kept on ice. As the temperature dropped in correspondence with the sun's descent toward the Gulf, we cuddled together under a second blanket. The heat generated by our conjoined bodies soon ignited the purging of one article of clothing after another until we found ourselves exposed and open to the elements—and each other—in perfect nakedness.

201

All the anxiety I'd felt about this moment prior to our New Orleans outing had dissipated. What did I have to lose?

If you've been feeling anxiety of your own, anticipating this scene might take a sudden turn for the worse, as has happened so often in my story thus far, you can breathe easy. Making love with Joy—for the first time and every subsequent time—offers nothing but complete fulfillment. In this case, gentleness and passion combined in a lighthearted but intense dance of generosity and receptivity climaxing in mutual surrender, with the afterglow from the internal fire we'd kindled matching that of the sunset in its splendor.

As dusk settled and Joy drifted into slumber, I gazed upon her profile for a while, sharing its sense of serenity. Then I tucked the top of the blanket under my arm and spooned her from behind. The tattoo on my upper arm just below the shoulder, which I'd gotten on New Year's Day as my first work of body art, drew my attention and reflection.

Getting inked was Jack's idea. What else to do in N'awlins the day after the one we'd just had? I agreed the circumstances felt right to finally take a leap we'd talked about for some time.

We'd even pre-chosen the images we wanted, each of us selecting a series of Viking runes—symbols from an ancient language once believed to possess magic power when inscribed onto objects. Neither of us had Scandinavian ancestry, but we shared an affinity for Norse mythology. He intended to name his firstborn son Thor. Growing up, I often fancied myself as Loki, who in the tales I read was a mischievous rascal and not the malevolent rogue of the Marvel Cinematic Universe.

The runes etched into my flesh form the points of a diamond, or compass. At the top, a slashing S—"*sowilo*"—represents the sun and its role in generating and sustaining life. Directly below that, a sideways hourglass—"*daguz*"—stands for daylight and the clarity that follows awakening. On the left, a Y with a third, center line branching up between the two outer ones— "*algiz*"—depicts a sanctuary into which a warrior can retreat to meditate on suffering and death before returning to the outside world revitalized by new insights. On the right, an angular C—"*kenaz*"—signifies an ability to reshape reality through creative vision and energized knowledge.

I've done the looking inward and contemplation part, I thought. At least some of it. Now all I need is a bit of illumination.

A moment later, the beacon in the nearby lighthouse tower came on, shining out into the darkness spreading over the Gulf.

I smiled at the timing. If only it were as easy as flipping a switch.

CHAPTER SIXTEEN

DEAFENING LUCIDITY

Six weeks later no cartoon light bulb had appeared above my head. I'd poured over every short story I'd written, evaluating whether they possessed enough substance for expansion as a full-length work. A few had potential but felt inadequate for the project at hand. I understood—thanks to Kessler's frequent reiterations—that a dissertation should be viewed as a means to an end and not as the pinnacle of one's achievement in life. But I wanted—*needed*—mine to reflect who I was—who I had *become*—as a writer and a man. Even the fiction I'd generated within the last year seemed outdated in that regard.

As a way to distract ourselves, Elijah, who was in the same boat in terms of his own lack of progress, and I traveled with our girlfriends—although I still didn't use that word for Joy—to St. Pete Beach, the name I used for the city even before the vote to shorten it from "Petersburg" a year later. My stepfather owned a condo there, which he'd made his home since leaving UMass for nearby Eckerd College while I lived in Seattle. This (sub-) tropical paradise had become a place of refuge for me whenever circumstances allowed me to take advantage of the open-ended offer of hospitality Bruce extended to me and any guests I brought along.

Upon completing the five-hour drive from Tallahassee, we went straight to my favorite tiki bar, conveniently located next door to the condo complex. As the four of us sat on the railing above a bench on the beach side of the hut, soaking up the March sun and sipping Rum Runners amidst a crowd of fellow spring breakers, other vacationers, and locals, I noticed Joy's attention linger on a hippie chick playing Frisbee on the sand nearby. So did someone else.

"She's cute," said Heather, whom I'd never known to hide her sexual interest in women.

"If I was ever with a girl, it'd be one like that—a free spirit," Joy responded. From her it came as a bit of a surprise, which apparently registered on my face. "Does that freak you out?"

"Hell no," I replied. "Two women. Hot." I looked at Elijah for confirmation, which he provided with a decisive nod.

"Maybe we'll put on a little show for you later," said Heather.

"Don't make promises unless you intend to keep them," Elijah answered.

"I said *maybe*." She leaned forward for a kiss, which he bestowed with a smile.

I often wondered about Elijah's sexuality and considered asking him outright a number of times, but I realized the question would almost certainly be flipped on me. And I wasn't ready to share my secret with anyone, even Elijah, regardless of how much I trusted him, especially if it turned out he was straight. I wasn't worried he'd condemn me for it—he was too accepting for that—but I suspected it would *change* things between us. I never considered admitting it to Jack, who I felt confident would exploit the disclosure as a running joke—through innuendo at least—whenever he needed something to tweak me as part of our gentlemen's rivalry.

Despite Elijah and I being in the same demanding

program, our relationship from the start had been wholly cooperative and not at all competitive, the first time I'd ever had such a friendship with a guy. I credited him for that, attributing it at least in part to his being the son of diehard political progressives, which—in my mind—compared favorably to my own parentage.

For a father I had a doctor who served in the Air Force—by choice—in the mid-1960s, as tensions ramped up in Southeast Asia (but who remained stateside); for a mother I had a graduate of a Baptist women's college founded as a seminary. Over time, both of them broke away from their southern upbringings and became less conservative. My mother in particular adopted a more liberal viewpoint as she turned into the "seeker" who found her way to the Bahá'í Faith. If she was born ten years later, maybe she'd have been a '60s radical. As it was, by the time of my birth in the latter half of that decade, she was on the wrong side of the mantra to never trust anyone over thirty.

I sometimes wished I'd been born twenty years earlier, so *I* could've experienced the revolutionary energy of that era. The closest thing my generation had to Vietnam was the first Gulf War, which did spark protests, including one I participated in along with a thousand others, marching from campus to the Florida State Capitol soon after the U.S. started bombing Baghdad in January 1991. But the conflict ended too quickly and decisively for much additional outrage to build. We'd also seen the fall of the Berlin Wall in November 1989, but that inspired celebration. If I'd been less self-absorbed and more aware of what was happening in other parts of Europe when I visited the Continent a few months earlier, maybe I would've hopped a train to West Germany instead of Spain.

As for race riots along the lines of Watts, Detroit, Newark, or in various cities following the assassination of the Reverend Martin Luther King, Jr., we had major ones across the country, including as close as Atlanta, after the

April 1992 acquittal of the Los Angeles police officers caught on video severely beating another Black King, named Rodney. Tensions in Tallahassee—home to historically and still primarily Black Florida A&M University and with a roughly twenty percent Black population overall—remained high for quite some time, especially over a possible change in venue to the city for the trial of a Miami cop who'd killed two Black motorists. During all this, I observed little white solidarity with our Black brethren.

"Hey!" shouted one of the bartenders, back in the present moment. "Look at me! Look at the sign!"

We all turned to the sign in question, attached to one of the tiki hut posts. *Don't feed the sky rats!* it read, above an image of a seagull dropping another kind of bomb as it flew through the air with its mouth full of garbage.

We looked out onto the beach where the bartender continued to glare. Dozens of seagulls battled for French fries tossed in their direction by a young child. The child's parents glanced back from their seats on lounge chairs a safe distance from the chaotic scene.

"He can't read," said the dad.

"He's only four," added the mom.

"Is that right?" replied the bartender. "What's *your* excuse?" He shook his head and rolled his eyes. "Idiots."

Before he could turn away, I stepped up and ordered us another round. *Look at the sign*, I heard his voice yell inside my head as he filled the blender with ice, both light and dark rum, and various fruit juices and liqueurs.

Then I heard another internal voice—one from my past—say, "People make it easier for gulls to eat, and that gives them an unnatural advantage over their competitors."

And then the whir of stainless steel blades pulverizing ice drowned out everything else.

Accompanied by the whir of the motor, the extruded

208

aluminum storm shutters rose along their tracks, and light flooded into the living room. Once the slats had rolled up and retracted into the storage box attached to the underside of the balcony roof, Bruce removed his finger from the toggle switch. Hurricane season wouldn't begin again until June, but he preferred to keep the shutters down to block out the direct afternoon sun and, I think, for privacy—although I'm not sure who he feared might see inside his top-floor end unit overlooking the Gulf. He opened the sliding glass door, and we all stepped outside.

I should mention how Bruce came to afford this mansion by the sea and on high. I can tell you from my own experience in academia it wasn't from his salary as a professor. Simply put, ever since he'd let go—for the most part—of the anger inside him, he'd had what John Lennon might've called "Instant Karma" after the former Beatle's 1970 hit song by that name.

He had tremendous luck in the stock market, but he also earned financial and other success through a research institute he'd co-founded—coincidentally in the year of my birth—to supply *Fortune 100* companies with data and strategies to help them more effectively manage their human resources. The institute filled a niche and a need in the field and by the mid-1980s brought in large sums of grant money from firms that supported and benefitted from its work.

I'd done some freelance writing for the institute over the previous couple summers. They mailed me hefty packets of research culled from an array of sources, which I read, synthesized, and then summarized for corporate executives. I sent in my reports as word processing files transmitted over phone lines via dial-up modem as part of the emerging movement toward "telecommuting"—which seemed almost as magical as telepathy.

The institute's goal was to be *the* one-stop source for analysis about anything impacting people management—in short, everything. The topics I covered encompassed

209

demographic trends, social issues, economic forces, political affairs, and legal matters. My immersion into this sea of information expanded my understanding of the world around me and contributed to my development as a thinker, writer, and person in a manner complementary—and perhaps equally valuable—to the learning I gained through my doctoral studies.

"Wow," said Joy upon taking in her first full view of the panorama. That said it all.

If you looked straight down over the railing, you saw the landscaped property of the condo complex, with a manicured lawn broken up by winding palm tree-lined sidewalks and a pair of swimming pools with hot tubs. Raising your gaze beyond the castle walls, you took in a ridge of dunes sprouting sea oats that provided a barrier to storm surges and beachgoer curiosity. Beyond that lay a strip of white sand and then water as far as the eye could see. To either side, sightlines stretched for miles without obstruction.

Bruce excused himself to return to what he'd been working on, and the rest of us stood there for the next hour or so mostly without talking or moving, except for my quick retreat inside to retrieve a round of beers for Elijah and me. The women felt no need for further inebriation. Neither of them had finished their second Rum Runner, leaving the remains for us to imbibe, lest we be guilty of "alcohol abuse" through wasting the precious commodity. Once the sun had set, the four of us shuffled inside to get ready to head out on the town for dinner and more drinks.

While the others were showering, I went to hang a few things in the bedroom Bruce had designated as mine after relocating there. When I opened the closet door, I noticed the chest of keepsakes I'd left in Bruce's care. I knelt down and lifted the lid, unleashing a wave of nostalgia from what I suspected, if I dug deeply enough, could prove to be a Pandora's box.

The first item I saw struck me in the eye like a pen,

which is exactly what it was. I lifted the fine writing instrument—a '67 "classic"—from the box and read the inscription: *Mightier than any sword.*

Only if you can get its "blood" to flow, I thought. This particular ballpoint remained virgin, as I had no desire to utilize it after my painful breakup with Tina. Seven and a half years later, here it was, still waiting for me to incorporate it into my crusade to change the world.

As memories from that fateful trip to Provincetown flooded my consciousness, I recalled our visit to Madame Cherie and how I scoffed at the notion I was predisposed to "promiscuity" and how I dismissed the notion I might be leading a double life.

Huh, I now thought. Nailed it.

Then I saw the beachscape print, the image of seagulls and piping plovers Tina had given to me as a reminder that "there's more than one way to be a bird." The message she intended to convey finally, after all that time, came through loud and clear, hitting me like a slap in the face.

By the time I finished cleaning up, Joy, Elijah, and Heather were dressed and ready to leave. I told them to head over to the seafood shack where we intended to dine and I'd join them there shortly. I needed to do something *personal* first. After seeing them to the condo unit door, I padded across the floor to another door, the one leading to Bruce's home office.

"Come in!" he called in response to my knock, in the same welcoming voice he always used to acknowledge interruptions many people would greet with less enthusiasm.

I don't remember exactly what I said to my ex-stepfather across his desk that evening as I rambled on—half-drunk, half-lucid—about how much I appreciated the respect, compassion, and generosity of spirit he'd shown me regardless of my often taking it for granted. I do know the message I intended to convey: *You've been a true father to me, and you've shown me the kind of man I*

211

want to become.

The wetness in his eyes verified that message had been received.

"I love you a lot, Drew, and I always will," he said with a quiver in his voice.

"I love you, too," I replied, meaning it in a way I never had toward him.

He stood up and opened his arms—and heart—to me, as he'd done constantly but not always so literally over many years. I stepped into the embrace with my full body and held him for what felt like hours.

If you think—like I did—the cathartic effect of this moment had exhausted my capacity for insight for one night, think again. I'd barely gotten warmed up.

"What's wrong?" asked Joy after I swooned and kept myself from falling by grabbing hold of the footboard in our bedroom. "Another seizure?"

"No. Nothing like a seizure." I straightened up and lowered my hand from my forehead. "Exactly *unlike* a seizure." Instead of locking up from an overload of activity in a single lobe, it felt like my brain was opening or expanding. "An un-seizure," I said.

I could sense unusual patterns form throughout my entire cortex, with what seemed like an awareness of individual neural impulses and an ability to trace each one from cell to cell. The effect at the level of normal consciousness was akin to non-linear cognition. I was thinking multi-dimensionally, in every direction at once.

It dawned on me I'd discovered—stumbled upon, really—the solution to *all* the world's problems. Humanity simply had to transcend the typical sensory perceptions and logical reasoning we learned to rely on for survival and advantage in a competitive and often dangerous environment, and we'd understand the whole, interconnected truth of our existence.

I realize that doesn't sound so simple. But I was

212

doing it, so I knew it was *possible.*

You're probably wondering what drug—or drugs—I was on. It's true I'd had several more beers while we were out and a couple little tokes of marijuana to round out the evening back at the condo. Even so, I knew then and still believe today my experience was not induced—although it may have been facilitated—by the chemical substances I ingested.

"Western culture got lost in the wheat field when it followed the path cut by Descartes and Newton," I said. "It wasn't The Enlightenment we needed. It was enlightenment." I reflected on that assertion. "That's not to say it's a mistake to be skeptical of traditional authorities, nor is it to deny there can be advantages to thinking rationally or to suggest we should reject scientific analysis. But we need to cease making rigid distinctions between the observer, the observed, and the observation."

"You're glowing," she said, looking on with wide-eyed magnetism. "For real. Radiating light."

I nodded, only mildly surprised she could see the field of energy I'd noticed surrounding the exposed skin of my hands and arms and could feel emanating from my entire body.

I should note, for anyone with lingering doubt, Joy had abstained from smoking pot that night and hadn't had anything to drink since our afternoon cocktails nearly ten hours earlier. She was completely sober.

Over the next thirty or so minutes, I tried to allow the heightened activity in my brain to unfold organically even as I attempted to witness it and explain it—usually in fragments—to Joy, searching for the right words to articulate what was happening to—for, inside, and through—me.

It occurred to me I was demonstrating, on a microscopic level (literally), the model for macroscopic revolution—in thought, not the violent kind—outlined by Michel Foucault. The French cultural theorist suggests radical transformation in human relations can be achieved through widespread change in beliefs and actions. The trick is accomplishing that before individual points of resistance are reabsorbed into existing power dynamics. The key is forming disruptive networks that shift and regroup in order to avoid identification and suppression until they coalesce in a strategic manner.

That's exactly what I felt happening in my brain. I saw this "rewiring" of my neural pathways, which I understood to be temporary—at least for the time being—as a potential way out of periodic bouts of cynicism and despair shared by Elijah and me. Much contemporary philosophy considers the feeling of having an independent and unified self to be an illusion. It views humans as disjointed—and often conflicting—collections of beliefs and behaviors determined entirely by our cultural conditioning, by the dominant modes of thought in our social structures. In doing so, it takes away the possibility of free will or any real agency.

I found particularly depressing the claim by Foucault's comrade Louis Althusser that people are *always already*—a phrase used in philosophy to denote an essential element of existence—constituted in and by ideology, whether they're conscious of their limiting beliefs or not. As with assimilation by the Borg on *Star Trek: TNG*, "Resistance is futile." One way or another, we have no choice but to answer, and thereby validate, the policeman—literal or figurative—who calls, "Hey, you!" In doing so, we subject ourselves to an authority outside ourselves.

I now realized I had a different call to answer. My "calling" was to bridge apparent gaps and seeming contradictions among my academic learning, my spiritual intuitions, and my in-the-flesh experiences, and to communicate my synthesis of all three to others through my writing. And that would require going beyond normal sensory perception and logical thought to grok—on a visceral, intuitive level—the entire web of connection.

I came back to "reality" enough to notice Joy's eyelids

flutter. The clock showed it to be nearly four in the morning. I tucked her into bed and kissed her forehead. Although the most intense lucidity had passed, my mind continued to race. I knew I wouldn't rest that night.

I opened the closet and my chest and lifted out my version of Excalibur's twin from the King Arthur legend: Clarent, sword of peace. Armed with that and a tablet of paper I liberated from Bruce's office, I sat in a rocking chair on the balcony and took the first step to answer the call.

By the time the sliding glass door opened and Joy sat down beside me, I'd filled almost the entire tablet with what Surrealists term automatic writing. I hadn't noticed the dawn come and go.

She picked up the pen's stainless steel casing, which I'd discarded when the button meant to extend and retract the ballpoint hadn't functioned, apparently stuck in place from years of disuse. I'd found it fitting to write with the bare ink cartridge—the core of the instrument stripped of its protective shell.

I set the tablet and cartridge down and looked at Joy with a sigh.

"You've been writing this whole time?"

"I think it's the start of my dissertation."

"Whoa. Whatever happened last night ... gave you an idea for a novel?"

"More of a memoir."

"Aren't you supposed to wait another twenty-five years for that?"

"I need to do it now. It's the only way for me to understand who I am."

"Cool," she said. "I can't wait to read it. In the meantime, I'll make coffee."

I gazed at the tablet. Somehow I'd never considered I'd have to let others actually *read* what I'd written.

CHAPTER SEVENTEEN
LOVER'S LOOP

I think Heather put it best when she told me, "For such a smart guy, you can be a real dumbass."

How was I being a dumbass? Let me count the ways.

For starters, I'd incurred the wrath of Kessler for refusing to let her read the pages I'd generated, and even more so for the manner in which I refused. I'd returned from spring break energized, and I submitted a dissertation prospectus—academic jargon for proposal—to her and my other committee members that same week, outlining my plan for interrogating my formative experiences, without yet mentioning they included sexual relations with men.

"A book-length memoir," she noted at the onset of my oral defense of the idea's merit. "Those are typically written from a more mature perspective."

Yeah, I thought. I know. Wait twenty-five years.

"Aren't you the one who keeps telling me the dissertation should be approached as a stepping stone?" I asked.

I knew what I was drafting would be only the start of a life's work to answer the call I'd felt in what Joy and I termed my "lucid moment." I further knew I'd be required to deposit a copy in the university library upon completion—and successful defense—of the project. Beyond that, I intended to exercise strict control over who laid eyes on the document. Absolutely no way would I ever publish it for a general readership.

"I more likely referred to it as a hurdle to leap," she replied. "But the point is the same."

Not exactly, I thought.

"In any case, I figured that's what you had in mind when you chose that genre for your comprehensive exams."

Not so much, I thought. At least not in my *conscious* mind.

"Quite frankly, I think working through that material will be a healthy process for you."

Once Kessler gave her approval, the rest of the committee acceded without debate.

More than a month later, I still hadn't shown any of them as much as a word of the actual manuscript, which numbered in the hundreds of pages as we reached the end of the term, a fact I'd made the mistake of letting slip during my semester review with Kessler.

"When might I read this grand tome of yours?" she inquired.

"I haven't been able to get my mind around what it all adds up to," I answered, which was not only an attempt to delay the inevitable but also true.

"Perhaps I can help you find focus. That is the usual role of one's advisor."

"I'll be prepared to defend the full work next spring," I said, weary of her pressure to prove my progress. "In the meantime, give me some fucking space to breathe."

"What the devil has gotten into you?" she asked in response to my unfamiliar—to her—language and tone.

The devil inside, I thought. *Every single one of us.* Could I exorcise mine?

Even before I'd prepared my prospectus, I'd sent an application and writing sample to the Bread Loaf Writers' Conference in Vermont, along with a petition to be considered for that summer's workshop despite having missed, by mere days, the official deadline. Sharing my personal story with strangers seemed safer than allowing Kessler or anyone who knew me to read it. Assuming I'd be accepted—something I wouldn't learn for almost another month, at the end of May—the session would be held in August, right before the start of FSU's fall term. Once I saw how the work was received there, I'd have a better idea how to move forward at home. That plan didn't strike me as at all foolish, even if my execution of it made me a dumbass.

Another way I *may* have been foolish was my reluctance to try to induce another lucid moment. The idea of such an attempt produced more double-bind anxiety in me. On one hand, I might fail and lose confidence in the legitimacy of my calling, or worse. Maybe the initial experience had been caused by a tumor the MRI didn't reveal. On the other hand, I might succeed, which could have undesirable implications or consequences of its own. Maybe I stood on the slippery slope of insanity and would lose my footing if I took another step. Besides, I didn't feel a pressing *need* for more lucidity. When I'm ready, I thought, the universe will call back.

In the meantime, I thought it sensible to study relevant materials. I took another pass at the *Bhagavad Gita* and understood it in a new way, although some parts remained beyond my grasp. For a more modern source, I turned to *The Varieties of Religious Experience*, a collection of early-twentieth-century lectures by Emerson protégée—and godson—William James. The introductory talk on "Religion and Neurology" inspired curiosity in me about more contemporary models of intersections between spirituality and cognitive psychology. The essential, or at least common, characteristics identified in the remarks on "Mysticism" lent credibility to what I'd undergone. In contrast to my insecurity about claiming veracity, questions of that sort of authenticity were of no

219

interest to the pragmatist James, who judges the value—and truth—of an experience based solely on its effects.

I also bought a copy of Hermann Hesse's *Siddhartha* and returned to Vasudeva's river for the first time in four years. It took me a few tries to make it through the passages Angie and I had recited to each other without breaking down in a fit of sobbing.

As I scanned titles on the spirituality shelf in a Tallahassee bookstore, a man introduced himself as James Redfield and handed me a copy of what he said was his self-published novel *The Celestine Prophecy*. I won't comment on the literary qualities of that book, which became a worldwide bestseller a couple years later. I did appreciate the author's indirect—albeit in some cases slightly vague—articulation of "nine insights" from an ancient manuscript discovered by his characters, especially the ones concerning synchronistic flow and the formation of a critical mass of awakened, purposeful beings evolving together to break free from their individual pasts and our collective history in order to bring about a more peaceful and loving vision for the world. I was more or less with him until I got to the part of the ninth insight about bridging the realms of life and death (or afterlife), which struck me as jarring the way some New Age sentiments still do. I objected in particular to his suggestion we pay our spiritual teachers—formal or not—for their insights, which I interpreted as a not-so-subtle call for readers to send Redfield money. He even listed his mailing address at the end of the book.

In my own manuscript, as I moved into the second stage of the Surrealist method, in which the power of reason is applied to material produced through automatic writing, I probed two lingering gaps from my lucid moment unrelated—or so I thought—to sexuality. The first, connected to what James calls the "ineffable" or indescribable quality of mystical experience, was how to get people to understand what I'd felt and known even when they *hadn't*—a question complicated by my own memory of it slipping from certainty to mere confidence. The second, connected to the cognitive psych aspect as well as to the transient nature of most mystical experience, was how to consciously and permanently rewire the brain to make multi-dimensional thinking—or, as I'd come to envision it, *linking*—our default or dominant mental mode.

I'd accomplished all this reading and writing, while still finding time to "hang out" with Joy, on several occasions accompanied by one or both of the couples we'd befriended, in part due to a diminished need for sleep. I could function on no more than three or four hours a night without any sense of deprivation.

Speaking of Joy, my most impressive and consistent display of dumbassery was in regard to her. I knew by then how good she was for me, how good we *could be* for each other. Alongside our similar interests and traits, we possessed complementary differences that brought us into harmonious balance. Her instinct toward moderation encouraged me to step back from lines I had a habit of crossing despite an awareness my recklessness often put me in jeopardy, while my impulse toward adventure inspired her to step outside her comfort zone and explore budding desires and new dimensions of herself. I sensed the potential for us to *see each other*, the way Tina had seen me and I'd seen Angie, but this time in a reciprocal manner.

In some respects that had already happened, in spite of—or even because of—the lack of expectations we'd placed on our relationship beyond enjoying the connection we felt. Ironically, our agreement to forego a future together may have enabled us to lay the groundwork for exactly that. With one notable exception on my part, we'd cultivated a bond based on honesty. Over the past few months, without ever losing myself in a mad rush of passion, I'd grown attached to Joy.

The situation reminded me of an adage my foster brother repeated on more than one occasion when we were in high school, which at the time seemed dispiriting and perverse. "You don't *fall* in love," Babak would say. "You fall in a well. Love is something you *build*."

His prosaic outlook now made sense but also conflicted with a strong idealistic thrust in his cultural lineage. I'd become familiar with several Persian romantic poets from the medieval era who influenced nineteenth-century Western Romantics. Chief among them, Omar Khayyám, a true (pre-)Renaissance man, achieved lasting impact through not only artistic works but by his efforts as philosopher, astronomer, and scientist. The Sufi mystic Rumi and the epicure Hafiz likewise had earned admiration from the world, including me.

The only alligators swimming near the lily pad safe harbor Joy embodied were inside me. I knew that. But my knowledge didn't help me avoid those devils, which—like their counterparts in the Frogger game—would float along with heads down until I neglected their danger and then snap their necks around and snatch me into their jaws. Even as this took place, it gave me some satisfaction to continue thinking of my inner demons as Gators, proud 'Nole that I'd become.

The first 'gator swam on the surface in recognizable form: my enduring pain from the treachery I'd felt at the hands (mouths ... genitals ...) of Angie and Scott. I was reluctant to open myself all the way to Joy, lest my trust again be betrayed, this time in a manner even more devastating and, perhaps, permanent.

A twin but better disguised and fiercer 'gator consisted of my shame about my secret bisexuality and, especially, my preference to bottom: to be penetrated in such unmanly fashion. My intellectual grasp of queer theory and understanding of how cultural ideology gets imposed onto the individual didn't help me curtail my self-imposed punishment for my transgressions against heteronorms. I'd ceased getting fucked once Joy and I started having sex, even though we hadn't taken a vow of exclusivity. But I knew that wouldn't—couldn't—last.

Whenever I felt I was becoming *too* attached, approaching the point of no return, I did something to push away Joy, usually during a state of drunken agitation. I'd apologize, with sincerity, the next day. And she'd accept the apology. Lather, rinse, repeat. We talked about the vicious circle and my genuine desire to break it—or, better yet, reverse it. But even with her support, I hadn't been able to execute my part in the drama.

That brings me to the specific dumbass behavior(s) prompting Heather's remark.

"Bull's-eye!" I shouted. A *double* bull, to be precise.

I branched my arms in a V centered around my head and strutted back and forth between our table and the darts alley, enjoying the sight of Jack grimacing. He knew bulls were my weakness, which is why he'd hit his three first—which led to him scoring points on me there with a couple "stray" darts as play progressed—while I'd followed standard Cricket decorum and worked my way from twenty down to fifteen, saving the heart of the board for last. I'd made up the points on twenties, so by closing bulls I'd won the game.

"*Bull's-eye!*" I repeated.

"Keep it up, and I'll stick a dart in your *brown* eye," he said.

I whirled and grabbed him by the throat as my other arm cocked back to deliver a potentially jaw- or nose-breaking blow. I felt a pair of hands catch hold of my raised forearm and twist it down and behind my back. I whirled that way, letting go of Jack's neck and balling that hand into a fist in time to smash it into Dave's temple. Unlike Jack, I'm not a leftie, but I had my rotating torso putting weight into the arcing swing, which connected well before full arm extension with the force of my follow-through behind it. The contact dropped Dave to the floor.

Hands dragged me through the tavern. A foot kicked against the panic bar and sent the door flying open, with

223

me flying through it close behind.

I landed hard on the asphalt outside. I heard the door close behind the bouncer. I rolled onto my back and stared up at the cloudy night sky.

Eventually Joy's face, showing a mix of concern and disappointment, appeared over me. "You want help up?"

"Perfect right where I am."

"Okay." She disappeared from my view. I heard the tavern door open and close.

"Still perfect," I said aloud to myself. My lifetime record in bar fights was two wins and zero losses. But my victory ratio fell fast if you included bouts at other venues, like frat houses.

Sometime later, I heard familiar voices as their speakers left the pub. I pressed myself up into a seat against the nearby brick wall. I saw Jack, Anna, and Heather standing off to one side as Elijah approached and crouched beside me.

"How ya doin'?" he asked.

"Been better."

"What happened in there? I thought you won."

"Nope. I most definitely lost."

If we'd had a chance to continue our conversation, my deep affinity with the other half of Drewlijah might've brought me all the way back into equilibrium and ended the ugliness right there. But then the door opened and Joy led Dave outside. He held a baggie of ice to his head and leaned an arm across her shoulders for support.

Come on, I thought. You can't still be woozy.

He gazed over at me, then grinned and pulled Joy tighter against him.

That's it, I thought. I knew nothing would happen between them, but I considered her offering him succor a violation, even though part of me understood she was trying to clean up my mess.

I scrambled to my feet and staggered toward them, Elijah shadowing me by half a step. "Gimme my fucking keys."

224

"You can't drive," said Joy.

"Says who?"

"The law, for starters."

"Fuck the law. Fuck the world. Fuck everything. Fuck *you*." Yep. I actually said it.

Her face now showed a different kind of concern mixed with something other than disappointment.

"Joy, why don't you give me Drew's keys," said Elijah, "and I'll get him home safe."

She tossed them down at my feet. "I'd like to know what the devil has gotten into you."

I seriously doubt that, I thought, as she and Dave started across the parking lot toward his car. You might *think* you'd like to know. But you wouldn't have any sympathy for *this* devil.

"Pleased to meet you," I called after them, rolling like a stone now, "Hope you guess my name!"

Then I heard the voice of Heather: "For such a smart guy, you can be a real dumbass."

CHAPTER EIGHTEEN

... A LOAF OF BREAD ...

The day after our end-of-semester blowout, and my out-of-proportion blowup, I'd once again performed an act of contrition to Joy. Walking from my apartment toward the residence she shared with two other master's degree students, I'd realized I should come bearing gifts. I stopped at the sole shopping outlet on my path, a convenience store, and bought a cheap bouquet of flowers and, for some reason, a cheap jug of wine—impractical not only because I had to carry it two more miles, but also because she didn't care much for cabernet, the only varietal in stock.

She'd refused the proffered bounty from the threshold without inviting me inside—at least not into the house. She said, "I get it. You're a work-in-progress."

An excellent way to look at it, I'd thought.

"But I'm not going to wait forever for you to get over yourself. Take the summer to think about it. Don't contact me again until you're ready to show me the real you." Then she closed the door, leaving me to bear my burdens—physical and psychological—all the way home.

I'd never felt like such a failure. I wanted more than anything to break the cycle.

Now it was do or die, which is why, as I stepped onto

the hallowed grounds of the Bread Loaf campus—what I hoped would be *my* Wimbledon—I felt immense pressure to succeed. I wasn't sure about everything that might entail, but I knew it required exorcising my devils.

My acceptance letter had included a rebuke for the tardiness of my application, which, the administrators noted, made me ineligible for financial assistance. They said they'd made an unprecedented exception by even considering me. They didn't say why.

I could afford the conference fees only because I'd inherited a little money from my paternal grandfather the previous year. He'd been an academic himself, earning a PhD at the University of Pittsburgh in the early '30s before serving on the faculty of North Carolina State University for more than forty years, including a reluctant six-year stint as Chancellor. I figured he'd support my decision to invest some of his bequest to me in my own pursuit of higher education. Sometimes fortune smiles through tears.

I'd spent the months of June and July laboring around the clock on my manuscript in order to send my best effort ahead of me so my conference mentor could read the full text prior to the workshop. Fortune smiled on me again when I was assigned to the sessions led by one of my literary heroes, and seemingly yet again when I received a call telling me he wanted to meet with me one on one as soon as I arrived, which, the administrator on the other end of the line told me, represented another unprecedented exception to normal protocol.

I had just enough time to drop my duffel bag and knapsack at my cottage and hustle over to the Inn—an expanded Victorian farmhouse—before the appointed hour. I stood by the door to the specified meeting room until the second hand on my wristwatch advanced three ticks past the specified meeting time. As I took in a breath and raised my fist to knock, the door opened.

"He's ready for you," said the woman on the other side, a soft glow radiating from her smiling, lotus-like face. She could have been anywhere from her late twenties to her late forties, an indeterminacy I attributed mostly to her petite build and Asian ancestry. But I sensed *something else* contributed to her apparent agelessness. As I stared at this human lotus, she closed the petals of her eyelids, bowed her blushing flower head, then floated down the passage.

Was that *real*, I wondered, or am I projecting stereotyped images of the exotic Orient onto someone who didn't really behave quite so much like they'd been sent to a film set by central casting?

"Well?" a voice from within called. "You coming?"

A moment later I stood before a man I'd admired for years.

"Have a seat," he said.

Not long after I'd complied, I started to fidget.

"Everything all right?"

"Sorry, Mister Wright," I answered. "It's just ... you're my second favorite living author. After John Irving."

"Hmm. I'll take that in the spirit you intended," he said. "I'm honored to be your favorite living author named Truman, which is what you can call me. I guess I'm lucky Capote's dead." His face turned serious, although possibly mockingly so. "Well then. The moment of judgment. By one of your idols, no less." He gazed down at the copy of my manuscript in his hands, then looked up and peered right at me. "Memoirs take courage. When you write a memoir, you open yourself to criticism not only of your writing, like all authors do, but of your humanity itself. No veil to hide behind."

He gets it, I thought.

"They also take perspective. Perspective you don't have yet. How could you at your age? You might not be ready to tell this story for another thirty years."

So everyone keeps saying, I thought.

"This draft offers no sense of resolution."

"I don't know how it ends."

229

"Sure you do. Same as everyone's story ends."

Point made.

"A working title would likely help you *focus* your reflections a bit. You'll need one eventually. Names imply so much."

I nodded. I considered titles one of my specialties. This one had me stumped.

"Might I offer a suggestion?" he asked.

"Please do."

"'Sex, Drugs, and Self-Denial.'" He leaned forward to study my perplexed expression. "You don't like it? Then change the story."

"How can I change it if it's true?"

"Well, one way would be to change your truth. That's easier said than done, of course." He sighed. "Listen. And I mean this as kindly as possible. You've done a lot of running. If all my years of living have given *me* any perspective, it's that running doesn't help when you're trying to escape yourself."

Wow. He really does get it. Far better than I do.

"Thank you," I said. I started to stand.

"Whoa whoa whoa. There you go again running away. I'm not finished with you. Unless you've had all you can handle."

I shook my head and lowered myself onto the hot seat.

"Another way you could change the story would be to concern yourself less with factual accuracy."

"Wouldn't that diminish its legitimacy?"

"On the contrary. What I mean is distill your experience to its essence. Then find a way to convey that essence in a less literal manner. I see you're a fan of Dalí and Van Gogh. To quote another great painter, 'Art is a lie that makes us realize truth.' Picasso proceeds to call on the artist to employ the appropriate methods 'to convince others of the truthfulness of his lies.'"

The truth within lies. Within lies, the truth. I pondered the implications.

230

"Besides," continued Truman, "this isn't wholly memoir anyway. It's part manifesto."

Indeed. I'd wondered what Truman would say about that aspect of what I submitted.

"You've got some fascinating ideas to share. I'm intrigued by the 'revolution in evolution' you envision."

"*Webolution*," I said, naming my invented term for the concept.

"Most readers don't like ideas. Not explicit ones anyway, or ones with a moral thrust. Unless you're George Bernard Shaw. He only gets away with it by being goddamn clever. If you're not that gifted with comedy, you have to find another way to make ideas engaging."

"Might you offer a suggestion about that as well?" I asked.

He smiled. "Allegory. Think *The Pilgrim's Progress*, *Moby-Dick*, or *Lord of the Flies*."

"Or *Siddhartha*."

He nodded. "I'm not suggesting you emulate those books to the letter, of course. But I believe your purpose would be well served by the incorporation of select allegorical elements."

I gazed out the window as I processed Truman's insights. I thought of *The Celestine Prophecy* and how its ninth insight rang false for me. Redfield's allegorical approach hadn't managed to convince me of the truthfulness of his lie. Could that be a matter of his literary skill and not any inherent flaw in the idea itself? Was its core—or its end point—really that different than the core of what I envisioned through *webolution*?

"If I can hold your attention a few more minutes ..."

I turned my gaze toward him. "Sorry."

"It's clear you come from a scholarly background."

And *lineage*, I thought. At least on one side. Following my grandfather's path, both my uncles earned doctorates and became university professors. I wondered if my dad's choice to become a "real" doctor—a distinction I've heard people make about medical ones—had been a

231

form of rebellion. Even my paternal grandmother had earned a master's degree, in the same scientific field, genetics, as her mate, a rare accomplishment for a woman of that era.

"Thanks," I said.

"I didn't mean it as a compliment." He smiled. "Don't get me wrong: It's a wonderful trait. But not for a creative writer. Let me explain. Would you agree the main goal of a scholar is, through written explication, to 'connect the dots' within the object of study? All of them?"

"As many as possible."

"That doesn't make for good art. The role of art is to express something beyond words. I believe that's a concept you understand."

I nodded. The *ineffable*.

"One way to do that," Truman continued, "is to connect *some* dots, enough to give readers a sense of a pattern—show them the outline of the map, or how a few stars combine into a constellation—and then leave the rest to them."

"They might not get the message."

"They'll get what they get, including things you never intended. It won't be the same for everyone. Nor should it be. Don't transcendentalists celebrate individualism and diversity?"

As I nodded, I had a bizarre flashback to my appearance on *Jeopardy!*, specifically the Daily Double I answered correctly to put myself in position to win my semifinal. I'd based my wager on my confidence in regard to the category, which was Literature. So I was momentarily thrown for a loop when asked to finish a quote from a book I'd never read: "In the opening line to *Little Women*, Jo grumbles, 'Christmas won't be Christmas without any' of these." I felt tremendous relief when the correct answer—easy enough to guess—popped into my mind.

But instead of "What are presents?" I said, "What is presence?"

Alex cocked his head at what sounded like a grammatical irregularity, but my homophone slipped past him, and I was awarded credit.

I now wondered if my slip of the brain had been a multi-dimensional neural linkage, an inkling of my own *webolution*. I'd been aware the book's author, Louisa May Alcott, grew up—as the daughter of transcendentalists—around Emerson and his circle of believers.

"I know I've thrown you for a loop today," Truman said before a pause. He seemed to be looking past my pensive expression into my soul. "To combine scholarly and artistic sensibilities at the level you aspire requires a special state of mind. You might achieve great things. Assuming you embrace, rather than reject, your hybrid identity. In all its dimensions."

My multi-dimensional hybridity.

"I don't know how to thank you," I said.

"I'm told it's a gift to be in my presence," he said with a wink.

I nearly fell off the chair.

"You okay?"

I nodded even though "okay" wasn't the word I would've used to describe myself in that moment.

"Good. Just one last thing then. Did you bring a computer?" Portable ones had been around for a while, but they'd only recently become commonplace and affordable.

"ThinkPad," I said, naming the brand-new IBM model I'd acquired with the rest of my grandfather's legacy.

He rose and handed me my manuscript. "Look through your files and find a more polished piece to workshop here. I think it would be a mistake to show the other participants your work-in-progress in its current form." He moved to the door, which he opened and stepped through.

I remained in the chair, surrounded by emptiness, for some time.

233

An earlier version of me would've walked out of that private master class feeling like I'd been reamed with a baseball bat by Truman. Instead, I recognized I'd been on the receiving end of an act of generosity, even if it left my ego sore. Some of what he said about writing and art I'd heard before, albeit stated so it cut less to the heart of the matter. In my role as a scholar, I understood it to be true about literature in general, if not about all *my* work as a creative writer.

I now realized my belief in the *significance* of this particular project had blinded me to how I'd come up short in terms of the most basic goal of my craft, and the very purpose I'd been obsessed with achieving: to communicate truth. My conference mentor—this creative-writing guru—exhibited miraculous powers of perception and imagination in seeing what I'd shown him for what it was *and* for what it might become.

Even so, the session left me with a problem.

Finding another piece to workshop wouldn't be difficult. I'd already thought of a story I considered developing as my dissertation—the sole entry in my body of fiction that even began to reflect my present interests—about a man named Frank Bodie, who, resolved to accomplish something meaningful before he dies of a brain tumor, struggles—Arjuna like—over the apparent need to commit violence for the sake of justice. I called it "Bodie's Sattva," a play on a relevant term from Buddhism I first heard in the similarly named Steely Dan song. I told you I have a way with titles.

My problem was this: What was I supposed to *do* with what I'd taken from my exchange with Truman? It's one thing to know what a situation requires. It's quite another to know how to bring that about. If it would be a mistake to show my fellow workshop participants my memoir-*cum*-manifesto in its current form, how could I conceive of showing it to my dissertation advisor and committee members? Never mind showing it to Joy, the only person expecting to see it who really mattered to me.

I needed another dose of lucidity, and I needed it NOW.

Over the next ten days, whenever I wasn't attending, somewhat half-heartedly, scheduled conference activities—the workshop meetings led by Truman, lectures and tutorials on craft given by him and other faculty, readings by faculty and students, and information sessions with editors and agents—I sought lucidity everywhere. I sought it while hiking in the surrounding mountains. I sought it while showering. I sought it while moving my bowels.

Although I never found what I sought, I did see Lotus seemingly everywhere I went on campus. We made eye contact over and over, exchanging smiles but no words. I saw her in the dining hall. I saw her sitting on the lawn in the shade of trees. I saw her when she'd appear with copies of student manuscripts and distribute them to the participants in our workshop meetings.

At the session on the final day of the conference, we finally got to "Bodie's Sattva." My peers and mentor alike offered insightful and constructive feedback. Maybe the piece had a core worth fleshing out someday. It might even serve as a substitute dissertation, if I opted to take the hurdle rather than the stepping stone approach.

But that still wouldn't resolve my issue with Joy.

"I hope you'll all attend my reading tonight," said Truman to the group while looking in my direction. "It's from my forthcoming memoir."

The sign taped to the Barn entrance declared only two words: Truman Wright.

I pushed open the door and stepped into the auditorium, already filled to what seemed like capacity. I guess I'm not the only one who considers him a genius, I thought. I wandered from the back of the audience area to the edge of the speaker area, gazing down each row in search of an empty chair. No luck. I paused in the corner not far from where Truman looked over notes behind a podium. As I surveyed the entire room from this fixed, angled vantage point, my eyes landed on Lotus, who sat in the middle of the front row.

She waved me toward her. "Drew!" She rose from her chair as I approached. "I saved you a seat."

"What about you?"

"I'll stand in back."

"You won't be able to hear."

"That's okay. I've read it." Before I could protest further, she glided away.

Over the next hour, Truman read from two chapters of his memoir. The first recounted his experiences, and later reflections on them, as an undergraduate student in the early '60s, when he participated in the Harvard Psilocybin Project led by Timothy Leary and another faculty member. The second did the same for his experiences as a soldier in Vietnam later that decade, a tour of duty for which he'd enlisted. The latter chapter included quite a "bombshell" of an admission. With the author's permission, I'm reprinting the final paragraph here:

> And so, at the age of twenty-five, I emerged from the jungle a sort of man-child. A man-child who'd killed other men. A man-child who'd fucked other men. I wondered: Was there any difference?

When he finished reading those words, he looked out into the crowd with a smile. "If you want the answer, *my* answer," he said, "you'll have to buy the book."

Talk about courage! Truman Wright had come out as bisexual to the literary world. And, as soon as the press got wind of it, he'd be out to the *entire* world.

But there's a big difference, I thought. He's a *top*. As

236

an adult man who fucks—or at least once fucked—younger ones, he's part of a masculine tradition going back to ancient Greece. Besides, he's *secure*, in his standing and his finances. I had my reputation—and entire future—to think about.

After the mix of enthusiastic and polite applause ended, I retreated to the nearby corner, where I watched Truman greet audience members and sign autographs. I noticed a few people glance askance in his direction and then murmur to their companions.

"He reads as sublimely as he writes," said Lotus from beside me.

I nodded. "Thanks for the chair."

She bowed her head.

"What's your name?" I asked.

"Guren."

"Guren," I repeated, to practice the pronunciation. "I like the sound of that."

"It's Japanese for crimson lotus."

Of course it is, I thought, shaking my head.

We stood in silence until Truman finished receiving the adulation of his worshippers and approached us. "I see you've connected with my wife," he said.

Your *wife*.

"We met overseas," he continued. "Early '70s. In the next chapter."

"I was merely a child at the time," she said with a smile.

"Guren and I have a cabin near here. On Lake Dunmore. Very quiet. Very romantic."

"Would you care to come with us there for an initiation?" she asked.

"Initiation?"

"Did I say initiation? I meant celebration. The two of you have had quite an experience."

"Sure," I said.

237

With one exception, Truman's description matched the cabin's characteristics to a T. It was indeed near the Bread Loaf campus, less than thirty minutes away by car—or, in this case, the Jeep Guren drove. The location was remote and, as promised, quiet. And it certainly satisfied the definition of romantic in the "idealized" sense: cozy, quaint, and serene. The only way he'd been inaccurate was to say it was *on* Lake Dunmore, which of course he hadn't meant literally.

Even if I'd expected a floating bungalow, I would've been pleased to find myself partway up one of the surrounding ridges, above and overlooking the surface of the water, rather than on it. As I stood on the deck gazing up at the clear night sky, I heard the sliding glass door open.

Truman walked over with a goblet of red wine. "I hope you like cabernet."

"I do," I said, as I accepted the offering. I looked at his now empty hands. "Shouldn't we toast ... something?"

"Recovering alcoholic. Chapter Nine." He smiled. "Please don't abstain on my account."

I nodded, raised the glass toward him, and took a small sip.

"I often wonder how different our culture would be if alcohol weren't the only drug we made legal and accessible," he said. "Seems to me it causes more destruction than most of the ones we prohibit."

I swallowed the larger sip I'd taken as he spoke, then set the goblet on the railing.

"I didn't mean to lecture. I really do wonder."

"I often wonder the same thing," I said.

"I know you do."

Right, I thought. He can read me like a book. My book.

He reached his hand around my head and fingered my ponytail holder. "May I?" he asked. Once I nodded my consent, he slipped the binder off me, letting my locks fall across my neck and upper back, fanning out between my shoulder blades. He stroked my full mane, then lifted a cluster of strands on his palm and rolled them against his skin with his thumb. "There is nothing unmanly about you."

"May I join you?" asked the voice of Guren.

I turned and saw her standing in the doorway, backlit, and without a stitch of clothing.

"There is no competition here," said Truman. "Guren and I are yoked as one, but we're not possessive of each other."

I found that concept, like the entire situation, so overwhelming I couldn't begin to say anything in response. Instead I grabbed my shirt at the waist and pulled it up and over my head, then tossed it aside.

We soon formed a stack of naked bodies in an Adirondack chair, with me on Truman's lap facing away from him, and Guren astride and facing me. In a physical sense, he penetrated me while I penetrated her, but it *felt* more like a reciprocal interpenetration of each of us by both the others.

I gazed up and spotted Cygnus—the cross-shaped stellar swan with various origin myths—positioned above Guren's head like a crown. I redirected my gaze to her face.

It blurred.

No no no, I thought. This is *good*. We're *connected*.

Before my panic could spread, her face refocused. But now it took the form of Truman.

I resisted an impulse to turn my head and verify he remained behind me. *Someone* was inside me.

The face blurred again, then refocused in the appearance of Joy.

After a moment of disbelief, I smiled and laughed a little as I felt a tear crest over my lower eyelid and trickle down my cheek.

Guren's face blurred and refocused as a series of visages: first Angie, Tina, and Gypsy, then Elijah, Heather, Jack, Anna, Scott, Melissa, Johnny, Sabine,

Kirk, Dina, Peter, Becca, and even the gentle giant Noel.

My tears and giggles flowed in a steady stream.

The circle of people I recognized in Guren's face widened to include my mom and Bruce, my dad and Betty, Adam and Diana, Babak, Billy, Bob and Ken, Stephanie and Calvin. Then it expanded again to include an array of other family members and friends.

I burst out in a flood of sobs and belly laughs.

As the intensity of our lovemaking increased, so did the pace at which the face of Guren blurred and refocused through a chain of other people I knew or had known or encountered—including Straightened Hair and Cornrow—and then sped through a succession of figures I'd never seen—including ones who appeared to come from faraway lands and long-gone eras. The impressions flashed across the screen filling the void of Guren's countenance faster than I could absorb.

A face I *thought* I'd never seen appeared and remained present until I recognized it—with a gasp—as Flora-Laura, the girl from Cape Cod all those years ago.

Just before I climaxed, I saw a face that somehow seemed to be every possible face at once. As I felt myself carried away in a torrent of physical and emotional release, I sensed Guren and Truman follow me over the edge.

Sometime later, after our stack of bodies collapsed into a heap and our heart rates and breath stabilized, we extricated ourselves from our intertwined posture and made our way into the shelter of their wilderness sanctuary, where we reposed in the king-size bed.

I half-awoke in the middle of the night to realize Guren and I were alone in the bed. I gazed through groggy eyes around the dark room until I spotted Truman, illuminated by a wide beam of moonlight, as he stood looking out the window.

He turned and spread his arms in a span that seemed to stretch the entire diagonal of the mattress. "*He no longer saw his friend Siddhartha's face; instead he saw other faces,"* he quoted, *"many, a long row, a streaming river of faces, hundreds, thousands, which all came and faded, and yet seemed all to be there at once, which kept changing and being renewed, and yet which all were Siddhartha."*

I nodded back into sleep with a smile.

When I awoke fully the next morning, a Sunday, I found myself alone in the bed. Alone, that is, except for two things.

The first was my dawning skepticism. How could Truman have known what I'd seen? He couldn't have. I must have imagined or dreamt his speech, accessing a subconscious memory of that passage from Hesse's book, as I likewise *must* have done—and seemingly linked in my neural web to the closing sequence from Michael Jackson's "Black or White" video—to produce the earlier hallucination. Neither Truman nor Guren, who'd been looking right at me, had shown any response to my crying and laughing, as though my sensations of those things had taken place at the interior level of my being without exterior manifestation.

Hallucination or not, its effects on me were undiminished. As William James concludes his scholarly explication of mystical states, "The supernaturalism and optimism to which they would persuade us may, interpreted in one way or another, be after all the truest of insights into the meaning of this life." I'd gotten the message of my vision—at least I'd gotten *a* message from it—regardless of where it originated. The faces I saw in Guren's, like those Govinda sees in Siddhartha's, were all my own face, reflections in the mirror of humanity. I felt immense love for every one of them, including and especially those I'd harmed and even those who'd harmed me.

I had no expectation of forgiveness from the former, but I extended it freely to the latter.

241

The second thing in bed with me was a note, apparently written by Truman. It read as follows: *I have to be somewhere now. Guren will see you off. Safe and peaceful flight home!*

I rose and padded into the bathroom, where I splashed water on my face. As I reached for a towel I glanced in the mirror and, for an instant, saw Truman reflected where I stood. *Whoa.* I hadn't expected residual hallucinations. The original wasn't even drug induced.

I wrapped the towel around my waist like a loincloth and headed for the kitchen on the hunt for coffee. I didn't find any of the magical brew waiting but then realized I didn't feel a need for stimulation.

Through the open sliding glass door, I heard music playing from the deck.

I stepped through the door and saw Guren, still naked, standing on an exercise mat, one leg extended back with the foot angled outward and the other planted with bent knee in front of her upright torso, her arms stretching up along either side of her head, her upper back arched so her face turned toward the sky. I'd never witnessed anyone do yoga before, and watching her shift her body from one posture to another with dancer-like grace, accompanied by a mix of New Age tunes and spiritual-minded songs by the Beatles and other pop artists, took my breath away.

At some point, I must've made my way to the Adirondack chair, for that's where I found myself when Guren finished the invigorating part of her routine and reclined onto her back. As she lay with her eyes closed and her arms slightly out to the sides and palms turned upward, her legs splayed apart, giving me a direct view of her vagina, which appeared to be emanating light.

I felt drawn to that light as if caught in a space-age tractor beam, which I knew—on *Star Trek* at least—most often served to tow a distressed vessel to safety. That's how I reacted to the attraction of Guren's beaming opening, surrendering myself to its gravitational pull.

242

The moment I brought my mouth to it, her entire body shook in the first of a series of increasingly profound convulsions as I explored this portal to the sacred origins of life with my lips and tongue. As much as I liked to think of myself as a "cunning linguist" (so to speak), I knew I couldn't take credit for her orgasmic response. Something she'd done in her yoga practice had contributed in a major way.

Eventually she grew completely still, and I withdrew to the Adirondack chair, where I sat, naked—having shed my covering somewhere along the way—and watched her bask in bliss.

After some time, her body began to undergo almost imperceptible movements, which developed into more noticeable ones as she reawakened. She rolled over onto her side and rested in the fetal position for a moment, then sat up cross-legged, with her eyes still closed and her palms pressed together in front of her heart.

"*Aaaaaauuummmmnnnnggg*," she chanted.

Then she rose, glided across the distance between us, and knelt in front of me, spreading my knees apart.

"No need to reciprocate," I said. "I'm satisfied." I truly felt no sexual arousal or desire.

She smiled and nodded, then took me into her mouth.

Much to my surprise, my penis immediately achieved its full expression of vitality. Between her hand around its base and her face obscuring the rest, I couldn't see an inch of it, but it felt more engorged than ever before.

Guren traced her other hand along my groin and pressed her fingertips between my genitals and anus.

My head snapped back from the intensity, and I saw stars—literal ones—shining against the crystal blue backdrop of the cloudless midmorning sky. Almost directly above us crouched the constellation of Leo, its neck and shoulders forming the familiar pattern of a backwards question mark known as "the Sickle."

I heard lines from a Blue Oyster Cult song: "Seasons don't fear the reaper / Nor do the wind, the sun or the rain / (We can be like they are)."

Partway across the heavens stood the hourglass shape of legendary hunter Orion, who, Greek myth holds, could be stopped from killing by only one creature: the scorpion.

I felt Pure Joy.

Guren released her death grip on *my* raised club—not a weapon but a fertility tool—and pressed that hand, her left, onto my lower abdomen.

A wave of emotion rolled through me.

Guren slid her hand to my solar plexus and pressed there.

A burst of flame shot through me.

Guren slid her hand to the center of my sternum and pressed.

I shuddered as *something* radiated outward from my core.

When I looked down at my chest, my skin turned translucent, as if my outer layer were dissolving. Beneath it ran currents of pure energy. At each spot she'd touched, I saw a colored disc pulsate: red, orange, yellow, and green in the order they climbed along my central energy channel from perineum to heart.

Guren floated her top hand from orange to yellow to green over and over as she pressed her bottom hand on the red disc and continued to fellate me, as if playing my body like a flute.

Before long, I heard a hum rise from my throat. As the vibrations spread into the chamber of my cranium, first reverberating in my cerebellum and then all through my cerebrum, I sensed a flash of illumination fill my entire being.

When I gazed around now, everything I saw—the cabin, the deck, the trees on the ridge, even the ether—transformed into pure energy flowing between forms, including into and through me and Guren, even as each

244

entity somehow retained its essence.

Guren paused her hand over the pulsating green disc of my heart and massaged it with energy from her palm.

The physical and other sensations built to a crescendo, and I felt myself release in every direction at once. A thousand laser beams of light blasted from my crown.

"Can you speak?" she asked, sometime later.

"... *Yeah*," I said.

"What did you see? What did you experience?"

I couldn't answer that. I had no words to describe what I'd experienced. There are no words to describe what I experienced: the *ineffable*—that which is beyond words—epitomized.

I'll try to put it into words all the same. It was everything and nothing. It was life and death. It was my self and my Self. It was *simply divine*—and I mean that literally. It was godly, and uncomplicatedly so.

Compared to this *un-seizure*, my lucid moment had been a spasm. I now knew things on a level deeper than thought or feeling but encompassing both. Even "deeper" gives a false impression, because one of the things I now understood was there are no levels—no hierarchies—in the true nature of reality. Those things exist only in our rational perception and comprehension of reality. I also now understood the universe isn't multi-dimensional but trans-dimensional.

Like Arjuna when Krishna reveals himself, I'd seen the entire universe. I'd traveled its infinite whole at beyond warp speed—in what I knew were mere seconds but felt like eternity—without ever leaving the Adirondack captain's chair.

And everywhere I'd gone I'd felt at home.

No logical explanation could convince me it had been anything less than absolutely *real*.

"You'd better go inside and collect yourself," said Guren.

245

"And your things."

I looked through the open window of the Jeep at my cottage on the Bread Loaf campus. I don't know how long we'd been parked there. The ride back from Lake Dunmore had passed in utter stillness.

"What did you do to me?" I asked.

"Nothing you can't learn to do for yourself any time. What you accessed today is *always already* within you."

I nodded. I knew she spoke truth, even if I had no idea how I'd learn to do it. And I liked her "always already" much better than Althusser's view of human subjects trapped in ideology.

"Are you familiar with Baba Ram Dass?" she asked.

"That's the spirit name or whatever of the guy Truman knows. The Harvard professor who led the drug studies with Timothy Leary. He changed it after going to India in the '60s."

"Nineteen sixty-seven, to be exact," she said. "The same year Truman went to Vietnam."

"The year of my birth."

"The year Richard Alpert was reborn as Ram Dass."

"Maybe Truman should've gone to India instead," I said. "Although then he wouldn't have met you."

"Our paths were destined to cross eventually. Anyway ... Ram Dass recently came out as bisexual. He says it 'isn't gay, and it's not not-gay, and it's not anything—it's just awareness.'"

Awareness, I thought. A good word for what I experienced at the cabin.

"Speaking of Truman ..." I said, a realization dawning on me as I stepped out of the Jeep and closed its door. "Do you have a second car?" I hadn't noticed one parked at the cabin when we arrived the previous night.

She shook her head.

"Then how'd he get wherever he had to go this morning?"

She smiled and shrugged. "I'll be back in an hour," she said, then drove away.

As I sat on the front step waiting for her to return—having showered, dressed, and stuffed my stuff into my duffel bag in about thirty minutes—two memories from my childhood popped into my consciousness.

As part of my mother's search for spiritual truth, she investigated Transcendental Meditation in the early '70s. When I was six, a college student who'd traveled to India and met the Maharishi Mahesh Yogi—guru to the Beatles and other celebrities—came to our house and gave me my very own mantra. I repeated it faithfully on my daily walk to school. For a week or so. That exposure, I now realized, even though it hadn't taken root right away, had planted a seed in me about the possibilities of achieving a transcendent state. (Thanks for that, and for so much else, Mom. I know you always had my best interests at heart.)

The other memory, a general one from about the same age, concerned coming home from school. Whenever my mom's parents would visit, my grandfather would ask me every afternoon, "What'd you learn at school today?"

"Nothing," I'd reply. "I already knew it all."

What he later joked about as a sign of my future academic achievement—as well as my, shall we say, *self-confidence* in that regard—I now saw in a different light, as if I'd intuitively realized all knowledge, at least all the knowledge that matters, was *always already* within me. I still got a similar feeling when ideas I encountered in cultural theory, spiritual philosophy, and poetic or narrative works—fiction or non—"rang true" for me.

In some cases, it seemed, I needed multiple unveilings of inner knowledge for it to stick.

That memory led me to think about my maternal lineage. My mom's father quit school at age twelve to help support his family during the Great Depression. He worked his way from sweeping the floor in a textile mill to operating machinery there before attending night school and earning a degree and a promotion to management, eventually retiring as personnel director. Throughout his

247

struggles to survive and thrive, he remained a voracious reader. I got as much—or more—of my love for literature from him as from my paternal lineage of academic and medical doctors. He'd given me many a book on birthdays and other occasions over the years.

My mom's mother, meanwhile, did graduate from high school, a high school for the deaf. (I'll tell you the remarkable story of their courtship and marriage another time.) I'd always felt like her hearing impairment kept us from true communication, but I now appreciated her in a new way. She'd taught me the sign language alphabet, including how to combine the letters I, L, and Y to say—in a single gesture—the only thing ever needed to be said.

Once the Jeep arrived, I carried over my duffel bag and knapsack and tossed them into the cargo hold. When I opened the passenger door, I noticed a book on the seat. I lifted it out of the way as I climbed into the vehicle.

"It's a gift," said Guren.

As she initiated the next leg of our journey, I studied the front of the book. *REMEMBER* appeared centered along each edge of the square cover. *BE, HERE,* and *NOW* repeated in varying order in a circle around the main image: a wooden chair inside a sphere of crisscrossed laser-like lines.

I opened the cover and read the handwritten inscription: *For Karuna Das: The light in you is so bright it's blinding.*

"Who's this Karuna Das?" I asked.

"No one, yet," said Guren. "It means 'Servant of Compassion.' Someday that will be you." She let that sink in before adding, "Karuna is more common as a girl's name. I hope that's okay with you."

I smiled and nodded.

Two days later I sat on a bench in Westcott Plaza as students streamed in and out of the nearby FSU administration building on the first day of registration. In

248

front of me, water flowed down the tiers of a fountain known for two main traditions. University officials take pride in one: being thrown in it on your birthday, especially the twenty-first. They talk less about the other: jumping into it, ideally naked, some time before graduation in a kind of baptism prior to the commencement of adult—or "real"—life. I had no idea, or much concern, about when, or if, I'd finish my dissertation and put myself in a position where the latter tradition would be applicable.

But another sort of self-baptism might be appropriate. The universe-ity that first came calling in my lucid moment had called back, and I'd received the message loud and clear. I had a new purpose, at least for now—the only time that matters—and I felt ready to dive in. Perhaps I'd be reborn like Richard Alpert twenty-six years earlier in India, where it was already, at this moment, my birthday.

I couldn't begin to summarize the contents of the book Guren had given me by Alpert's altered ego Ram Dass. What he calls its "Core" consists of drawings and text—including quotations by William James and others—printed in different fonts and layouts in an artistic attempt to express the ineffable. It's filled with images, visual and verbal, that point toward truth.

The most powerful part for me on my initial reading had been the introductory section, a reflective narrative account—or memoir—of the author's transformative journey from PhD to Baba, a term of honor given to wise men in Asia from India to Persia. Despite major differences in the details of our experiences, I developed a deep affinity for him as I read his description of his struggles to find his place in the world. Like him, I'd long felt I was faking my way through life, anxious about breaking free from social structures, and sensing there was more to it all if only I could grasp it. His story was my story was our story.

I flipped open the book and turned to the last page of

249

that section, in which he outlines the commitment he'd made to work out his karma by returning home:

> Part of this commitment is to share what I have learned with those of you who are on a similar journey. One can share a message through telling 'our-story' as I have just done, or through teaching methods of yoga, singing, or making love. Each of us finds his unique vehicle for sharing with others his bit of wisdom.
>
> For me, this story is but a vehicle for sharing with you the true message ... the living faith in what is possible.

As I read those last words, a shadow fell across the page.

And Thou, I thought after looking up at the source of the shadow, completing a famous line from Omar Khayyám's *Rubáiyát*.

The lengthy poem divided into stanzas of four lines is among the books my mom's dad gave me. I'd rediscovered it on my shelf upon return from Vermont.

In my mind, I now recited the entire stanza:

> A book of Verses underneath the Bough,
> A Jug of Wine, a Loaf of Bread — and Thou
> Beside me singing in the Wilderness —
> Oh, Wilderness were Paradise enow!

And indeed, at that moment, Joy stood within arm's reach.

"I hoped I'd see you here," I said.

"Does that mean there's something you want to share with me?" she asked.

I nodded. Then I gazed into the two shimmering blue-gray pools before me, and I took the scariest—and most rewarding—leap of faith in my life.

"I have a story to tell you."

CODA

ODE TO JOY

Today's self-portrait of a middle-aged man
Once known as Drew, and who, for many years,
Was at best a sketch of who he would become,
Looks something like this:

He awakens early and gazes upon,
Then caresses with a fingertip,
The face of the woman beside him,
Whose beauty remains constant.

He rises, then meditates,
Or goes for a run,
Which, for him at least,
Is nearly the same thing.

Next he makes her breakfast,
Puts together her lunch,
Sends her off into the world,
With a kiss and a smile.

He also does the laundry,
And most domestic chores,
In deviance from (and defiance of?)

Established gender norms.

He used to be a teacher—
Perhaps, in a way, still is.
But he's a student, too,
In this classroom without walls.

"If you live long enough,
Life teaches you how to live,"
Schooled a documentary film
Called *Amy*, after Winehouse.

He remembers River Phoenix,
Kurt Cobain, and many more,
Who never reached the point
Where wisdom outweighs pain.

Much of his life's learning
Parallels favorite books,
Which encompass fact and fiction
And in between, much like his story.

The Tibetan Book of the Dead,
Bhagavad Gita and *Tao Te Ching*,
The Yoga Sutras, and *Shiva Sutras*
Fill a high level in his case.

Another holds memoirs by men
Whose journeys ring true for him:
Ram Dass, Bhagavan Das,
And the (Ultimate?) Peaceful Warrior.

Works by critical theorists
Who opened up his mind,
As others opened his heart,
Secure their place as well.

Judith Butler, Michel Foucault,

Derrida and Baudrillard,
bell hooks and Audre Lorde ...
To name just a few.

Among his novel treasures are
A Prayer for Owen Meany,
In the Skin of a Lion,
And, of course, *Siddhartha.*

When inscribing truth through lies,
He sets the mood with music
From tunes he's compiled
As the soundtrack of his life.

He soaks up mantra chants
By Deva Premal and Krishna Das,
And he loves to belt along
With Jai Uttal's *kirtan!*

He still likes to rock-'n'-roll—
To classic, alt, and pop.
At times he feels an urge
To jazz things up a bit.

His personal yoga mix—
For on and off the mat—
Incorporates all those
To stimulate his chi.

His inner flute reverberates
When he listens to Madonna
Sing "Shanti/Ashtangi"
From her *Ray of Light* album.

"Awakening the happiness
Of the self revealed," intones
The Virgin *cum* Material Girl
Cum Free Spirit, in Sanskrit.

When he looks in the mirror now
He sees his true Self shine
Through the windows of his eyes
And the skylight on his dome.

His Agassi-like conversion
Shows more than in appearance.
No longer rebel or grinder,
He's found his place in the world.

The tattoos on his body
From more recent years
Express some of his views
About that special place.

An Om where his spine
Joins his ribcage to his skull
Shows he knows his voice can speak
In harmony with all.

Six-petaled Svadhisthana
At the chakra of his sacrum
Opens a path for the sacred
To rise upward from his root.

On one arm an infinity
Signifies his sense
Of limitless potential
And ever-lasting flow.

That loop further embodies
Principles of yin and yang—
Forces that *seem* opposed
In balance in one whole.

A quill pen on his other wing—
The one he calls his "sword arm"—

Denotes his aim in battle
To let fly righteous words.

The nib points to his wrist,
To point that when touching you
He writes things beyond words
From his soul onto yours.

A peace sign on one hand
And a heart on the other
Reflect the energies
Flowing through his palms.

One way he touches others
Is through tantric massage,
Which isn't what you think,
If you think it's all about sex.

Although for recipients
It provides profound release,
For him it's spiritual practice—
Turning desire into love.

The bodies he massages
Range quite a bit in type:
Petite to substantial;
Female, male, and trans.

He neither penetrates
Nor gets penetrated.
The unions go much deeper,
To the divinity at their core.

His partner respects his yen
To cultivate in others
Bliss that in him bloomed
Above a lake, like a lotus.

Eventually she'll return (she always does),
Greeted with a kiss and a smile.
They'll break bread together
And pass the evening in repose.

They enjoy their quiet nights
But go on adventures, too.
Jointly they've explored
All manner of terrain.

They've mounted heavenly peaks,
Discovered hidden caverns,
Survived the wilds of jungles,
Add trekked through desert sands.

They've encountered many rivers.
Some they followed.
Some they crossed.
And some they sat beside.

On this night they'll retire
To the queen-size bed they share—
Quite suitable for them ...
And occasional third musketeers.

They've accepted all along
Monogamy isn't their way.
The bonds they form with others
Pose no threat to their own.

Nearly three decades have passed
Since the day he seized the day
And the lifeline she threw
For him to drag himself ashore.

They may someday reach a fork
And follow separate paths.
But in spirit they'll remain

Forever yoked as one.

He's still a work-in-progress
And knows he always will be.
But his brain's been seizure-free
Since he let Joy into his heart.

He no longer tries to save
Others from themselves,
Accepting he can only—and only he can—
Save himself from his self.

He stood on a lofty bridge
Not so many years ago,
Drowning in despair
As deep as the water below.

As the river called his name,
An Angel(a) came to remind him
Of his sole (soul) purpose to live:
His boundless power to love.

He knows another river
Will beckon him one day.
He hopes the ferryman
Accepts his savior-fare.

'Til then all he can do
Is fully *Be Here Now*,
Letting go of the past and
Embracing what unfolds.

He's had his natal chart read;
Much like with his palm,
The stars unveiled inner truths.
If you believe in that sort of thing.

He tries not to moralize

In *Poor Richard* style.
Others must find their way,
The way he's found his own.

Above all else, he'd tell you,
Take one thing to heart:
We *all* are works-in-progress,
And we always will be.

What we might think are flaws
Are what truly make us art.
So be kind to yourself
As you re-vision your form.

What seem like contradictions—
In the world, in others, and in our selves—
Are actually connections
Waiting to be made.

Peace and love to all beings!
Even if you don't believe in that sort of thing.

Karuna Das

AFTERWORD

I often refer to this novel as a fictionalized memoir. The story is true—in essence—to the arc of my journey toward self-acceptance, my long struggle to reconcile characteristics of my embodiment with societal and self-imposed models of masculinity. I ultimately lost that struggle. I could not reconcile them. That left me a choice between two kinds of death: the literal death of my body-mind through continued self-destructive behavior or the figurative death of the identity I'd constructed through my conditioning. I chose—and continue to choose—the latter, embracing the process of writing myself into existence, being the author-ity for my own life's story.

It wouldn't surprise me if readers are curious which aspects of the narrative—which of the events, relationships, and other details—are true to my real-life experience. I'm not particularly interested in identifying them. But I probably will if you ask politely and without judgment. I'm more interested in which aspects *ring true* for you. I hope enough of them do for the story to offer flashes of insight and inspiration on your own journey through this life. Some of the events that probably seem most likely to be invented actually happened as described, or as close to that as I can find words to articulate my experience.

That being said, Drew is not an accurate representation of an earlier version—or earlier versions—of me, nor are any other characters intended to accurately represent corresponding figures in my life, even when they say and do things those people really said and did. Think of the characters as *inspired by* more than *based on* people with whom I've interacted. The most important word in "fictionalized memoir" is the first one.

ACKNOWLEDGMENTS

Where to begin expressing gratitude for the countless people who've contributed to this project? I suppose with the folks who inspired characters or aspects of them. Regardless of the nature of our interaction and how I felt about it at the time, you helped me become the man I am today, and there's no one I'd rather be. I love you all.

This book grew out of material I conceived and developed as drama. I initially wrote a purely autobiographical solo show, which I performed as readings in some friends' living room in Stevens Point, WI, then at the University of Wisconsin - Stevens Point, and later at a now defunct Pittsburgh tea and coffee house called Your Inner Vagabond. I subsequently mounted a production in Pittsburgh's Bricolage Theatre space. Thanks to the audiences at those events for their support and feedback, especially Jane Graham Jennings, who responded to the first of them with a rare and brave degree of honesty that benefitted me and the project greatly. Thanks also to the individuals who helped make those presentations happen: Shannon and Wayne Semmerling, Becca (Hengstenberg) Van Bockern, Jeremy Larson, Andrew Barrett Watson, Jeffrey Carpenter and Tami Dixon, Jackie Baker and David Bielewicz, and Tyler Hodges. I love you all.

I began the process of fictionalizing the material when I adapted it as a screenplay. Thanks to the judges at three industry competitions where it was a finalist for the encouragement that provided and to the readers at three other contests who offered constructive coverage. Thanks also to three young men—Michael Kaup, Timm Romine, and Andrew Baer (RIP)—for their insightful feedback and for the suggestion, as with *Kat's Cradle*, I adapt the story as a novel to have a broader canvas on which to paint with more depth, detail, and nuance. I love you all.

The first few chapters of the novel were critiqued by Jonathan Auxier and Tom Sweterlitsch. The latter later read the complete manuscript, and his advice in regard to shopping it was invaluable, as has been his support of my writing in general. Arianna Garofalo likewise read the early draft, as well as various revisions, and offered always-constructive comments. Feedback from additional beta reader Michael H. M. Brown included a particularly helpful observation about a key element. I love you all.

I got additional encouragement from the editors at Stillhouse Press, where the manuscript was a semifinalist in the Mary Roberts Rinehart Fiction Contest, and from readers at several other small presses who praised the work even though it wasn't quite right for their catalogs. Thanks also to Elizabeth Macduffie, publisher of *Meat for Tea: The Valley Review*, for including a standalone version of the last chapter in the magazine's Lotus Blossom issue. I love you all.

Special thanks to Daniel Willis for accepting the manuscript and guiding it through the publication process at DX Varos and to John David Kudrick for his generous, perceptive, and reassuring editorial review. I love you, Dano and JD.

I'll conclude by acknowledging the unconditional support I enjoy as a perpetual work-in-progress from my long-term nesting partner Tiffany Wilhelm, to whom this book is dedicated and to whom I can never express the extent of my gratitude. I love you beyond measure, Ti.

ABOUT THE AUTHOR

Karuna Das (Sanskrit for "servant of compassion") is the pen and spirit name of Kyle Bostian. Born in Wisconsin, he grew up in Massachusetts and presently resides in Pennsylvania, but he lives wherever he happens to be at that moment, feels at home everywhere in the universe, and steps through almost any door that opens to him. He holds a BA in English (UMass), an MFA in Playwriting (UW - Seattle), and a PhD in Theatre and Dramaturgy (FSU). His short piece "Irony of the Second Degree" appears in *24 Gun Control Plays* (NoPassport Press) and has been performed around the world. In addition to his dramatic writing, he's published the sci-fi novel *Kat's Cradle: Webolution Book One*, short fiction in *Meat for Tea*, *Catalyst*, *Pif Magazine*, and *ActiveMuse*, and creative nonfiction and poetry in *The Wayfarer*. Projects in development include *Solar Max: Webolution Book Two*, a follow-up to this novel called *More Sex, Drugs & Spiritual Enlightenment (but still mostly the first two)*, and a nonfiction memoir about his relationship with his mother, *Finding Our Way Home*. He and life partner Ti share their house with five wonderfully wacky cats.

OTHER EXQUISITE FICTION FROM
DX VAROS PUBLISHING
www.DXVaros.com/catalog